THE GREAT BIG GEORGE BOOK OF STORIES

ERIC PRINGLE

Illustrated by Colin Paine

BLOOMSBURY

LONDON BERLIN NEW YORK SYDNEY

Bloomsbury Publishing, London, Berlin, New York and Sydney

This omnibus edition first published in Great Britain in August 2011
by Bloomsbury Publishing Plc
36 Soho Square, London, W1D 3QY

Big George first published
by Bloomsbury Publishing Plc in 2001
Text copyright © Eric Pringle 2001
Illustrations copyright © Colin Paine 2001

Big George and the Seventh Knight first published
by Bloomsbury Publishing Plc in 2002
Text copyright © Eric Pringle 2002
Illustrations copyright © Colin Paine 2002

Big George and the Winter King first published
by Bloomsbury Publishing Plc in 2004
Text copyright © Eric Pringle 2004
Illustrations copyright © Colin Paine 2004

The moral rights of the author and illustrator have been asserted

A CIP catalogue record for this book is available from the British Library

ISBN 978 1 4088 1521 2

Printed in Great Britain by Clays Ltd, St Ives Plc, Bungay, Suffolk

1 3 5 7 9 10 8 6 4 2

Featuring

Big George

Big George
and the Seventh Knight

Big George
and the winter King

Big George

contents

Foreword

This book is about England's very first visitor from outer space.

It is the story of how he got his name and how, helped by the smallest of girls, he became the Biggest Hero England Ever Had.

These things happened a long time ago, in the Year of Our Lord 1103.

Close your eyes. Imagine that time ...

The Norman Conquest happened only thirty-seven years ago, and now a Norman, King Henry the First, sits upon the throne of England. He has two and a half million subjects, most of them as poor as church mice.

England is full of dark places. There are deep, dark, trackless forests roamed by deer and wolves and wild boar. There are dark mountain regions where people are afraid to wander and wildcats hiss in the mist. And everywhere the people believe in the dark power of magic, in wizards and witches and the power of potions.

In this half-civilised land, mighty barons hunt in the forests by day, for sport. At night, hungry poachers steal through the trees looking for food.

This is everyday life in the Year of Our Lord 1103.

Nothing extraordinary is happening. But it's about to.

Listen!

Do you hear that noise?

Something is approaching very fast. Heading for England.

Here it comes …

chapter one
The Stranger

The noise of the crash was heard at court, a hundred miles away.

King Henry looked up, cocked his head and listened for another bang. His courtiers listened too.

When a second tremor did not arrive, Henry nodded wisely and said, 'Meteorite.' (Which was not a bad guess, really.)

His courtiers bowed low and replied, 'Thank you, Your Majesty, for telling us. How wise you are to know such things!'

They all believed it was a meteorite because the King was the King and Kings Know Everything.

Five minutes later the bang was forgotten and Palace life carried on as though nothing had happened.

9

*

But something *had* happened – something big.

The Stranger had arrived.

Deep in the dark forest, a hundred miles from the King and his courtiers, a machine lay shattered and smoking at the bottom of a vast hole.

Moments earlier it had resembled a shooting star, fire bright, hurtling through Earth's atmosphere in a swizzle of dazzling light. When it smacked into the forest the star went out. Now little green lights fizzed and sparked like glow-worms, and spat puffs of smoke.

Somewhere in the hole, inside the wreckage, in the middle of the sparks, a noise crackled and a panicky voice spluttered gibberish on and off, on and off. Gradually the voice grew fainter, as if it was losing strength, then with a sigh it stopped altogether.

Pieces of the machine lay scattered far and wide among the trees. They too smoked and glowed in the dark night of the forest.

Suddenly the voice returned, screaming. It gave a final command and at once the machine and every scattered piece of metal shone with a blinding light.

Then one by one they shrivelled, the way cotton wool shrinks on a fire, twisting and dwindling until

the machine was no more. The voice died too.

All that was left was a hole in the floor of the forest, and trees were flattened to twigs all about.

But there was nobody to see these things.

That is how the scene remained for weeks. Still nobody came to see.

Then one night the silence was broken.

Something stirred in the undergrowth, not far from the hole.

Something had been left after all.

It was big.

It was very big.

If anyone had been watching they would have seen something like an arm raised to scratch what looked like a face – a face covered at its top and bottom with something like hair, only this hair was striped blue and green.

A second arm reached out and pressed against the ground, pushing upright an object that looked very like a body – except that this body was at least as big around and as tall as a tree. The face rose above it and kept on rising. Something like a neck, like a swan's neck that seemed to go on for ever, uncurled slowly and achingly.

As it did so, what sounded like a groan escaped from a mouth hidden inside the blue and green beard. In the silence of the forest the groan sounded as loud as thunder and it made the leaves shiver all around.

Very slowly, with many more groans to make the trees tremble, the whole thing rose up on two enormous legs. Up and up it surged, thrusting through the branches until its head was out in the clear air, towering against the sky and blotting out the stars.

Now at last the Stranger stood upright.

Rocking unsteadily on feet the size of boulders, he looked about him, blinking his eyes in the darkness.

If anyone had been watching they would have thought him the most extraordinary being they had ever seen.

The Stranger was almost human-like, apart from the blue and green hair and the giraffe neck.

Very like and almost a man, but not quite. He was bigger than the biggest tree in the forest. But the oddest thing of all was his face.

It was definitely a face and in many respects it was like a human face. But it was almost white and almost green – a pale greenish white – and it glowed in the dark. It nodded up there against the sky like a full moon.

Actually, it isn't surprising that the Stranger looked like a man in so many ways. Because where he had come from, astronomers had been searching the universe for thousands of years, seeking a star like their own. It was like hunting a needle in a haystack, but in the end they found it.

Earth seemed so similar to their world that those

astronomers thought that everything on it might be similar too. This made them very excited, but it was only guesswork. They had to find out if it really was true.

They decided to send an explorer, a messenger. So they built a spacecraft and aimed it at their discovery, with an astronaut inside – the Stranger.

It worked. Here he was.

But there was an unforeseen problem. The Stranger had no idea who he was, where he was, or what he was doing there.

In the crash of the landing he had been thrown clear of his craft, bumping through the forest and banging his head so hard that now he could not remember anything. And when his craft destroyed itself, there was nothing left to remind him.

He had no past, only a new beginning on an unknown world.

The Stranger had another problem too. He could not get his neck down.

His neck was supposed to fold like a swan's but one of the bumps had locked it fast and now his head was stuck up high and shining like a lamp on a lamp-post.

After teetering on his shaky legs for a while, the Stranger thought he might as well go somewhere, although he had no idea where. So he staggered off, leaving his direction to chance.

As he went, he cut such a swathe through the forest that hunters riding there afterwards thought there must have been a hurricane.

All this a watcher would have seen, if there had been anybody there to see.

And there was.

chapter Two
A Shock for Simpkin Sampkins

There was a poacher.

His name was Simpkin Sampkins, and he was very, very frightened.

Simpkin had pale, watery eyes and no hair and trembling knees. They had been shaking ever since the moment when, setting a rabbit trap, not far away he saw a tree rise up in the darkness and scratch its head.

That had scared Simpkin so much that he almost caught himself in his own trap.

'Jumping fleas in a jam jar!' he muttered, making the sign of a cross on his ragged tunic. 'Bless my toes with honey!'

Simpkin Sampkins lay flat on his back on the

ground, hardly daring to breathe, while what looked like more trees moved and merged into the biggest tree he had ever seen.

'Oh, Mother, forgive me, for I must have been drinking,' he moaned, 'although I don't remember it.'

Gazing at the enormous tree that swayed high above his head, looking as if it might topple on him at any moment, Simpkin began to cry and he began to pray.

He cried that he was sorry for every wicked thing he had ever done. He was sorry for stealing the miller's flour and his daughter Tilly Miller's honey, and for trapping Baron Lousewort's rabbits.

'I will be a poacher no more,' he sobbed. 'And bless my boots with beer but I will never drink alcohol again, for I am being punished with walking trees.'

The Stranger still hovered above him, so Simpkin Sampkins began to pray for a miracle.

'Lord,' he begged, 'if I promise to be good for ever, will you please make this tree go away? *Please?*'

The moment the thought babbled from his brain, the tree moved.

It thumped down a boot as big as a hut, missing Simpkin by a hair and trampling his rabbit trap six feet down into the soft earth.

Next the tree stepped over him and thudded away through the forest, squashing everything in its path.

Simpkin Sampkins lay shivering, rigid as an icicle, for an hour. At last he got up. Peering into the grave where his rabbit trap was buried, he cried again.

Then he ran for his life, watched by a nearby rabbit that rubbed its face with its paws and grinned, glad of its lucky escape.

Chapter Three
The Girl at the River

Simpkin Sampkins ran until he thought he could run no more, and still he kept on running. He ran with a stitch in his side and his breath rasping. His legs bled and his hands stung from the briars and nettles that tried to hold him back.

He ran until he reached the edge of the forest and came to the first building on cultivated land. It was a mill, standing sturdily beside the looping bend of a winding river. Simpkin Sampkins had never been so glad to see anything in his life as this mill.

When Simpkin arrived, the night was over and gone. The sun was up and the river shone and the mill-race sparkled as it pushed and dripped over the mill's great turning wheel. The water drove the wheel outside, and the wheel turned, grinding stones inside, and the stones ground corn into flour.

Across the river, inside the mill, Simpkin could hear the miller working beside the noisily grinding millstones, shovelling corn and flour. As he worked, the miller was whistling a happy tune.

Outside, the miller's daughter Tilly was washing his clothes in the river.

The girl was young and small and pretty. She slapped the clothes on flat stones at the water's

edge, and rubbed and shook them. All the time she sang too as she worked, but the song she sang was a sad song.

Tilly looked up from her washing as something appeared out of the forest on the other side of the river.

What she saw looked like a bundle of clothes falling about. It croaked and wobbled and sucked in air. It flapped its arms like wings. Then it sat down and cried.

'Simpkin, is that you?' Tilly shouted.

She carried on washing her father's clothes. She dared not pause because she knew that the miller would have a hundred other things for her to do afterwards.

'Of course it's me!' Simpkin Sampkins wanted to shout back at her. 'Who else would be out in these wild woods at this time in the morning?' But the only sound he could make was a croak like a tired frog.

So he sat on the bank to get his breath back, and looked across the river at Tilly Miller.

Simpkin liked Tilly. He liked watching her. He liked her long yellow hair and the way she tied it back with a band of blue cloth. He liked her smile. He liked the way animals and birds trusted her. That, he knew, was a good sign. They didn't trust

23

him as far as they could spit, but that was natural, for he poached them mercilessly.

Simpkin wished Tilly was *his* daughter. He told himself *he* would not work her so hard if she was. He would take care of her far better than that greedy miller, who was so busy making money that he hardly bothered to speak to Tilly, except to give her orders.

And Simpkin knew that if Tilly had been *his* daughter, *he* would not have promised her in marriage to Baron Lousewort's horrible son Bones when she grew up, as her greedyguts father had done. No, sir.

Simpkin had no children.

He had no wife, either.

Simpkin Sampkins had nobody.

People said it was because he was a loner, as if this had been by choice. But Simpkin had not chosen it at all, it was just the way things had worked out.

Whenever he felt lonely Simpkin talked to his friend Tilly. But he had no time to talk to her now because there was a tree on his heels.

Tilly was wringing out the cold washing when finally he came plunging across the river towards her.

'What's up, Simpkin?' she asked.

Simpkin staggered up the beach with water dribbling from his armpits.

'I'm sorry I stole your dad's flour,' he babbled. 'Here, have it back.'

He hauled his poacher's satchel off his back, dragged out a soggy bag and dumped it splat on the ground.

Tilly's blue eyes opened wide with horror. 'Simpkin, how could you!' she cried.

'It was easy,' Simpkin wanted to say, but instead he said, 'And I'm sorry I stole your honey, Tilly.' He pulled out a dripping honeycomb and dropped it squelch on the stones.

'You stole my honey? Why?'

Simpkin wanted to explain that stealing things was what poachers do. But instead his eyes filled with tears. He scratched his bald head. 'I – I'm sorry, Tilly,' he stammered. 'I won't do it again, I promise. Never ever. I've been punished – oh, how I've been punished!'

Tilly examined him closely. 'Simpkin, have you been drinking?'

'Not a drop has touched my lips, Tilly, and never will again. Now I have to go. There's something I must tell people. I have to tell everybody. The forest is alive, and on the move!'

With that he ran away down a track that led

alongside the river to the village, with his arms waving and his bald head bobbing in the sun.

Tilly Miller carried the clean washing into the mill house, where her father was waiting impatiently with a list of jobs for her as long as her arm.

'Simpkin Sampkins is drunk, Father,' Tilly said and smiled. 'He thinks trees are chasing him.'

'Trees will be chasing you if you don't hurry up,' the miller snapped, heading for the door, 'and *I'll* be behind them. I'm off to the village now to deliver flour. If you don't finish that list before I get back you'll be sorry. Understand?'

He banged the door shut behind him without even waiting for his daughter to say yes.

chapter four
worse than Dragons

The miller did not get far. In fact, he got nowhere at all.

He had just finished harnessing his horse and was loading up the cart with sacks when he heard the sound of hooves.

Looking up he saw a cavalcade of horses approaching along the river track. And what horses they were!

They came trotting up the lane two abreast, fifty, sixty – the miller blinked – there must be a hundred of them at least, he thought. Their teeth gleamed, their eyes flashed, their harnesses jingled and twinkled. Each horse was decked out with coloured saddle-cloth and ribbons and had a rider perched on top, clad from head to foot in dazzling chain mail. The procession glittered like hundreds of mirrors in the early-morning sunshine.

But the miller's heart sank when he saw, bringing up the rear, two horses that were much bigger than the rest. Jerking up and down on them, like two cardboard puppets, were two figures he recognised. They were Baron Grimshanks Lousewort and his weedy son Bones.

The miller swallowed nervously. He guessed what they wanted. The Baron and Bones were coming to look at Tilly, to make sure she was still there. Keeping an eye on their property.

Tilly had also seen them coming, and she too guessed what they wanted. With her heart thumping, she backed into a corner and stood twining her apron strings in her fingers. She wiped a tear from her eye and whispered, 'Oh, please, won't somebody save me from that dreadful boy Bones?' But there was nobody to listen.

When the horsemen arrived, Tilly was kneeling with her face in her hands, praying.

This did her no good at all.

'There's no use pretending this isn't happening, Tilly,' snapped her father, pushing open the door and leading in two of the ugliest, most revolting, nastiest-looking bullies you or England could ever dread to see.

Picture a bursting warty boil with hairs sprouting out at all angles, twisted and wiry and black. Think of a hole in the middle, filled with brown and broken teeth. Now imagine this horror stuck on top of a roly-poly, podgy body like the ugliest balloon in the world.

When you have done this, you will have some idea what Baron Grimshanks Lousewort looked like as he followed the miller into the mill.

Tilly felt sick just to look at him.

She felt even sicker to look at the Baron's son.

Bones Lousewort was thin – thin as a stick insect, thinner than a skeleton – and he looked as if

he didn't have any blood in him. His hands were almost transparent, with pale hooks for fingers. Except for the spots which erupted like a scaly disease all over his skin, his face was white as a sheet. Inside it his eyes glinted like black buttons, his nostrils flared like black holes and his mouth sagged like a dark cave.

Bones looked barely alive.

Worse than that, he looked as if anything he touched would wither too.

And Bones wanted to touch Tilly.

He wanted to hold her hand. He wanted to kiss her. He wanted to *marry* her.

This was because one morning a year ago, returning from a hunting expedition with his father, Bones saw Tilly brushing her long golden hair beside the beehives in front of the mill. He fell for her on sight.

Unfortunately for Bones, no one could possibly fall for him, even though he was the Baron's son and heir and one day would be very rich.

The thought of marrying him filled Tilly with horror and made her want to retch.

Now here he was coming towards her, clicking his stick legs and grinning his death's-head grin.

'Hello, Tilly,' he piped in a thin voice that made the teeth rattle inside his skinny mouth.

Tilly screamed.

'Gadzookles!' growled the Baron, with a grimace that made the hairs jump all over the bursting boil of his face. 'That wench has a good pair of lungs in her. That's a good sign. But you'd better say hello to my son, Tilly, or it will be the worse for your dad, gadzookles in a piecrust if it won't.'

'I will *not* be nice to him!' Tilly shouted. 'I hate him! I can't stand him! I'd rather marry a turnip! Take him away!'

This only made Bones want her more, for although his body was meagre, his skin was as thick as a crocodile's.

But it made the Baron angry and the miller scared.

'Miller!' Grimshanks roared, with his face reddening and swelling until it looked as if it might explode all over the mill. 'If my son wants to marry your daughter he will, gadzookles in a moonbeam if he won't. I'm allowing her to stay here with you only until the time is right, but when I say so you'll hand her over and no messing. Do you understand?'

'I do, my lord,' the miller quaked, and fell to his knees.

The Baron rapped him on the head with his fist. 'If I have any trouble, you'll be out of this mill

faster than you can put your shirt on, and your life won't be worth a fried shrimp. Do you understand *that*?'

'Yes, sir, my lord,' the miller babbled.

The Baron nodded. 'I just hope you do, because

I've had enough nonsense for one day already and it's still only nine o'clock in the morning. We passed that thieving fool Sampkins on the way here, blathering about marching woods. It'll be singing skies next. If Sampkins isn't poaching my game he's drinking himself silly. I gave orders for him to be clapped in jail. That'll cook his goose.'

All this time Bones was smiling at Tilly. His grin struck cold as a knife into her heart.

'Please, Father,' she whispered, 'don't do this to me.'

'Shut up, you, and listen,' the miller hissed back. 'A year ago I promised you to the Baron's son for five sovereigns. Would you have me lose my gold? You'll do exactly as you're told, my girl, and be grateful.'

'Grateful for what?' cried Tilly.

'Grateful for me!' shouted the Baron, coming so close she felt dizzy. The Baron had extremely bad breath.

'Grateful for *me*!' squealed Bones, slithering towards Tilly like a snake. His breath was so nasty it burned like fire.

'Father,' Tilly sobbed, 'this cannot be! These men smell worse than dragons!'

'Dragons!' the Baron roared. 'Ha ha! Ha ha ha!'

'Dragons!' chortled his son.

'Dragons!' chirruped the miller. 'Well, you're intended for this dragon, my girl, so you'd better get used to the smell. What a joke!'

They laughed again, shovelling stench over Tilly like dollops of manure until she fainted clean away.

At that moment, in the trees across the river, something stirred.

chapter Five
How to Be George

The Stranger had been wandering all night.

He had no idea where he was, even less where he was heading, and where he had been he could not remember. As he wandered, he made a chuntering sound, halfway between a mumbling and a humming, very soft and low. He might have been talking to himself or seeking comfort in a song of home. Who knows?

There was no one to hear him, except the animals who lived in the forest. The noise warned them of his coming so that they were able to skip out of the way and avoid being crushed. The Stranger could not even see where he was going because it was dark.

He had not experienced night before. In the world he had come from it was always day. Its inhabitants stayed awake for the length of nine hundred Earth years, then slept for another nine hundred, silent behind the curtains of their closed eyelids. Which, when you think about it, is almost like living for ever.

The Stranger could not recall any of this, of course. Nor, with his memory gone, could he know that his journey to Earth had lasted eight hundred and ninety-nine years, although he was beginning to feel a little tired.

As he rambled through the forest, he cut a swathe like a maze, which people would spend years trying to get out of afterwards.

At last a new day dawned, and the Stranger began to see where he was.

Then he smelled the river.

He was thirsty and the smell drew him like a magnet, but instinct told him he must be wary. So he got down and crawled along on his great stomach, as carefully as he could between the trees.

When he saw the glint of water ahead, he stopped and pushed out enormous arms to part the undergrowth. Then he probed his giraffe neck about, pushing his head forward until it was just hidden by bushes.

Peering through the twigs, the Stranger saw the river and the mill. And people. Small people!

They seemed to him *very* small people, compared to his own size. Midgets with short necks.

Most of the midgets he saw were sitting on dwarf horses, riding away. The two at the back were laughing. Behind them there trundled a cart laden with sacks, driven by a surly-faced man.

Soon they had all disappeared round the bend of the river.

The Stranger's way seemed clear.

So he crawled out of the bushes and lay down on the beach and drank his fill.

*

Inside the mill, Tilly, who had collapsed only to get rid of the two dragons, decided she had lain still long enough. It was time to start the jobs her father had left her. She jumped to her feet and looked at the daunting list.

She was to seek wood from the forest and chop it.

She was to fetch water from the river and boil it on the fire.

She was to clean the house and set the mousetraps.

She was to cook dinner.

And so on.

Etcetera.

There was no end to the work.

Tilly sighed, but she knew that sighing wouldn't help and so there was no point doing it. The only thing to do was make a start and tick the jobs off one by one.

So she picked up a pail and opened the door and went outside to collect water from the river.

And that was when she saw it.

She saw Whatever It Was, spreadeagled on the bank, stretching out of the forest to halfway across the river, guzzling.

'By George,' Tilly exclaimed in an astonished voice, 'you're big! You're *very* big, by George.'

Whatever It Was lifted its head at the sound.

Water streamed in rivulets from its blue and green beard.

'By *George*,' Tilly said again, 'has someone been painting you?'

The ears of the Whatever It Was twitched. It seemed to be concentrating. Its eyes glittered. Its mouth formed a shape, and, making a chuntering sound like a soft, low humming, it said, slowly and carefully, 'G-g-g-e-e-e-o-o-o-r-r-r-r-g-g-e.'

Tilly was a bright girl. Not a lot passed her by, and she was an athlete at jumping to conclusions.

'Is that your name?' she asked. 'Is it George, by George? What a coincidence!'

The Stranger smiled the biggest smile Tilly had ever seen. She was on a level with its teeth and from where she stood its mouth looked as if it could swallow the world.

The Stranger was smiling at Tilly's bright musical voice. It sounded friendly. It was the first friendliness he had come across since he found himself lying on the floor of the forest, a Stranger without a history.

'I'm Tilly,' the very small person across the river was saying now. 'How do you do?'

'T-illlll-llll-yyy.'

'That's right. Want to shake hands?' Tilly held out her hand.

George pushed himself up on one elbow, making a wave that surged out of sight down the river. Then he stretched out his other arm towards her.

And stretched.

And stretched.

The arm seemed to be made of elastic. It kept coming until it was within a hair's breadth of her face. Then it stopped. Tilly, who was not a girl to scare easily, grasped a finger in both hands and shook it.

'Pleased to meet you, George,' she said, smiling.

The Stranger liked her smile. He liked the way it lit up her face. He grinned back.

'Hello,' he said. In his own language.

To Tilly it sounded like 'G-r-o-l-y-h-o-o-m-p', and straight away she raced to another conclusion.

'Is that what you are?' she asked. 'A grolyhoomp? Do you know, I've never met a grolyhoomp in the whole of my life before! I've never even heard of one, by George!'

chapter Six
Listening to the Sky

If you are thinking that Tilly is taking this very casually, remember that it is happening in the Year of Our Lord 1103, when people believe absolutely in every kind of wonder. And if you believe in fairies and witches and boggarts and goodness knows what else, why not in a grolyhoomp?

Actually, Tilly was very excited, because it isn't every day a girl gets to meet a grolyhoomp. In fact, she had never heard of anyone meeting one before.

But it is one thing finding a grolyhoomp outside your door and quite another knowing what to do with it. That is what Tilly was pondering now.

'Excuse me for asking, George,' she said very politely, 'but would you mind getting out of the river? You're making a dam and in about five minutes my father's mill will be flooded. *If* you don't mind. Thank you so much.'

Although he had no idea what the words meant – it sounded to him like a kind of melody – George seemed to understand.

He stood up.

And up.

Waterfalls cascaded from his armpits and the holes in his tunic, soaking Tilly from head to foot as in two strides he crossed the river and stood towering above her.

She looked up at him until her neck ached. Blinking at the bright stripy face perched on top of that long neck, she said, 'Oh, George, you must be forty feet high!'

The grolyhoomp grinned down and repeated, 'F-f-f-o-o-r-r-t-i-f-f-y. Four-t-i-fy.'

'Close,' said Tilly. 'You're getting there.'

But she was thinking, Now what?

Because up to now, conversation didn't seem to be getting them very far, and at this rate her father would be back before she had even started on her chores. Then she would be for it.

Tilly thought hard. What on earth was she going to do with Big George? (It never occurred to her to wonder what Big George might be going to do with her.)

She could hardly take him visiting. Try as she might she could not see herself turning up at a friend's house and saying, 'Look, I've just found this forty-foot grolyhoomp called George. Can I bring him in for tea?'

In the end she decided that the best way through the puzzle was to be logical. To put things in order. First things first. And the first priority was to get those jobs out of the way.

'Why don't you go round the back and hide, George?' she suggested. 'Make yourself scarce for a bit. I'll hurry my chores and when I've finished, I'll come round for a chat. How does that sound?'

It sounded like magic to George – all jiggy and sing-songy, like the kind of music that makes your feet tap. It made him happy to hear it.

So, chuntering gently, he followed Tilly's pointing finger and wandered round to the back of the mill.

Here trees had been cleared to make a wide yard where the miller stored grain at harvest time. Now in spring most of the grain had been ground into flour and sold and the clearing was almost empty.

George lay down in the open space. He stretched out and waited for Tilly.

He had to wait for a long time.

He felt tired, though not sleepy, for it was not yet his time to sleep. His nine hundred years of waking were not quite used up.

His neck was bruised and stiff. A bump on the back of his head felt as big as his boot. He touched it gently and groaned.

He tried to think things out, but that made his head ache even more, so he stopped.

To take his mind off his troubles, George thought about Tilly. That did not hurt, because he liked her. He wanted to be her friend.

He practised her language so that they could talk to each other. 'G-e-o-o-r-r-g-e,' he hummed. 'Ff-o-rrt-i-fy.'

(Tilly, hurrying through the chores on her list, heard the sound inside the mill and thought her bees were all swarming at once.)

Now George lay back and looked straight up at the sky.

Fleecy clouds floated across it like fish swimming in a blue sea.

But there was something strange.

The sky was singing.

George strained to listen, but could make no sense of it. It seemed to him that he should be able to look through the clouds and see what lay beyond, but trying to do that made his head ache again, and failing to do it made him want to cry with loneliness.

The sky seemed like a friend calling him, but he couldn't quite hear it, and he could not answer.

He tried to imitate the sound, opening his lips and whistling. His whistling was a wind that shook the branches of the trees all around the clearing. Birds flew startled from their nests. Insects scurried

and darted into holes. Miles away, owls hooted with surprise.

Inside the mill Tilly heard a hurricane.

Where on earth did that come from? she wondered. I hope George is all right.

The wind dropped as suddenly as it rose. Everything grew hushed and still. Breathless.

In the clearing George was crying.

chapter Seven
The Tilly Bird

Even though she worked her very quickest, when Tilly had finished her tasks, the day was already ending. Her father must be home soon.

She felt tired and frightened and sad. The Baron's visit had reminded her of the fate she had been trying hard to forget, for just the idea of being married to Bones Lousewort was more than she could bear. She felt like running away, but there was nowhere for her to run to.

The worry was still on Tilly's mind when at last she was able to visit the grolyhoomp.

She paused at the rim of the clearing and looked at him. The very sight of George cheered her up, he was so astonishing. He nearly filled the clearing all by himself. With that amazing neck, his striped, tufty hair and beard, his elastic arms and knobbly

hands and boulder-sized feet, he hardly looked real.

But he was real all right. Why, he was turning his head towards her now, and smiling!

What a smile that was! It wafted over her like a blanket. It warmed her up. It comforted her.

But even so, she still felt sad.

George saw her pain and frowned. 'What's the matter, Tilly?' he asked.

Tilly heard, 'Trlllleddibbbileppolyubftsatilly,' which made no sense whatever. Yet the sound comforted her because it was so friendly.

She moved up close and looked the grolyhoomp in the eye. That brought another surprise, for it was like looking into a deep black pool in which she could see herself swimming.

Tilly had the strangest feeling that she had swum right inside the grolyhoomp's head. She felt sure he was inside hers, too.

It was like being best friends with somebody, so close that you each know what the other is feeling. Tilly thought there wasn't anything about her that George could not guess and understand.

So she poured out her troubles. She told him about her life and her father's promise to the Baron.

'I'm too small to marry, aren't I?' she cried. 'Look

at me, I'm a midget. It makes me scared to grow up, thinking about that skinny bonebag waiting for me with his smelly breath. Bones is a monster! One puff from him and I'll die! I know I shall!'

George winked and jumped to his feet, making the trees shiver and the ground tremble.

Tilly nearly fell over.

'You're not going away?' she cried.

George was not going anywhere. He had something else in mind.

He had understood not one word from his small friend, but the sound of her voice had moved him like sad music. How unhappy she was!

Well, he was going to make her happy.

From his great height he looked down on the top of Tilly's head. She looked very tiny and delicate. He would have to be careful.

'Larklyggwocavvuiotpvnmjnms,' he said. It meant, 'Watch this.'

Slowly, like a giraffe nibbling short grass, he spread wide his legs, bent his long neck and lowered his head to the ground.

Once again his eye was level with Tilly's, and once again she saw herself inside it.

'Ffffbbiggley,' he said. He waggled his head. 'Ffffbbiggley!'

'You want me to climb up?' Tilly gasped.

'Mmmnnn. MMMnnn!'

'All right, George. If you say so.'

She grabbed hold of the grolyhoomp's tufty beard. It felt like a handful of wire.

'Blue and green should never be seen, George,' she said. 'That's a basic rule of colours. But I expect grolyhoomps haven't been taught – wheeee!'

George lifted his head and Tilly swooped upwards. With legs dangling she hung on to the wiry beard with all her strength.

'Wheee!' she shouted again as George straightened his neck and back and brought his legs together.

She was swinging back and forth like the pendulum of a giant clock. Trees and sky rocked dizzily about her.

Then her kicking feet found a hold on George's bottom lip. 'Is that all right?' she asked breathlessly. 'I'm not hurting you?'

'Qqqwwallopmid,' George laughed, and Tilly bounced up and down.

Now that she felt safer, she dared to look about. What she saw made her cry out with excitement. 'George, this is the most wonderful thing I ever did!'

Suddenly she was no longer a miller's daughter, promised in marriage to a dragon.

She was a bird. A bird flying above the treetops.

Tilly had never seen the tops of trees before. It was amazing, like looking down on enormous cushiony mushrooms.

She laughed out loud. She was a bird soaring in a blue sky, so high she felt that she only had to reach out to touch the clouds.

Then George began to turn and now she was a bird winging above the mill and the shining river. Far below the turning waterwheel splashed a million sparkling diamonds of water. On the river, swans with necks like George's swam like little stately boats. Tiny cows grazed the fields. From up here she could see how the river ran, on through field and forest towards the village where her father lingered.

Now Tilly heard a strange noise. It was like humming, a deep strong droning somewhere between a shout and a murmur. It made the air tingle and it made Tilly feel very happy.

George was singing.

Then, shockingly, the world moved.

It went down and up and down again, and up and down and up, faster and faster. Trees rocked before her eyes. The sky lurched.

Holding tightly to George's beard, Tilly rose

and fell and spun and swung until she hardly knew
where she was.

George was dancing.

He danced and sang and the world whirled and Tilly shouted for joy.

George heard her and laughed. His plan had worked.

As dusk fell, the girl and the grolyhoomp jumped about in the forest clearing and were happy.

That is how they were when the miller saw them.

chapter Eight
Nightmares

The miller had delivered all his flour by the middle of the morning. Then, because his daughter was taking care of all the work at home, he went to the alehouse.

And stayed there.

He drank some ale.

He drank some more ale.

Villagers trickled in and out of the alehouse during the day. The miller drank with them all, and told each one how he was to be related to the Baron, because his daughter was going to marry the Baron's only son.

'I'm celebrating,' he said. 'Have some ale.'

'Have some more ale.'

The day grew hot.

At three o'clock in the afternoon the miller

staggered out of the alehouse. Across the shimmering dusty square he spotted Simpkin Sampkins watching him through the bars of the jail.

'You'll never get my daughter, you putrid poaching piewacket!' the miller shouted. 'She's for Bones-Worse-Than-a-Dragon!'

Roaring at his joke, the miller reeled back into the alehouse.

A tear rolled down Simpkin Sampkins's cheek.

When the miller had spent all his money, the sun

had sunk low in the sky. By this time he was so drunk he could no longer stand up.

So somebody brought his horse. Somebody else fetched his cart. Somebody connected the horse to the cart and somebody else carried the miller out of the alehouse and dumped him in it.

Then all four somebodies shouted, 'Go home!' to the horse, and watched the cart trundle away with the miller snoring noisily on top.

Then they turned to each other and said how sorry they felt for Tilly, and wasn't it a pity that nothing could be done about it, because the Baron's word was law.

Simpkin Sampkins heard them.

'If I was out of this jail,' he said to himself, '*I* would do something about it. Though I don't know what, just at this moment.'

The horse pulled the cart and the cart carried the miller towards his mill, along the track beside the river.

Evening had arrived and the light was fading fast. Midges nipped the miller's face. Bats zipped past his ears.

Although the miller could hardly hear anything because of the noise of ale sloshing in his stomach, and although he could hardly see because of the dying light and the pink mist which had formed in front of his eyes, as the cart neared his mill he thought …

He certainly thought …

He was almost sure …

Was there singing?

Was there laughing?

And what on earth was that huge shape bobbing against the sky above the mill roof, with a midget dangling from it?

The miller shut his eyes. Was it something … or nothing?

He opened his eyes again and the shapes were still there. Dancing.

The miller's heart turned upside down. His stomach slipped sideways.

'Mother,' he moaned, 'I'm seeing things!'

Then the good horse stopped outside its stable and the miller stared up from the cart at his worst nightmare.

Out of it his daughter's voice cried, 'Hello, Dad! Look at me!'

With a cry of fear the miller staggered to his feet and fell off the cart.

By the time Tilly reached him he was snoring again, fast asleep beside the waterwheel which was churning water all over him.

Tilly helped her father to his bed. She took off his boots and covered him with a blanket, praying that when he woke he would remember nothing of what he had seen. Because if he did, there would be trouble.

There was always trouble where the miller was. He was that sort of man.

When this last weary task of the day was done, Tilly headed for bed herself. She was very tired. It had been a hard day and a strange day, but it had ended up being the most exciting day of her life.

Tilly slept on a heap of old sacks at the very top of the mill. As she climbed up the stairs towards it, she paused to look through a window. She rubbed away dust and cobwebs and peered out into the night.

In the dim starlight she could just make out the line of trees where the forest began behind the mill. Low down beneath the branches a pale light glimmered, as if the moon had come down to Earth and was resting on the ground for a while.

'Goodnight, Big George,' she whispered.

The Stranger lay across the clearing. Unfamiliar darkness covered him, except where the glow from his face cast a ghostly pallor on the ground beside his head.

He was looking at the sky and listening. The stars were singing.

The Stranger did not know why this should be, but he felt the music run through his veins and into his heart.

It haunted him.

chapter Nine
Sludge, Bog and Grolyhoomp

In the morning Tilly rose early.

She knew that this day she must set the mill grinding herself, because when her father finally woke he would have an ache in his head like a blacksmith's hammer thumping an anvil, and a moan in his mouth like a bleating sheep. He would be useless for hours.

This had happened many times before.

Tilly had another reason to be about early. She wanted to see her grolyhoomp again.

Still excited by that amazing dance, she sang as she washed her face in a bucket of cold water and brushed her long hair.

She was singing as she ran down the stairs, but when she entered the milling floor, the song died on her lips. Somebody had risen even earlier than she.

Two somebodies.

They were standing on the millstone like warts on legs, waiting for her.

Silas Sludge and Bartholomew Bog were as alike as two peas from a very nasty pod. They were short and leery and the skin of their faces was like wrinkled paper, furrowed into scowls and frowns and grimaces. Both had pointy noses and pointy feet and pointy hands.

The only difference between them, the only way you could tell them apart, was this.

Silas Sludge had crafty, slidy, slippy, grey eyes that were hard as stones and mean as mousetraps.

Bartholomew Bog had rolling, yellow, jaundiced eyes that were never still. He looked like a fever in motion and he was as prim and sniffy as a pedigree cat.

They were bad news, as vile and pitiless a pair of characters as you could ever dread to meet on a dark night, and they looked even worse perched on a millstone pointing their sharp fingers at you at six o'clock on a spring morning.

The Sludge was Baron Lousewort's steward. The Bog was the Baron's bailiff. They were always together, but you could not say they were friends because they were always arguing.

'Don't point your fingers at me, it's rude,' Tilly

said when she had got over the surprise of seeing them there.

'*I* wasn't pointing, *he* was,' said Bog, pointing at Sludge.

'No, he wasn't, *I* was,' Sludge argued, pointing back. For a moment he looked doubtful, as if something wasn't quite right, but he changed the subject and said, 'The Baron sent us.'

'He sent me,' said the Bog.

'No, he didn't, he sent you,' snapped Silas.

The warts moved around their faces like counters.

'What didn't he send you for?' Tilly asked.

'To keep an eye on you, that's what,' Bartholomew sniffed. He was manicuring his nails with a stick and his eyes rolled with concentration.

'To report on your doings,' hissed Silas, stepping off the millstone and waddling across the dusty floor to Tilly. He stopped just in front of her, glared at her with his slippy eyes and pointed a jabbing finger into her face. '*That's* what.'

'No, it isn't,' said the Bog.

'And what's more,' growled the Sludge, 'we're to stay here and watch you until you marry Master Bones.'

'No, he isn't, *we* are,' corrected the Bog.

Tilly's heart sank. If these two horrors were going to spy on her every minute – and she knew they would, right up to the moment Bones Lousewort slipped a ring on her finger – how would she be able to see George?

How would she have any freedom?

It would be worse than being in prison, and with a life sentence waiting at the end of it.

Bartholomew Bog swayed forward to stand

shoulder to shoulder with Silas Sludge. They were both so close that Tilly could see the red veins snaking across their eyes, the hairs sprouting out of their noses and the dirt in the nails of the fingers that stabbed the air in front of her.

She screamed with fright.

Tilly was never certain exactly what happened after that, because she had her back to the mill door and Silas and Bartholomew were facing it. All she knew was that one minute they were threatening her and the next they were whimpering, backing away with eyes popping and warts leaping like jumping beans.

'Take it away!' babbled Bog.

'*You* take it!' gabbled Sludge.

'No, *you*!'

'Yes, me – no, not me, *you*!'

Tilly turned to look and saw an arm, massive as a tree trunk, filling the doorway. From its hand a huge finger probed. The finger was moving across the floor, pointing, pushing and hopping like a leg towards the intruders.

'Aaahh!' screamed the steward.

'Aaahh!' yelled the bailiff.

For once they were in agreement, but it was much too late.

The finger flicked.

65

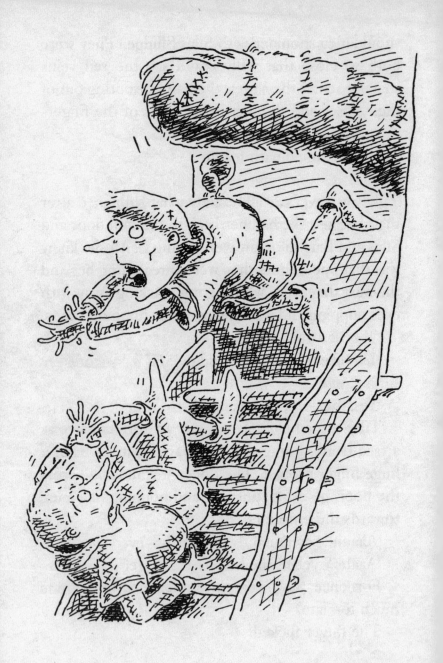

It caught them square on and flipped them head over heels towards the back stairs.

Down they tumbled, waving their short arms and yelling.

At the bottom they picked themselves up and ran for their lives, bursting to tell the Baron about the Great Pointing Finger of Tilly's Mill.

Their tale, and the finger, would get bigger every time they told it.

Inside the mill another door opened and the miller staggered through. He gazed blearily at Tilly.

'Did I hear a noise?' he asked.

Then he saw the finger.

It looked as big as his horse, and it beckoned to him. *Beckoned.*

The miller's face turned to ashes. 'No,' he whispered. 'Oh, no. Please, no.' He closed his eyes.

When he opened them again, it was no better. If anything, it was worse, for now he could have sworn his daughter was sitting on a hand – a hand that filled the mill. *His* mill.

'Slap me with an elephant if I ever touch ale again,' the miller whimpered, staggering back to his bedroom and shutting the door firmly behind him.

*

'Now look what you've done, George,' Tilly Miller said, smiling at the dark shining eye beyond the doorway.

The eye winked at her and a deep voice hummed.

'Grolyhoomp,' it said.

She understood that he meant, 'Good morning, Tilly.'

chapter Ten
The walking Tree

As Silas Sludge and Bartholomew Bog hurried towards Lousewort Castle, which stood on a hill high above the village, an extraordinary noise came sounding towards the mill.

When Tilly heard it she was frightened, for already it was too close to give her time to hide George.

The noise was made up of many different sounds, all borne along the river on the morning breeze.

There was a sound of men talking and shouting.

There was a sound of women and children laughing and singing as if they were going to a fair.

There was a sound of dogs barking.

There was a sound of cats miaowing.

There was a sound of tramping feet, as if the whole village was marching to the mill.

Above all this Tilly heard Simpkin Sampkins's squeaky voice.

'I *did* see it,' he was shouting. 'A walking tree! I saw a whole forest on the move! Wait until *you* see it, you won't believe your eyes!'

The moment Simpkin Sampkins had been freed from jail he had told his story to anyone who would listen. And just about *everybody* had listened, as you would if somebody offered to show you a walking wood.

Now the villagers were coming to see this miracle for themselves.

Tilly gave George a brave smile.

'Stand up, Mr Grolyhoomp,' she said and gestured.

Her voice was sweet as a violin to George's ears. He smiled back at her and rose up like a tower in front of the mill.

Tilly stationed herself in front of his feet, folded her arms and waited.

George folded his arms too.

They stood very still.

'This way!' they heard Simpkin Sampkins shout. 'This way to the place where trees run and branches fly!'

Around the bend of the river they came, Simpkin swinging his arms in front, the people marching behind and the dogs and cats running about their feet.

And they saw.

Their mouths fell open.

They stopped in their tracks.

They saw Tilly Miller, but she was no surprise because they knew her already. The surprise was the thing behind her.

Behind and above her.

Way above her.

When they saw the thing, they laughed.

It's a curious fact that when people come up against something they don't understand, they either laugh at it or they fear it. Or both.

If they fear it they hate it for scaring them, and attack it.

And when they laugh at it, they often attack it too.

That is what happened now.

When the villagers found their voices again, they turned to Simpkin Sampkins and demanded, 'Is *that* your marching tree?'

Simpkin wasn't sure, but he decided to make the most of it. 'Didn't I tell you!' he squealed, looking so wild with his wide, watery eyes and shining, bald head that somebody began to snigger.

Then they all laughed together, and snorted, 'What's that stripy turnip, Tilly? Does it *do* anything? Does it *say* anything? Is it *real*?'

'Say something, George,' Tilly murmured.

The Stranger gazed down at the giggling people. He supposed that since they were Tilly's people they too must be friendly, so he smiled happily and opened his enormous mouth and slowly and carefully spoke the words he had learned from her.

'Ggg-e-e-o-o-r-r-r-g-g-e,' he said. 'Ffo-r-r-rtti-fy.'

'What's that?'

The villagers frowned and muttered to each other.

'What did it say?'

'What was that all about? George fortify? Fortify George?'

'What does it mean?'

'The thing must be an idiot.'

Big George grinned. 'Grolyhoomp,' he said, though he meant, 'Hello'.

'Grolyhoomp!' they laughed.

'Grolyhoomp!' they sneered.

'George is a grolyhoomp,' Tilly explained gently, 'and my friend.'

The villagers roared, but when George did not say anything else or do anything else, their laughter grew bored and bad-tempered.

'We don't want strangers here,' snarled the fat barmaid from the alehouse who had served the miller with ale all the previous day.

'Especially grolyhoomps!' snapped the alehouse keeper. 'He'll drink us dry!'

He threw a stone at George.

That began it.

Suddenly the villagers were all snatching stones from the river bank and hurling them at the grolyhoomp. They bounced off him like peanuts.

'Stop it!' Tilly screamed.

She ran to stop them but the fat woman grabbed her by the shoulders and turned her round.

'Tell that thing to go away!' she hissed. 'Whatever it is, we don't want it here. Tell it to go away!'

Tilly looked up at George.

George looked down at Tilly.

Although the stones were not hurting him he could see that these people were angry. Their voices were harsh and unpleasant, quite unlike Tilly's.

And Tilly was crying now.

George stooped to her.

'Spriglerwkaiytebiooltilly,' he said, meaning, 'Don't cry, Tilly.'

At his movement the villagers shrank back. Now they had laughed and thrown their stones they didn't know what to do next.

'What did he say?' a man shouted.

'Spriggle something,' a lame, ragged woman replied. She waved her stick at George.

'Kityboothingy,' a boy yelled. 'Or something.'

As they stood scowling and muttering, George leaned low and touched Tilly's cheek, wiping away her tear with his finger.

'Friend,' he said in his own language.

One word.

It made no sense to anyone else, but Tilly understood.

She sniffed.

'George,' she said, and smiled through her crying, 'you're a big softy.'

Watching the grolyhoomp and the girl smiling at each other made the people restless. They wanted action. They wanted something to happen.

And something did happen.

In fact, *three* things happened very quickly, all of them bad.

chapter Eleven
OFF WitH HiS HeaD!

The first thing happened when George looked up and saw a tiny shape circling high in the blue sky.

All at once it dropped like a stone and landed on his head.

A crow.

The crow cawed and flapped its black shiny wings. It shuffled about as if making a nest in George's striped hair, and settled down.

'Grolyhoomp,' said George.

'Caw,' said the crow.

The villagers didn't like this one little bit, because it looked like a sign. In those superstitious days people looked for signs or portents everywhere, and crows were signs *and* portents. Crows were bad luck.

It followed that a crow making itself at home on a grolyhoomp's head meant that the grolyhoomp must be bad luck too.

They backed further off and murmured anxiously among themselves. What they murmured amounted to one thing: the grolyhoomp must be got rid of, fast.

But how?

The grolyhoomp was big, very big. It was much too big for them to deal with. They would need help.

That was when the second thing happened. The miller opened his window and looked groggily out at the morning.

As his throbbing eyes looked from left to right, this is what he saw.

First he saw what looked like the entire population of the village huddled by the river, whispering.

The miller didn't like the look of that.

Then he saw that all the dogs and cats of the neighbourhood were there too, frozen like statues with their eyes on stalks and their hair standing on end.

The miller liked that even less. That looked scary.

But it was nothing to the sight that hit his eyes next.

He saw his daughter sitting with her arms folded on the biggest boot he had ever seen. Above the boot was the biggest leg, and above the leg was the biggest body, and above the body was the longest neck, and at the end of the neck was the oddest-looking head you could imagine, striped blue and green.

On the top sat a crow, like a black cherry on a cake.

'Oh, my,' said the miller.

He blinked. Twice.

'Oh, my,' he said again. 'I'm still drunk. I've never been this drunk before.'

As he hung out of the window, the miller prayed that he *was* drunk and that none of this was real.

He was disappointed.

'Good morning, Father,' his daughter called.

'Grolyhoomp,' said the giant with the crow on his head.

'Oh, my,' the miller groaned. 'Oh, my, oh, my, oh, my.'

He started to cry.

Just then thundering hooves, and shouts, and a jingling of harness could be heard. And that was the beginning of the third thing happening.

This third item was very bad news for George.

Into sight galloped a dozen horses. Eight carried soldiers, two bore Silas Sludge and Bartholomew Bog, and the last two brought the Baron and Bones Lousewort.

Silas Sludge and Bartholomew Bog were waving their arms and squealing excitedly. They had not stopped squawking since, puffing and blowing, they had reached the Baron's castle and poured out their incredible story.

They were still pouring, and the Baron was heartily sick of it.

'Finger big as the world,' croaked his steward, who was growing hoarse.

'Not at all,' argued his bailiff, in a piping squeak which was all the voice he had left. 'Big as the sky.'

'Bigger,' croaked Sludge.

'Bigger than everything there is,' squeaked Bog.

'Bigger that that.'

'Bigger, bigger, bigger.'

'Shut up!' yelled the Baron.

It was only to stop their nonsense that he had agreed to come on this fool's errand.

'If you don't stop gabbling,' he threatened, 'I'll cut out your tongues and swap them over.'

The thought of each having the other's tongue and arguing with himself to the end of time closed their mouths tight.

But then the mill came into sight, and the Baron saw what he saw.

He saw the miller hanging out of his window and he saw all his people white as ghosts, and he saw Tilly and he saw …

'Oh, my,' the Baron said.

'What did we tell you?' said the Sludge and the Bog. They spoke with their mouths closed, so that it sounded like, 'Waaaaaaaaiiieeeeeoooo' – which is exactly what the Baron was thinking.

But the Baron wasn't a baron for nothing. He

pulled himself up and pulled up his horse. Then he said, very politely for him, 'Good morning, Tilly.'

'Good morning, Baron,' said Tilly.

She looked very small and very determined.

'Hello, Tilly,' said Bones, baring his teeth in a smile like sick in a bucket.

Tilly gave him a stare which would have melted him off his horse if he hadn't been so dense.

'Come here, Tilly,' ordered the Baron.

'No,' said Tilly.

'Do as you're told.'

Tilly folded her arms tighter and said, 'Why don't you come and make me?'

The villagers gasped, because nobody ever argued with the Baron and lived.

The Baron swelled with fury, for even his highest noblemen did not dare to speak to him like that. Yet here was this chit of a girl … he'd have to sort her out.

But maybe not just at this moment.

'What's *that*?' he asked instead.

'He's a grolyhoomp,' explained Tilly.

'Yours, is he?'

'I think he belongs to himself,' Tilly said.

'Don't be cheeky.'

The Baron rode a few careful paces forward, then stopped and gazed up at George.

'Look here, you,' he snarled. 'I am Baron Grimshanks Lousewort of Lousewort Castle. Get that?'

'G-e-e-o-o-r-r-r-g-g-e,' said George.

'And you are George. All right. Well, George, this is my land and you can't stay on it, so clear off. And, ahem, I'd go quietly if I were you, get my meaning?'

While he was talking, the Baron was eyeing the

grolyhoomp and calculating how much he would eat in a day.

'By George,' he said to himself, 'he'll eat me out of house and home! In a week I'll have no cows or milk left. In two weeks he'll clear me out of pigs and sheep and rabbits and rivers. In three weeks I'll be starving. Well, I'm not having that, thank you very much.'

Frowning, he rode back to his men. 'Chase it away,' he ordered. 'Clear the grolyhoomp out of my territory.'

'Don't even think about it!' Tilly shouted. But

she was growing anxious, for the villagers had lined up behind the soldiers and there seemed such a lot of them against one gentle grolyhoomp.

It wasn't fair.

'Well, get on with it!' the Baron barked, making Bones jump in his saddle.

The soldiers rode a few paces forward, then stopped. Their horses refused to go any further, for which disobedience the soldiers were deeply grateful. None of them was keen to be within grolyhoomp range.

The Baron saw their reluctance and snarled, 'All

right, kill him instead. You can do that long distance.'

'No!' screamed Tilly. 'Don't you dare!'

'Yes!' shouted the villagers. 'Finish him! Off with his blue and green head!'

Tilly looked at George with tears in her eyes and put her arms around as much of his leg as she could manage.

'I'd get out of the way if I was you,' said the Baron with an evil chuckle. 'Unless you want to be splattered as well, of course.'

He squinted at his men.

'Are you ready?' he snapped. 'Right, then. Ready, steady …'

chapter Twelve
A Marriage is Arranged

George was no fool. He knew there was a problem. So he leaned down towards the little squirt on a horse who was doing all the talking and said, 'Hifflethwackserrumptermiff.' Meaning, 'Push off.'

'Beg pardon?' said the Baron, astonished. The hum of George's voice echoed round his eardrums and he had to smack the side of his head to get rid of it. 'Say that again?'

'Ticktockthwackyrote,' George said, meaning, 'I'm warning you.'

'That's just nonsense,' the Baron snorted. 'I won't listen to it.'

Once more he turned to his men.

'Kill him again,' he commanded. 'Kill him twice! Three times if you like.'

But when the soldiers looked up at George, he did not seem quite so friendly as he had before. So instead of advancing, they backed away.

'You bunch of sneaks!' the Baron screamed. 'You panload of cowardy custards! I'll have you shovelling manure for the rest of your days, see if I won't!'

He was so worked up the warts on his face squirmed like ferrets. But when he turned to his son, he smiled encouragingly.

'*You* do it, Bones,' he said. 'Show these jellies how it's done.'

Bones turned a paler shade of white. 'Do I have to, Dad?'

'Of course you do. This is your chance to show Tilly what you're made of.'

'But I feel sick, Dad.'

The Baron foamed at the mouth. 'Is everybody in the world useless?' he ranted. 'I'll give gold to the first man who rids me of this – this *thing*!'

'Hang on!' the miller shouted from his upstairs window. 'I'm coming down!'

The villagers had forgotten all about him, but now they remembered that this miller was the greediest man alive. Why, he would do anything for money, even sell his daughter to a dragon.

So they weren't surprised when he ran among them piping, 'I'll do it! Let me do it!'

'You wouldn't dare, Father!' Tilly screamed.

'Mind your own business, you,' her father hissed. 'You should be getting on with your work, not hugging boots.'

Borrowing a bow and arrow from the nearest soldier, he walked forward, craned his neck, squinted and took aim at George.

'Cover your face, George!' Tilly shouted. 'Guard your eyes!'

George raised his hands, but too late. The arrow bounced off his nose. It hurt.

'Ow,' George said.

'I understood that!' the Baron shouted, jumping up and down for joy. 'I understood a grolyhoomp! Well done, that miller. Kill him some more!'

Now the miller collected a whole sheaf of arrows.

The soldiers, noticing that the miller was still alive, grew bolder and fitted arrows into their bows too.

The villagers also grew brave and gathered stones.

Silas Sludge and Bartholomew Bog loaded catapults.

The Baron drew his sword.

Bones sucked in air and breathed it out again.

This was all too much for Tilly. She knew what

would happen. In her imagination she saw the arrows thudding into George's eyes and the stones flying into his face, and his blood spurting.

He would be hurt, and he was too gentle to fight back.

Tilly couldn't bear it.

She ran into the river, shouting, 'Follow me, George!'

George hesitated.

'Come on!' Tilly pleaded. 'Hurry! Please hurry!'

She swam through the water and climbed up the opposite bank.

Just as the arrows were released and the stones thrown, George turned to follow.

The crow flew away squawking and the weapons bounced harmlessly off George's back as he forded the river and followed Tilly into the forest.

Soon they had both vanished from sight, although for a long time the people at the mill could hear undergrowth crashing and trees splintering. Then that, too, faded away.

'That's got rid of him!' cried the Baron with a self-satisfied smirk. 'He won't come back here in a hurry.' Then he shouted, 'Go home, everybody! The fun is over. Get back to your work!'

Now only the Baron and Bones and the miller were left standing there.

'I want Tilly,' Bones whimpered.

'Stop snivelling,' the Baron snapped. 'You'll have her sooner than you think.'

He frowned at the miller. 'That does it, miller,' he said. 'We've waited long enough.'

The miller was feeling that if he did not get his hands on some gold soon, he would burst.

'So have I,' he grumbled. 'When do I get my money for seeing off that grolyhoomp?'

'The only time you'll see gold,' said the Baron, 'will be when my son marries your daughter. It had better be soon, too, because I've had just about enough of her disobedience and cheek.'

'All right,' said the miller. 'He can have her tomorrow. I'll see to it personally.'

'Done,' said the Baron, spitting on his hands and slapping them across the miller's face. 'A promise is a promise, mind. If you don't keep it, you die.'

'I'll keep it!' the miller cried.

Now at last they were all happy.

Grinning with satisfaction, the Baron and his bony offspring rode away.

The miller watched them depart. As soon as they were out of sight, he ran into his mill, dancing and singing with happiness at the thought of the pieces of gold he could already feel in his hand.

Seconds later Simpkin Sampkins emerged from where he had hidden himself behind the waterwheel, half-frozen, with water glistening on his bare head and oozing from his pale eyes.

chapter Thirteen
Down in the Forest Something Stirs again

Simpkin Sampkins was following the typhoon trail through the forest. He had been tracking it for hours, scrambling over toppled trees and hooking himself on splinters, and he was worn out. But still he kept going, because he was a man on a mission.

Simpkin was a very unhappy man, though. He was unhappy because by trying for once to be a hero instead of a fool, he had led the entire village to see his walking wood and so he had caused Tilly and the grolyhoomp to run away.

Now there was a curious thing, Simpkin thought. He had no idea what a grolyhoomp was and couldn't understand a word it said, but he had liked the look of it very much. He had enjoyed its smile and its sing-songy humming voice, and the warm way it looked at you when it was trying to understand you.

Simpkin was not surprised that the grolyhoomp had failed in its attempt to understand *him*, because he couldn't understand himself.

Mostly, though, Simpkin Sampkins liked the grolyhoomp because Tilly so obviously liked it too.

Yet he had caused it to be stoned and chased away.

He was determined to make up for that mistake, and he also had to warn Tilly about the fate that the Baron and her father were cooking up for her.

He was desperate to *save* her from it.

Simpkin had no idea how he was going to achieve this, but there was no point in worrying about that yet. He had to find Tilly first.

So on he ploughed, over tree and under bush and through the tearing briars.

At last he could go no further. His exhausted legs gave way and he collapsed on a mess of squashed toadstools and hung his head between his knees.

He did not know how long he had been sitting there – he thought he might have fallen asleep – when suddenly a sound made him wide awake.

By this time it was almost dark.

Simpkin had no idea where he was, but that did not worry him because he knew the forest better than anybody and he was sure he could find his way out of it.

What *did* worry him was the whispering.

It came skittering like a little breeze among the dead leaves under his feet. It hummed in the new green leaves over his head. And it came from somewhere very near.

Silent as a poacher – which of course he was – Simpkin crept towards the sound.

The branches of a fallen tree spread in front of him like a hedge. Softly – so quietly that he could have caught an unsuspecting rabbit in his bare hands – Simpkin moved the leaves aside.

This is what he saw.

On the other side of the tree there was a clearing in the forest. In the clearing, in the dim evening light, the grolyhoomp was sitting. Lying on his arm was Tilly.

She was looking anxiously at the grolyhoomp's stripy face and whispering, and he was humming gently back at her.

Now Tilly reached down and scooped up some soil, then reached up and rubbed it over the grolyhoomp's face.

'One of your problems, George,' Simpkin heard her saying, 'is that you have a luminous face. Your enemies will see you a mile off. This will make that harder.'

'Enn-emm-eyys,' said George. 'Ha-a-rrr-dd-errr.'

'Exactly. Another trouble is, you're the wrong size. I mean, you're probably the right size for a grolyhoomp, but around here you stand out a bit.'

'S-t-a-an-dut.'

'Nearly.'

Tilly picked up some more soil, spat on it and kneaded it in her fingers. Then she flung the mud at George's forehead, where it stuck like a small currant on a large cake. She regarded him seriously.

'Have you any idea what I'm doing this for?'

George shook his head.

Listening to this made Simpkin Sampkins feel so guilty that he wanted to stick himself back in jail. But he dared not make a sound, so he stayed crouching in the undergrowth with leaves up his nose and his legs starting to cramp.

'What am I going to do with you?' Tilly murmured, smearing George's enormous nose. 'Everybody wants to hurt you just because you're different. And I'm in trouble too, so what are you going to do with me? What are we going to do with each other?'

George was quiet. He seemed to be miles away.

'You're not paying attention, are you?' said Tilly. 'Here, George, look at this.'

From the depths of her skirt she produced a small, battered but brightly polished spoon, and waved it in front of his face.

She might as well have been waving a matchstick at a tree. George squinted at the tiny shiny thing.

'Ymmylllochmidtilly? What's that?'

'This,' Tilly explained, 'is a spoon. You use it for eating. But you can also use it to see yourself. It's metal – very precious. It's my treasure, see?'

'Tttrrree-eee-szerrr.'

'You're catching on.' Tilly breathed on the spoon and rubbed it with her sleeve, as she had done every day for years. 'This is my mirror, George. Here, have a look and see what I've been doing to you.'

She held up the spoon in front of George's face.

He smiled, looking at her instead.

'Of course,' said Tilly, 'you look a bit twisted in a spoon. Staring into water is best, but you can't carry water in your pocket, can you? Go on then, look at yourself.'

George closed his eyes for a moment. He was beginning to feel very tired. It was a long, long time since he had last been asleep.

Tilly shook her head. 'I can see you're not interested, but one day you will be. So you can have my treasure. It's a present.'

George made no effort to take it, so Tilly pushed it into a pouch as big as a cave in his tunic. 'There, George. From my pocket to yours. Because we're friends.'

'Fffrrenndss.'

They grinned at each other.

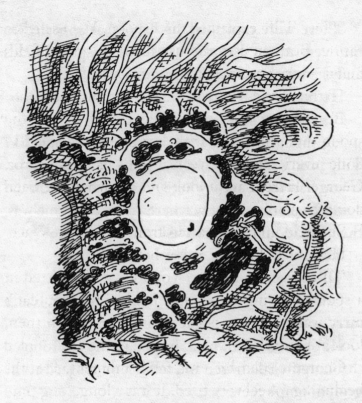

'I wonder what you think of us?' Tilly sighed. 'I wonder what you think of England? Not much, I expect, after today.'

But George was thinking something very different. He was thinking that perhaps the trouble was simply that he did not know these people enough yet to understand them. There had to be a reason why they grew angry and shouted and threw things, and laughed or cried at the drop of a hat. It was just that so far he could not see it.

There were things in this land that appealed to him very much, like the trees and the green fields and the winding sparkling river.

He had liked the crow that sat on his head, too.

But most of all George liked Tilly.

He thought that if there were more people like Tilly in this place, then it was not a bad place to be. If you had to be somewhere – as of course you did – and if you didn't know where your real home was, then this would do very well.

'E-nn-g-ll-a-nn-d,' he said softly.

Tilly laughed.

Cramp gripped Simpkin Sampkins's leg like a vice.

He shrieked with pain, leaped in the air, toppled through the fallen tree and fell flat on his face at the grolyhoomp's feet.

Chapter Fourteen
The Star Man

In the Year of Our Lord 1103 people's lives were shorter, so they hurried things up a bit. For example, they married at a much younger age than they do now.

Even so, Tilly Miller considered that she was far too young to think about marriage. And it was her belief that even if she had been alive a thousand years, it would still be too soon to let herself be hitched to a stinking, scaly, scrawny dragon like Bones Lousewort.

That was why, when the three of them had got over the surprise of meeting like that in the middle of the dusky forest, and Simpkin had told her the Baron's vile plan, she began to think long and hard about what she could do.

Only one idea came to her.

'I could ask the Baron for mercy,' she said.

Simpkin Sampkins shook his head.

'That's a waste of time, Tilly. People like the Baron make rules to suit themselves. They love power and they *never* have mercy.'

Tilly sighed. 'Then what can I do?'

'You could ask your father to change his mind,' Simpkin suggested. 'He *is* your dad, after all.'

'He doesn't act like it, does he?' she said mournfully. 'But it's worth a try. I'll ask him in the morning – it's too late to go back now.'

Simpkin agreed, and soon he and Tilly had settled themselves against the grolyhoomp's side and closed their eyes to get some sleep.

George did not sleep. It was still not his time for rest, although he could feel it coming closer.

With his friends quiet, he lay back and looked up at the sky.

Once again, as on the night he arrived, stars shone down through the forest canopy.

Slowly the galaxies wheeled through their courses.

Shooting stars swooped.

And once again, so deep inside his ears that the sound might have been coming from his own head, George heard the universe singing.

Tilly was not asleep either.

Lying close to George, she could sense his excitement. She felt his arms tremble, heard his great heart beat faster.

She looked up and saw how intently he was scanning the sky. In the starlight his eyes glittered.

Then slowly his arm rose, with a finger outstretched. Up and up his arm reached, up and on until the finger had cleared the topmost branches and was pointing at …

At what? Tilly couldn't tell.

George's arm stayed raised for a long time. Then Tilly felt his body heave a sigh. His arm withdrew and his finger folded in, and he was still again.

Tilly tugged at Simpkin's sleeve.

'W-wha-what is it?' the poacher stammered, startled from a dream of rabbit stew.

'Could you lead us past the mill in the dark?' Tilly whispered.

'Am I the poacher of poachers or am I not?' asked Simpkin. 'And hasn't this grolyhoomp left a track like a highway? Of course I could.'

'Good. Because I want us to go back now,' Tilly said. 'I want to see a man.'

'What man?'

'The star man.'

Simpkin gasped. 'The star man is a crazy man!'

'I want to see him anyway,' Tilly said, in a determined voice that left no room for arguing. 'Can we go now, please? We haven't much time.'

She nudged the grolyhoomp.

'Come on, Georgie, we're going. But move quietly, please. Try not to flatten the whole forest.'

The star man lived in a lonely mud-roofed hovel in the middle of an upland heath which rose swiftly beyond the mill. Gorse and bracken and heather stretched away on all sides as far as you could see.

Tilly had always thought this a very boring landscape, but that did not bother the star man. All he was interested in was the sky, and the night sky at that.

He was a long, lanky fellow with a straggly white beard and a habit of talking to himself. He hardly ever spoke to anybody *but* himself, for the simple reason that whenever anybody was about he was looking upwards and didn't see them.

So far as people could tell – and they did tell, making up new stories about him every day – the star man never ate and never washed and spent his life with his head sticking out of his roof, talking to the sky. So they said he was mad.

But the star man wasn't mad at all. He was just ahead of his time.

Mad or not, Tilly wanted to see him. And she wanted George to see him, crazy though that also seemed.

Because Tilly had a crazy idea.

Simpkin went along because he liked her company and was determined to protect her from harm if he could.

But he was afraid.

It was still dark when they arrived at the hovel on the heath, and the stars were still shining.

As they approached, they saw the star man's head poking out of the roof. He was gazing up in a dreamy sort of way and muttering what sounded like a spell.

'Gemini Cassiopeia Betelgeuse Orion Jupiter Mars.'

The words floated down to them on the night air, fluted in a high, piping, sing-songy voice as reverently as if they were holy scripture.

The sound frightened Simpkin witless.

But to Tilly it sounded like music and it sounded like poetry, even though, like grolyhoomp language, it made no actual sense.

She coughed to attract the stargazer's attention.

'Excuse me, sir.'

Startled, he let his eyes rove the starlit heath until they rested on a small girl and a bald man and the unbelievable bulk of George.

'Great suns in the universe,' he cried, 'what's that?'

'Please, Mr Star Man,' said Tilly, 'this is George. He's a grolyhoomp, and he wants –'

'He's a *what*?'

'A grolyhoomp, sir. I found him – or he found me – and he – no, we – that is, we have a question.'

'A question? A *question*? You want to ask me a *question*?'

The star man grew instantly excited. 'You mean you're *interested?* Well, that is wonderful. Wonderful. That is truly the most wondrous thing. Nobody ever wants to ask me a question. Nobody has asked me a question in years. And I *like* being asked questions, I *long* for it. Hold on, don't go away!'

The head disappeared and there was a crash as if he had fallen off a chair.

'This is madness,' Simpkin Sampkins moaned. 'I can't believe I'm part of it.'

The door of the hovel creaked open and the stargazer appeared, limping. He hobbled towards them. Twitching his beard like an exotic bird ruffling its feathers, he looked warily at Tilly, sharply at Simpkin Sampkins and astoundedly at George.

Since it was impossible to view George all at once, the star man examined him bit by bit, working up from his boots.

As he did so, his expression changed.

The sharpness vanished. The wariness disappeared.

Instead, as his eyes roved on and up over the huge trunk and the gigantic shoulders and the neck that went on for ever, there entered into them a look of wonder.

When he arrived at George's striped head it became a look of awe. Because from his point of view George's head appeared to be in the sky.

Starlight shone upon it. It was surrounded by twinkling lights. It was part of the universe. And most amazing of all, it shone itself, like a grubby star somebody had thrown mud at.

I am a star man, the stargazer was thinking, but this is a man of stars – if he is man at all, which I doubt. The girl says he's a grolyhoomp, and a grolyhoomp he may very well be. Whatever he is, I'm glad to have seen him. This is the very greatest moment of my life.

He blinked and swallowed and tried not to cry, but the thought that this miracle wanted to ask him a question was too much.

'He wants *my* opinion!' he sobbed. 'He has come to *me*!'

It was almost too much to bear.

'Oh!' he cried. 'Ask away! Ask me that question!'

Tilly nudged George. 'Go on, George, ask him,' she whispered. And she looked up at the sky.

'What's that supposed to mean?' cried Simpkin.

'George knows,' said Tilly.

To Simpkin's surprise, George appeared to understand. Slowly his arm lifted and stretched like unending elastic.

A finger unfolded and pointed deep into the blue-black, speckled bowl of the sky.

Simpkin closed his eyes. He could not believe what he was seeing, and preferred not to. It was too scary.

But the star man was so excited that he took the wonder of George's never-ending arm in his stride. He hurried round to where he could gaze up the long line of arm and pointing finger, dimly lit by the glow from George's face.

The star man drew in his breath. 'Is that the question?'

'Yes, that's the question,' Tilly said. 'At least, I think it is. Can you answer it?'

'Certainly I can,' the star man said confidently. 'Do you know, I am *glad* to be asked this question. In fact I am happy to be asked *any* question. I'm *here* to be asked questions, though nobody bothers. It's very frustrating.'

'Answer it then, please,' said Tilly politely.

'Well,' said the star man, 'if your friend is asking the question I think he's asking, he wants me to tell him what he's pointing at. And my reply is that he is pointing at the constellation of Ursa Middling.'

'Ursa what?'

'Ursa Middling. It lies halfway between the constellations of Ursa Major, or the Great Bear, and Ursa Minor, or the Little Bear. But further back.'

'How far back?' asked Tilly.

'Much further back,' said the star man. 'So much further that only I have seen it.'

'Is it far from here?'

The star man nodded. 'It is so far that it is for ever,' he said. 'For ever and ever and ever, that is how far it is.'

'Is there any way of getting there from here?' asked Tilly. 'Or to here from there?'

'That is the best joke I ever heard,' said the star man, though his smile was rather sad.

'Well, thank you very much,' said Tilly. 'We won't bother you any more.'

'Any time,' said the star man. 'I enjoyed that. Any time you think of a question, come and ask it. Ask me another. I like questions.'

Mumbling to himself, he limped back inside. The door creaked shut.

Tilly felt disappointed. She had been hoping for more. But maybe more was impossible to get.

'What was that all about?' Simpkin asked as they picked their way down from the heath towards the shining river below.

'I don't know,' replied Tilly. 'And I don't think George knows either. But I'm sure it was about *something*.'

'Well, that clears it up,' Simpkin said.

Then he nodded towards a faint light that was beginning to show in the eastern sky.

'Here's another something, Tilly. You're getting married today.'

chapter fifteen
Trick or Treat

Nobody was allowed to sleep in Castle Lousewort that night, for the Baron had commanded that everything be made ready for the immediate marriage of his glorious son Bones to Tilly Miller. It was to be the grandest of weddings.

Messengers were dispatched far and wide to invite guests from all corners of the countryside.

The castle musicians were ordered to rehearse their most rousing wedding music.

The cooks in the kitchens were charged to produce the tastiest wedding fare ever tasted.

The maids were commanded to scour the castle from top to bottom and then scrub it all over again, until not a speck of dust remained and everything gleamed so brightly that it made your eyes hurt.

The grooms were required to polish the wedding carriage until they could see their faces in it more clearly than in a mirror.

The result of all these commands was that everyone ran round in a panic and got in everybody else's way.

And the bridegroom?

Well.

Bones Lousewort was getting nervous.

'Do you think this is such a good idea after all,

Dad?' he squeaked as a bevy of barbers snipped and shampooed his hair into curls and manicured his nails and massaged his cheeks until they were redder than a reindeer's nose. 'Am I not too young?'

'Too young?' yodelled the Baron, admiring his new wig in a pewter mirror so dull it made him look almost presentable. 'How can you be too young? Listen, Bones, do you want Tilly or not?'

'Of course I do. But –'

'I don't want any buts. It's lucky for you her father is such a greedy guzzler and I have the money to satisfy him. So be happy, my boy, be happy! I'm preparing for you a wedding feast you wouldn't believe!'

Bones smiled. He felt reassured. There was nothing he liked better than getting his own way, especially when someone *persuaded* him to have it.

The Baron smiled too. This wig was magic, he thought. It would do wonders for him at the feast. Those country ladies would think him the handsomest baron in the world. He was almost happy.

Almost.

There was one cloud on the Baron's horizon. The grolyhoomp.

He had felt uneasy about that strange creature

ever since it had seemed to look right through him. Try as he might, he could not get it out of his mind.

That was why he had commanded his steward and bailiff to get rid of the beast permanently, once and for all and for ever. They were seeing to it right now.

Afterwards there would be no grolyhoomp and no clouds anywhere.

The Baron heaved a sigh of satisfaction.

'I think of everything,' he said out loud. 'I'm marvellous!'

Silas Sludge and Bartholomew Bog were also pleased with themselves, because they had worked out a foolproof plan for geting rid of the grolyhoomp.

They were going to murder him.

They were going to kill him with poison.

Reasoning that George must be getting hungry, they had prepared an enormous platter loaded with every kind of meat, sweetmeat, vegetable, cake and biscuit known to man in the Year of Our Lord 1103.

It looked tempting. It smelled irresistible. It was mouth-watering and scrumptious.

But inside the food, Silas and Bartholomew had hidden every kind of poison known to man in the

Year of Our Lord 1103, from hemlock and deadly nightshade to poison ivy and the venom of toadstools.

Chuckling with happiness and staggering under its weight, they carried the dish to the edge of the forest across the river from the mill.

'This will blow that grolyhoomp's belly sky high,' chortled the Sludge. 'I'm glad I thought of it.'

'It will toast his tonsils. It will grill his gizzard. I'm glad *I* thought of it,' the Bog sniggered.

'No, *you* thought of it.'

'Not at all, *you* did.'

Laughing at their triumph, they placed the platter under a tree above the beach, and retired to watch.

It looked like a picnic.

Soon after this, Tilly and her companions arrived at the mill.

While the others waited outside, Tilly went in to ask the miller to let her off the wedding.

'Please, Father,' she begged, 'I don't want to be married.'

'Tell me you're joking,' he replied jovially. 'Why ever not?'

'Because I don't like Bones,' Tilly said.

The miller gaped at her. 'You don't?'

'I can't stand him. His breath chokes me.'

'Well, hit me with a corncrake,' her father snapped, growing angry now. 'What has that got to do with it? Who cares what you like? You'll do as you're told, my girl, or else! Believe me, marrying Bones will be a walk in the park compared to what will happen to you if you don't.'

Tilly began to cry, but her tears had no effect on the rock-hard miller. Twisting her hair with trembling fingers, she sobbed, 'I'll hang myself!'

'Not until I have my five gold coins, you won't,' growled the miller. 'You can do as you like afterwards.'

'I'll run away then,' Tilly cried.

'Where to?' the miller shouted. 'Where would you go? For miles and miles there's nothing but wolves and wildcats and tusked boars. You'd be breakfast before you got five miles.'

But he tied Tilly's hands just in case, and roped her to her bed.

Outside, morning was breaking. Mist rolled up the river. There was a hint of rain to come.

Simpkin Sampkins snored beside the water-wheel, dreaming of mermaids. They were flicking water at him with their tails, and he loved them in his sleep.

George, hungry and thirsty, sucked water from the river.

As he drank, a delicious smell wafted across his nostrils and made his stomach twist inside him. He had eaten nothing since the crash and he had never felt so hungry.

Following the scent, he forded the river and sniffed his way to the line of trees where he saw a platter heaped with food, lying under the branches as if it was waiting for him.

He was too hungry to ask questions.

Picking up the platter in one hand, he leaned back his head and tipped the food into his mouth, soup, nuts and piecrust.

Silas Sludge and Bartholomew Bog watched him from their hiding place. They patted each other on the back. What a wonderful idea they'd had! In no time the grolyhoomp would be history.

Laughing and skipping they headed back towards Castle Lousewort to tell the Baron that his troubles were over.

There was nothing to stop the wedding now.

chapter Sixteen
The Sacrificial Bride

At six o'clock in the morning, when it was still not fully light, a carriage arrived at the mill.

From it stepped six sleepy maids, each carrying equipment designed to transform a humble miller's daughter into a bride fit for a baron's son to marry.

One maid carried a golden wedding dress.

Another carried golden underwear.

A third bore a silken cushion on which stood a pair of golden shoes, sparkling with precious stones.

The fourth maid held high a golden comb to dress the bride's hair and a diamond tiara to adorn it.

The fifth brought a box padded with silk, containing jars of the finest perfumes of Araby.

The sixth maid lugged a casket studded with

rubies and stuffed with half a hundredweight of jewels, to hang round Tilly's throat and waist and wrists and ankles.

When he heard the carriage approaching, Simpkin Sampkins squeezed himself into the niche in the wall supporting the waterwheel. He lay there curled up and trembling like a sodden mouse in a very wet hole and watched with awe this parade of attendants led by a fat coachman with a squint.

The coachman hammered his fist on the mill door.

Inside the mill, the noise rattled the roof timbers and sent dust falling down in streams. Rats scuttled into their holes. Spiders fled to the furthest corners of their webs.

The miller opened the door and with cringing respect scraped the ground with his head as the maids paraded by.

'Up the stairs, my beauties,' he wheedled, 'go on up, my daughter eagerly awaits you. Do what you like with her.'

When she saw them coming with all this finery, Tilly cried, 'Take it away! I don't want any of it! You'll make me look like a princess and I don't want to be a princess! I don't want to be the Baron's daughter-in-law! I don't want to be married at all!'

Nobody took any notice.

The maids did what they had been commanded to do.

They doused Tilly in freezing water, scrubbed her thoroughly and anointed her with the perfumes of Araby.

They dressed her in the golden underwear and the golden dress.

They brushed her hair till it shone with a golden sheen, and fastened in it the golden comb and dazzling diamond tiara.

They put silk stockings on her legs and fitted the sparkling shoes on her feet.

Lastly they fastened a necklace of rubies round her throat, a belt of silver about her waist, and jewelled bracelets on her wrists and ankles.

Then they held up a mirror so that she could see herself.

Tilly wept.

'I'm not Tilly Miller any more,' she sobbed. 'I'm a sacrifice!'

Now she was dragged kicking and screaming from the mill, lifted on top of the carriage and made to sit there in full view of all the people she would pass on her momentous journey.

For the carriage was to make a triumphal progress about the countryside and then parade through the village to the church where the bridegroom would be waiting.

The Baron had decreed that *everybody* was to see the bride on her wedding day.

Now Tilly could scream her head off and nobody would hear her, because in front of the carriage there marched sixteen trumpeters in scarlet livery, and the sound of their trumpets split the air and made the birds fly off in fright.

As the carriage rolled away, the miller brushed a tear of joy from his eye. He thought he might raise his daughter's price because she looked so beautiful.

As the carriage left the mill yard, Simpkin Sampkins squeezed out of his mouse hole. Wringing water from his clothes and shaking it from his ears, he sighed bitterly to see Tilly looking so lovely, only to be wasted on a ninny like Bones Lousewort.

Simpkin followed the procession at a safe distance, and wondered if there was anything that anyone could do to save Tilly from her fate.

But in his heart he knew there was not. The Baron was too powerful.

And as the carriage began its fateful journey, across the river George blinked at the light filtering down into the cool shade of the forest.

Looking over the water, he thought he saw a carriage leaving the mill with an angel sitting on top, but he could not be certain.

George could not be certain of anything any more.

Because now his waking time was really up. He was already half-asleep. His limbs were sluggish and growing heavier every minute. It was time for him to be in bed.

But there was something else as well.

Something worse.

Something terrible.

There was pain.

The pain was like nothing George had ever felt before.

He felt sick, and every part of his body hurt.

Shivers of agony shot through his arms and legs

and sped like arrows up his neck, where they changed into hammers to beat his skull. His stomach had swelled like a gigantic balloon, and it was still rising. Torture was going on in there.

George rubbed his eyes and blinked and squinted. He could hardly see for drowsiness and pain.

Was it Tilly sitting on top of that carriage disappearing around the bend of the river, or was it not?

Was that her voice he could hear?

If it was, was she crying?

With grolyhoompian effort he struggled to his knees and rocked there, wheezing and groaning.

The trees held hands and swung round him in a ring.

They began to move more quickly – faster and faster until they whirled like a tornado.

And slowly, slowly, slowly, like a tree falling in slow motion, George toppled forward, rolled over on his back and lay still.

The spring weather had changed in the night. There was a dampness in the air.

Now, very gently, with a touch as soft as feathers, rain began to fall.

The drops made circles on the river.

They whispered on the leaves above George's head.

And feathers of rain drifted down on his unconscious face, on and on.

chapter Seventeen
A Wedding Like No Other

Two hours after setting out, at the end of a triumphant procession along a route lined with cheering peasants waving flags and flowers (they had been ordered by the Baron to applaud or else), Tilly finally arrived at the church for her wedding.

The church was a small, simple wooden building set in a green field below the rocky hill on which the Baron's castle stood.

The priest, chubby and smiling, waited at the door while the bride was helped down from the carriage.

It was raining hard now and everyone except Tilly was very wet. All through the journey the maids had leaned out of the carriage doors to hold umbrellas of plaited sackcloth and grass over Tilly's head, keeping her dry while they themselves got soaked to the skin.

They were not happy about this.

Nor was the miller, who, dripping steadily, was waiting outside the church to lead his daughter up the aisle to her bridegroom.

Simpkin Sampkins, squelching along behind the procession, was oozing rain from every pore. It seemed to Simpkin that he had spent days getting wetter and wetter, and that if this went on any longer he would turn into a fish.

Inside the crowded church the bridegroom and his father were dry but growing impatient.

The Baron wore his brightest suit of armour and looked very manly and splendid.

Bones, on the other hand, had been dressed up like Tilly.

He wore a tight, white, choking ruff around his scrawny neck, a scarlet jerkin, short, puffy, blue trousers and a pair of long, yellow tights which clung like a second skin to his bandy legs.

Bones looked a twerp, but a dangerous twerp.

He had a nasty gleam in his eye, and since he had feasted on garlic for breakfast, his breath was more fearsome than ever. Some weaker guests unfortunate enough to be within whiffing range had fainted away, and lay flopped over their pews or in heaps on the floor. Every time they came to, another breath from Bones knocked them out again.

Only the Baron seemed immune, but that was probably because he smelled even worse himself.

At last a bright halloo of trumpets was heard outside, and the church door swung open. The trumpeters marched slowly in, followed by other musicians.

'Father!' Bones gasped in a fit of nervous excitement. 'Oh, Father!'

The Baron slapped him on the back. 'This is your hour, my boy,' he laughed. 'Now's your time!'

They watched eagerly as the procession moved at a stately pace up the church. Musicians, trumpeters, choirboys, pageboys and maids of honour all followed each other, like the animals entering Noah's Ark, two by two.

They were all dressed in the grandest finery, but even so, nothing prepared Bones for the vision of his golden bride.

Tilly clung nervously to her father's arm, but even though she was pale and terrified, she still looked glorious.

Bones's heart flipped inside his meagre chest. 'Ahh!' he cried, heaving a sigh which felled four rows of the congregation. He swaggered into the aisle to greet his bride.

Tilly would not look at him.

The miller pushed her towards Bones, and Bones took her soft fingers in his skeletal fist, but still she would not look at him.

'Look at your bridegroom, Tilly,' said the priest.

But she would not.

'Look at my son, you ungrateful little beast!' the Baron hissed.

But Tilly would not. Instead she turned her face as far away from him as she could.

Bones stamped his foot. 'Look at me, Tilly,' he pleaded. 'If you don't, I shall get in a temper, and I'm not nice in a temper. You wouldn't like it.'

Still Tilly refused to look anywhere near him. She was shaking from head to toe and her eyes had filled with tears at the thought of all the freedom and adventure she might have had but would never get now.

The congregation began to grow restless. They started to whisper to each other and hiss.

'For heaven's sake, look at him, Tilly Miller!'

'Look at Bones!'

'Smile at your bridegroom.'

'Whatever you do, don't put him in a temper.'

'Please don't make the Baron angry, or we'll all suffer.'

'Oh, look, Tilly, for heaven's sake!'

'Look! Look!'

The hisses grew to a shout, and the shout swelled to a roar, and the roar raised the timbers of the church roof, which was quite flimsy.

Tilly shut her ears and tried not to hear any of it. 'I hate them,' she told herself. 'All they can think about is themselves, so I hate them all!'

The noise was extraordinary.

The trumpets brayed.

The viols screeched.

The people screamed and shouted.

The rain hissed down outside.

There was a rattle of thunder.

Altogether there was such a din that nobody heard the strange new sounds enter in.

There was a sound of creaking.

There was a sound of wrenching.

There was a sound of splitting.

Nobody realised what was happening until half the church roof disappeared and rain poured inside on to the heads of the wedding guests.

Then all noises stopped at once.

As one man the entire congregation looked up and saw a grolyhoomp looking down.

The rain had woken George from his sleep-sodden torpor.

He had squeezed rain from his eyes, licked it from his lips and wiped it from his face.

He had gripped his bloated belly to still the pains that writhed in it like snakes.

Then he had heard music.

Somewhere a long way off, trumpets were playing. High and shrieking, they sounded like a girl's screams.

Was it Tilly?

George remembered her cries on the carriage.

What was happening to her?

Like a drunken man he had pushed himself to his feet and staggered towards the noise. Across the countryside he reeled like a sick giraffe.

At last, tired and tormented to distraction by the devils inside him, he arrived at the church. He heard the trumpets inside. The viols. The shouting. He understood none of it.

But then, deep inside the din, he heard Tilly crying.

George understood that. He understood that inside this building something terrible was happening to his friend. But he could not see what it was.

So he raised the roof.

For a moment everyone inside the church was speechless, except Tilly.

'George!' she cried. 'Oh, George!'

George was trying to take it in, but the film of sleep kept slipping over his eyes and the snakes were wriggling along his arms and legs and up his neck into his head, making him giddy.

Through the film and the snakes he looked down at Tilly.

'G-ee-o-o-r-r-g-g-e,' he said. 'Ff-orrt-i-ff-y!'

To the people in the church this sounded like a rallying cry. 'Fortify yourselves!' they thought the grolyhoomp was saying. 'Fortify yourselves against this evil baron and his reeking son, who keep you in poverty and make your lives a misery! Shake off the yoke that has made you their slaves. Fight them!'

'Ff-orrr-ti-ffy,' said George again.

He hardly knew what he was doing. Blinking and

squeezing his eyes, he tossed away the roof timbers and probed down a finger.

Bones thought the finger was coming to get him. He yelled with fright and ran to hide behind the altar.

But Tilly knew the finger was coming for her. She grabbed hold of it and George lifted her right out of the church.

When he saw his son's bride soar into the air, the Baron's face swelled like an overripe pomegranate.

Speechless with rage, he beckoned to his steward and bailiff, and when they crept close, sweating with fear, he swiped them off their feet with two blows of his fists.

Then he signalled to his trumpeters to play the fighting fanfare.

This fanfare was a pre-arranged signal. The day he came to power, the Baron had laid plans to protect his lands and castle if ever they should be threatened by an enemy. Now those plans were to be put into practice.

The fanfare was a message to the Baron's troops.

It was a call to battle.

It was a declaration of war.

Inside the castle, as soon as they heard the silvery squeal echo faintly from the valley below, the

Baron's soldiers gathered their weapons and leaped on their horses.

All the machinery of war, for attack and defence, was made ready in double-quick time.

With a deafening clanking of chains, a drawbridge was lowered over the slimy, stinking moat that surrounded the castle.

And out of the castle, over the drawbridge, into the unsuspecting world, there rode the Baron's invincible army.

chapter Eighteen
Into Battle

The people ran from the church prepared to rally to the grolyhoomp's cry and rise up against their oppressors.

But when they looked towards Castle Lousewort they changed their minds.

This is what they saw.

They saw a hundred horsemen clad in chain mail riding down the steep slope towards them. Each horseman carried an axe and a sword and a spear and rode high upon an armoured steed.

Behind them the wedding guests saw more horses and riders pulling enormous catapults and hauling cauldrons of boiling oil that steamed and hissed in the rain.

Behind those they saw two hundred footsoldiers

pushing a battering ram made from the biggest tree that ever grew in the forest.

The people saw flags waving and pennants flying and armour flashing, and they saw the snorting nostrils of the horses.

They saw Death marching towards them down the hill.

These people were simple and unarmed and unprotected, and the sight scared them silly. They were so terrified that they climbed over each other to hide behind the church for shelter.

The Baron and Bones, followed at a ragged trot by Silas and Bartholomew, jumped on their horses and galloped to ride at the head of their army.

From its leading rider the Baron snatched his great flag embroidered with the Lousewort arms, a scarlet dragon breathing fire. He shook it furiously and roared vengeance on the grolyhoomp and every person in Lousewort land who had the nerve to stand at his side.

The Baron was a terrifying sight.

Bones was less so. He rode behind his father, keeping out of the way.

And the rain rained down.

When the soldiers reached the bottom of the hill, they fanned out into a line and advanced steadily. Right in the middle was the battering ram, and on each side of this there rolled a catapult loaded with boiling oil.

Forward they came. Forward and onward, closer and closer.

George screwed up his eyes at the sight of the approaching army. It was all very hazy, but even so he was fairly sure that these people were not friendly.

He was still holding Tilly in his fist.

Tilly no longer looked like a princess or a bride. Her hair dripped, her tiara hung askew, her dress was smudged and torn and she had lost her golden shoes.

'George!' she cried anxiously. 'They want to kill you. You must protect yourself – you'll have to flee!'

'Grolyhoomp,' George answered.

He tried to smile at her but a terrible cramp was gripping his stomach and the smile didn't come out right.

It looked like a frightening lunatic grimace.

The nearest of the Baron's horsemen saw it and trembled. This was the first time most of them had seen the grolyhoomp that everyone was talking about, and it was even worse than they had imagined.

They looked at the colossal mound of his belly and quaked, for it was *still* swelling. It was growing so enormous that now they could hardly see what lay above it. Then suddenly George's ostrich neck and head were hidden from view altogether.

'Heaven knows what's going on up there,' the horsemen groaned.

The Baron's army halted, twenty paces from the grolyhoomp.

George reached out his arm and put Tilly gently

down behind the wall of the church with the rest of the congregation.

'Stay there,' he said in his own language. 'Fyjkvoatkif eishnnmufpikel.'

Simpkin Sampkins put his arm around Tilly. 'I'll look after you, my girl,' he said.

'Poor George,' Tilly whispered. 'Poor George.'

The Baron and George looked at each other.

'Go away, ugliness,' the Baron sneered. 'This is your last chance.'

'Fortify,' said George. And he belched.

Now a grolyhoomp belch is an awesome thing. It blew the helmet clean off the Baron's head and the flag from his hand.

The catapult captains saw the flag falling and took this to be their signal to action. At a single barked command, the heavy horses winched back the huge hammers.

The catapults creaked and trembled under the strain.

Their wheels nearly lifted off the ground.

The cauldrons teetered.

'Look out, George!' Tilly screamed, running from her shelter to stand at George's feet.

'Leave him alone!' she shouted to the Baron. 'Five hundred to one isn't fair!'

Simpkin Sampkins, with more courage than he

had ever dreamed he possessed, scuttled out like a frantic crab, snatched Tilly and dragged her back behind the church.

Just in time.

The catapult captains shouted their command.

'Fire fire!'

Immediately soldiers tossed flaming torches into the cauldrons to set the oil alight.

Axes cut off ropes.

The flaming cauldrons were catapulted into the air, spraying molten fiery fat in all directions.

At that moment a bell clanged inside George's brain.

Far away, on his world in the constellation of Ursa Middling, a day the length of nine hundred Earth years had ended and an evening curfew was tolling the citizens to their beds.

The curfew had tolled for so long that it had become like a bell ringing deep inside their heads to send them into trance-like sleep.

No one could resist.

And although George was light years away, the bell still rang in his ears, and he could not resist it either. His eyes closed and he began to nod just as the cauldrons came sailing through the air towards him.

One whistled harmlessly past his ear.

The other hit him square on the chin, spitting scalding oil over his face and setting his beard alight.

George's eyes jerked open.

'Ow!' he cried, spinning away from the source of the pain.

'Bend down!' he heard Tilly screaming. 'Duck, George!'

Dimly he saw Tilly and Simpkin beside his feet,

waving their arms. Flames roared in his ears, making such a noise he could not hear what they were saying.

He bent right down to listen.

'Stay there,' Tilly cried. 'Don't move!'

Tilly and Simpkin and the villagers grabbed buckets from the church and raced to fill them from puddles the rain had made all over the field. Then they ran back and tossed the water into George's face.

His beard hissed as the water hit the flames. He spluttered and spat and sighed with relief.

In all this excitement George did not hear the captain of the battering ram shout, 'Forward!'

And because he was looking the other way he did not see the great ram, pushed by two hundred men, come trundling towards him.

Faster and faster it rolled.

Neither did George hear the Baron's command to 'Charge!', and he did not see the cavalry come galloping at him waving axes and swords and spears.

Tilly did.

She shouted a warning but it was too late.

The battering ram hit the crouching George on his backside.

The blow had a most unexpected effect.

The poisoned platter prepared by Silas Sludge and Bartholomew Bog had filled George with billowing poisonous gas. It was this that had blown him up like a balloon.

When he bent down to have his beard extinguished, George compressed the gas to danger level. He became a volcano ready to erupt.

The battering ram was the detonator. As *Crash!* the tree smacked into his rear, so *Crack!* with a noise like a thunderclap George exploded.

Afterwards nobody could remember exactly the order in which things happened next, because they all seemed to happen together.

At the explosion, George's tunic billowed outwards and a wind like a hurricane, stinking a hundred times worse than Bones Lousewort's breath, blew the batterers clean off their ram and the catapult men to kingdom come.

The stench caught Silas Sludge and Bartholomew Bog full blast and wiped them out in a whiff.

The gale tore through the horsemen and hurled them off their steeds. Coughing and spluttering, with their eyes streaming, they staggered blindly about.

In no time the Baron's entire army was reeling and gasping for fresh air.

A grolyhoomp passing wind is an awesome thing.

George himself felt a whole lot better. As the wind wafted across his enemies, he experienced a delicious relief. He rose to his full height and yelled, *'Grolyhoomp!'* with such gusto that it caused a second eruption.

That finished what the first had begun.

Everybody left standing in that invincible army, including the Baron and Bones, passed out on the spot.

Tilly clapped her hands.

'Hooray!' she shouted. 'Hooray for Big George!'

'Three cheers for the grolyhoomp!' yelled the villagers, who could hardly believe their eyes or their noses. 'Hip hip, hooray! Hip hip, hooray! Hip hip –'

They stopped in mid-cheer. They gasped, because something strange was happening to their saviour. Something ominous.

'Look!' they whispered. 'Look, his eyes are closing!'

George's eyes had shut tight. He was swaying from side to side and backwards and forwards and round and round. The triumphant smile seemed to have frozen on his face.

'George!' Tilly cried. 'George, what's the matter?'

Inside George's head the curfew was clanging hypnotically. Like a drum it was beating out the same message over and over.

'*Time to go to sleep,*' it insisted. '*Go to sleep, George. Sleep …*'

George leaned further and further backwards.

Tilly screamed.

'Look out!' yelled Simpkin Sampkins, and everybody ran for cover.

George toppled over.

He hit the ground with a force like an earthquake, and beneath his body the Baron, Bones, Sludge, Bog, the miller and half an army were flattened and buried six feet under.

chapter Nineteen
Goodnight, George

Never had England seen such an astonishing victory.

As George fell, the rain ceased, the storm clouds rolled away southward and the sun came out to shine warmly upon the field of battle.

But there was no celebration.

Tears rolled down Tilly's cheeks as she looked at her fallen champion and felt her heart breaking.

Simpkin Sampkins's watery eyes ran like the mill race.

The villagers doffed their hats in respect for the extraordinary saviour who had sacrificed his life to rid them of a tyrant. They looked at him sprawled on the ground and wondered how they were going to bury him.

It would take weeks to dig a big enough hole.

Then suddenly, with a heave of his enormous chest, George drew a deep breath and blew it out again in a snore like another hurricane.

'Hooray!' they all cried. 'Our great champion is alive! He isn't dead but only sleeping!'

Weeping for joy, Tilly gripped George's finger in her hands and whispered, 'My hero!'

Now they all waited for the grolyhoomp to wake up.

And waited.

They waited until it grew dark, and then they set watches through the night to guard their deliverer against marauding wolves.

They set them again the next night.

And the next.

Still they waited, and still George showed no sign of waking.

It seemed unbelievable, but no matter how much noise they made, or how hard they prodded him, he slept on like a dead man.

Days multiplied into weeks.

One by one the villagers gave up and returned to their homes.

Finally only Tilly Miller and Simpkin Sampkins were left.

Then even they had to give in.

Sadly they turned their backs on George.

Gradually life in the village returned to normal. That is, normal except for the fact that now there was no wicked Baron to bully them. Normal except for the grolyhoomp that lay snoring below the castle in the meadow beside the church.

Rain fell on him, and the wind and sun dried him again.

Everybody was sure that before long he would catch cold, or else the King's spies would come snooping and find him. Goodness knew what would happen to Big George then.

But what could they do about it?

It was Tilly's idea to make a shelter.

Building the shelter took months of labour and noise. George slept through it all.

It was Simpkin Sampkins's idea to make the shelter look like a hill, so that no one would suspect there was anything of interest inside.

So huge earth walls were raised on each side of the sleeping Stranger.

Tall trees were felled and hauled and planted like massive pit props, and over these a roof was spread.

Cunning holes, which could not be seen from the outside, allowed fresh air inside.

At first when the structure was complete, it resembled an enormous dome. But when the people had covered it with turf and sown flowers and shrubs and small trees, it really did look like a hill.

Tilly planted the last flower of all. She planted a wild briar rose and called it Big George.

Underneath the rose she buried a stone tablet. On it she had written, in old Anglo-Saxon so that no Norman conqueror would be able to read it, *'Here sleeps the biggest hero in the world.'*

The flowers of spring and summer, the falling leaves of autumn, the snows of winter came and went, and came and went again.

Big George slept on.

At Tilly's request, Simpkin Sampkins took over the running of the mill. He gave up poaching and looked after Tilly like his own true and much loved daughter, and they were very happy together.

Later, when she grew up, Tilly married and had

children of her own. Then her children had children, on and on, generation after generation.

And as the generations arrived and departed, gradually people forgot all about the hero under the hill.

Big George knew nothing about any of it. He slept quietly, settling deeper and deeper into his nine hundred years' rest.

All this happened a long time ago.

But although Tilly and the villagers faithfully kept the secret of the grolyhoomp so that George could remain undisturbed, with the passing years an extraordinary tale began to be whispered throughout the kingdom.

It told how in a remote village at the edge of a forest, a Stranger had rescued a beautiful girl from the clutches of a monster. With each telling the story grew, until the Stranger became a knight in shining armour and then a saint who had killed a dragon – a real dragon breathing fire.

And so a legend was born.

afterword

Three things remain to be said.

The first may concern you, and it is this.

As the centuries wheeled by, many of Tilly's descendants became travellers and settled across the world.

Today they are living at all points of the compass, north, south, east and west, anywhere and everywhere.

So wherever you are, it is possible that you may be one of them.

The second thing concerns Big George.

Because his secret was kept so well, all knowledge of his whereabouts faded from memory. Nobody now knows where he is, just as nobody ever knew just where he came from in the first place.

But he's somewhere around, peacefully sleeping inside a dome that looks like a hill. Perhaps it is that curious-looking hump near you.

Better go and take a closer look. See if it has a wild briar rose growing on it.

The third thing concerns both you and George, and it is this.

The inhabitants of a star hidden deep inside the constellation of Ursa Middling sleep for exactly nine hundred Earth years.

The events of this story happened nine hundred years ago, more or less.

You know what that means.

It means that unless something unexpected broke into his sleep and woke him early – always a possibility – then any moment now Big George will be waking up and bursting from his shelter like a chicken from an egg.

Some chicken!

Unless, of course, he is awake already.

And that means that any minute now you could see your first grolyhoomp. So keep your eyes peeled. You wouldn't want to miss Big George.

And who knows, you may even be in his next adventure.

Big George and the Seventh Knight

Contents

Foreword
In Days of Old when Knights were Bold

For two hundred earthly years the Stranger slept inside the hill. From time to time, his rest was disturbed by dreams – glimpses of a vast, barren landscape of mountains and stones, lit by a colossal, cold sun. The place meant nothing to him, but it bothered him. Even in his sleep it bothered him.

Then the dreams would fade and the Stranger would sleep undisturbed for another fifty years, while outside his sanctuary history moved on and the world slowly changed.

It is the Year of Our Lord 1305.

Tilly Miller and Simpkin Sampkins, who built a shelter over the Stranger's massive frame and planted grass and trees and bushes and flowers, so that the giant structure looked just like a hill, are dust.

Whole generations with their kings and queens and wars have come and gone. Even Richard the Lionheart and the Crusades are only memories, and now King Edward I – called Longshanks because he has legs like stilts – sits upon the throne of England.

But in the countryside things haven't changed very much. There are more people around than there were in Tilly's time, but even so there are three times as many sheep. More ground is cultivated, but there are still great forests and wastes for hunters and poachers and wild animals. And everywhere people still believe in magic.

Daily life in these 'Middle Ages' moves rather slowly. The horse is the fastest transport, and most people don't even possess a horse. All they have to carry them about is shanks's pony, so they don't travel far from home.

Life could do with a bit of a jolt, really. And it's going to get it, because on this warm June evening something exciting is happening.

Listen!

Do you hear that noise?

Do you hear the shouting and barking and neighing as men and dogs and horses go charging through the greenwood? Can you feel the drumming of hooves on the ground?

And look! Who is this running before them, racing out of the undergrowth like a terrified rabbit and making straight for the Stranger's sleeping ground?

Look! Listen! Helter-skelter, here he comes . . .

chapter one
Surprise For Two

When Walter broke free of the forest he had no idea where he was going. His only purpose was to evade capture, for capture would mean trial and punishment – terrible punishment.

The boy's hands bled, and below his short tunic his legs had been torn in a fall. But he didn't care about that. He felt no pain. There was no time to feel pain.

Daylight was fading as he scanned the wasteland ahead. He saw heath and bog and beyond that open fields and a distant village. Nowhere to hide. He needed somewhere to hide.

A small hill on the heath caught his eye. It was curiously rounded – more a hump than a real hill – and it was clad in bushes and low trees and covered by an enormous briar rose in full bloom. The sun setting behind the hill made its flowers blaze like a hundred fires.

There seemed something magical about that, and Walter, whose head was crammed with stories of wizards and warlocks and witches, needed some magic right now. He thought, perhaps the hill will offer me sanctuary. If it doesn't, I'm done for.

He heard the hounds baying close behind him – too close – and the sound of galloping hooves and the excited voices of men and of women, too. His lord was there, and his lord's lady, enjoying the pleasures of the hunt. But there was no pleasure for him, because he was the quarry.

Walter's heart cried out to the hill and he ran towards it as fast as his aching legs would carry him.

Its sides were as steep as walls. They were too steep for dogs and horses, which was good, and he had to grab the bushes to pull himself up. Under the shrubs it was already dark, but there was not enough cover for complete safety.

The men might see him, the dogs smell him.

Fear gripped his throat like a fist.

I must go higher, he thought.

He reached for a bush above his head, but to his dismay its roots lifted away from the ground. For a frantic moment he thought he would fall. Then, as he began to slide, his scrabbling feet with their

pointed shoes found a stone embedded in the hillside.

The stone held.

Sobbing with relief Walter looked more closely at the straggly bush and noticed a narrow cleft beneath it. He tugged at the surrounding grass and, wonder of wonders, the grass peeled away to reveal a hole wide enough to take the body of a slim boy like himself.

Walter breathed a prayer of thanksgiving and slipped through the gap like a fox going to earth. He vanished just as the first hound burst out of the greenwood.

Now the hunters appeared. There were a dozen of them, with hawks at wrist, swords at side, longbows slung across their shoulders and peacock–feathered arrows sheathed at their backs. While the dogs spilled about their horses' legs, they looked out across the darkening wasteland. All they saw was a mound, black against a bloodshot sky. And all they heard was a blackbird whistling goodbye to the day.

Walter plummeted down the hole like a stone.

Mother save me, he thought, I'm falling into hell.

But he hadn't dropped very far when he was stopped short by something strange. It was neither hard nor soft but something in between, and under his winded body he felt it rising, and falling – slowly, slowly – like waves waxing and waning on a beach.

He thought it might be some kind of quaking bog. He had better move carefully.

It was black as pitch inside the hill, except that away to his right there glowed an eerie greenish light. Swallowing his fear, Walter crept towards it.

The ground beneath his knees felt curiously like fabric, and then – oh help – as he reached out a hand towards the glow his fingers touched something like wire, like bristles, like a beard!

Walter recoiled. He was sure now that he had fallen into the lair of one of the monsters the minstrels sang about in his lord's hall after dinner. But there was no snarl here, no convulsing leap, no terrible snap of slobbering jaws to tear him limb from limb.

Instead, warm gusts of air alternately sucked and pushed him like a wind that couldn't make up its mind which way to blow. And then there was the merest hint of what might have been a snort.

Was the monster sleeping?

Curious, Walter inched forward again – and with a start saw that the greenish light was coming from a face.

But what an extraordinary face! It was

surrounded by hair shaded blue and green and it sent out a light like a lantern.

On top of which, it was enormous – bigger than any face he could ever have imagined. But the strangest thing of all, the thing which made Walter hold his breath with fear, was that although in many respects it looked like a man's face, it wasn't human and never had been.

Walter realised now that he was kneeling on the creature's chest, just below its long – its very long – neck. And to his surprise he noticed a piece of paper pinned to its tunic.

He peered closely in the green glow and saw that it was a note, in scratchy, uneven writing.

It said, simply, 'If found. This is George. He is a grolyhoomp.' Signed, 'Tilly Miller.'

Walter gulped and made the sign of a cross on his chest. What on earth was a grolyhoomp? Was it fierce or friendly? Was this one half alive or half dead? Asleep or unconscious?

He reached for the quiver behind his back and plucked a small feather from one of the arrows. Then, warily, he crawled up the giraffe-like neck, climbed through the wiry beard, skirted the enormous mouth and, taking care not to touch the creature's skin, leaned forward and held the feather under its nose.

He held his own breath and waited for a sign. When it came, the sign was entirely unexpected. The grolyhoomp snored, and in a chain reaction the feather vanished up its nose, produced a sneeze like a thunderclap and Walter, blasted by the explosion, sailed through the air and landed spread-eagled on a foot the size of a very large horse.

Slowly, the feather drifted down and landed on his stunned face.

And the grolyhoomp sat up.

George, who had been immersed in a very deep sleep, blinked and looked about him.

He could see nothing.

George did not understand darkness. For a moment he thought he must be dead or blind, but then he remembered a battle and pain and a small man called Simpkin and an even smaller girl whose name was Tilly.

The thought of Tilly cheered him.

He blinked again to clear the sleep from his eyes and saw two other eyes staring at him from where his toes should be.

It would be hard to tell whose eyes were the most surprised.

George leaned forward and in the reflected light from his face saw yet another very small person.

This one had black wavy hair and wore a short, embroidered, wide-sleeved tunic above scarlet stockings and black, pointed shoes. He looked rather fancy, though knocked about a bit.

For his part, Walter drew his sword. Although he had little faith in its ability to do more than irritate this strange giant, or pick the bared teeth that were bearing down on him, Walter was determined to fight.

Then, with a shock, he realised that the mouth was actually smiling at him. And speaking.

'Gg-ee-oo-r-r-g-g-g-e,' it said.

Walter bowed courteously. 'Walter of Swyre, at your service, sir.'

'Grolyhoomp.'

George was saying hello, but Walter thought

they were exchanging information. He decided to be honest.

'You're a grolyhoomp,' he sighed, 'and I'm an outlaw. Until yesterday I was page to a great knight, but now I have a price on my head.' His lip trembled.

George frowned. 'Ooothmadderwiggley!' he said.

Which meant, roughly, 'But what the blazes are we doing in here? Where *are* we?'

chapter Two
An Outlaw called walter

Something – maybe that toothy smile – made Walter decide to confide in George. So, making himself as comfortable as possible on George's knee, he told the grolyhoomp his story.

'My father, sir, is Robert of Swyre, cousin to my lord Sir Neville de Magott. Until recently he was also his steward and I thought his friend.

'For myself, three years ago on my eighth birthday I was sent to live in Sir Neville's household, to be his page and faithful servant. At first I was content enough – although his rages were frightening and I soon found that he could not be trusted to keep his word.

'I learned how to serve and dress my master and carve at table. I studied manners, and how to read and write, and I was learning the duties and accomplishments of knighthood when . . .'

Walter's voice gave way and he broke off his story to compose himself.

George, who had understood not a word, felt the boy's sadness. He also liked his polite manner, so he leaned forward and said encouragingly, 'Hhrobboonglotl,' meaning, 'Tell me more.'

Walter pulled himself together.

'We were all happy,' he continued. 'Sir Neville had confidence in my father and, I thought, in me, too. But then something happened. My lord Sir Neville's bailiff, one Jeremiah Wormscrode – a treacherous weasel who would tear out anybody's throat if it suited him – was envious of my father's position. So he worked against him by stealth, whispering lies accusing my father of treachery, and turned Sir Neville against him.

'My father was tried in the Shire Court, and because the justices were in the Wormscrode's pay he was proclaimed guilty. Luckily, though, before sentence was passed he escaped with the help of friends and went into hiding. Now he's an outlaw. He could be anywhere. Oh, sir, I fear for his safety, for he's a mild man, and gentle!'

It was anger that stopped Walter's story now. He lifted his head and George saw such a fury blazing in his blue eyes that he was startled.

'My father is not guilty of those crimes!' Walter cried. 'He's an honest, true man! But see how fate has turned against us. The name Robert of Swyre is so disgraced that even to speak it is forbidden. His goods are forfeit. My mother is left alone with no one to protect her – she has nothing and is forced to beg for food and shelter. Meanwhile, Jeremiah Wormscrode is promoted to steward and smiles out of his own backside.

'And I . . .' Walter swallowed. 'I too am in great

danger. "Like father, like son," the parson preached, and Sir Neville believed him, too. He sent men to arrest me but I had word beforehand and fled with the few things I carry. Now I'm being hunted to death, although first Sir Neville will try to use me as a pawn to catch my father.'

The boy looked at the grolyhoomp with the light of destiny shining in his eyes. 'But his men won't catch me,' he cried, 'and they won't catch him! I shall save him – his son will clear his name!'

Even as he spoke, Walter's brain was working overtime, and already an idea was forming in his head. Meeting this grolyhoomp was the most tremendous luck – if he could enlist its help on his quest, why, anything might be possible.

But he was tired and, as they looked at each other in the pool of light from George's face, he felt himself slipping into sleep. He must have dozed for some time before he was woken by cramp gripping his leg, yet when he opened his eyes he found the grolyhoomp still looking at him, unblinking, and he had the strangest feeling that somehow, during his sleep, a kind of understanding had arisen between them.

'Will you help me, sir, in my quest?' he ventured. 'I must warn you there will be great danger.'

'Gug,' George answered.

Puzzled, Walter followed George's gaze, which seemed to be fixed on something behind him. As he turned, the bag around his neck moved and something protruding from the top glinted and caught his eye.

It was his pipe.

'Do you like music, sir?' he asked. 'Is that it? You wish to hear the pipe? I have a tabor drum as well.'

'Gug.'

Somewhere in the back of George's mind the landscape of his dream was gathering again. It hovered hazily – stony mountains, a great, cold sun and, nearer, a dried-up oasis.

Nearer still – just in front of his eyes, so close he felt he could reach out and touch it – the mouth of an instrument gave sweet sounds, and above it the fingers of the player moved constantly. But George couldn't hear the sounds and he couldn't tell whose the fingers were. He was flooded with such longing that tears started in his eyes.

'I asked if you like music, sir?' Walter insisted gently. 'If you come with me I will play for you. I plan to earn my living by performing with the pipe and tabor.'

George focused on him again.

'P-p-l-l-a-a-a-y-y,' he mimicked.

Walter reached behind for the pipe, then hesitated.

What if the sound carried outside? His hunters would have given up the chase by now, but it would be foolish to take a chance on anyone else hearing.

Besides, he might persuade the grolyhoomp to leave his shelter by *promising* music. And, once outside, he might be persuaded to go further.

'My journey will be a crusade for justice and truth and my father's freedom,' Walter said bravely. 'I should be glad of your company if you would give it, and we would see the world together.'

Walter watched the grolyhoomp's eyes narrow as he tried to understand. He held the pipe halfway to his mouth and waited.

'P-p-l-l-a-a-a-y-y.'

Even though he had enjoyed less than a quarter of the rest required in his own world, George was no longer sleepy. He felt curious about this boy, and edgy too, for Walter's urgency had communicated itself to him. 'P-p-l-l-a-a-a-y-y,' he said again.

Walter nodded. 'Outside, sir. I'll play outside.' He slid down George's leg and jumped off his boot. 'But first we have to find a way out of here. I wonder, could you bend this way, please?'

He beckoned. George leaned forward. As he moved, his face lit the shelter like a swinging lamp, and in that instant Walter spotted a row of wooden hinges on the wall near George's feet.

He pressed his shoulder to the wall and heaved. The earth was cold against his sleeve. He pushed again, straining. 'Help me!' he gasped.

'H-e-e-l-l-p-p.' George raised a knobbly finger and laid it against the wall and the wall moved.

'Gently. Do it gently. We don't want to attract attention.'

George pressed again and slowly the wall opened. Stones clattered down. Stems of grass appeared.

Outside it was night, but there were stars and, in the eastern sky, the first glow of dawn. As they looked out a thrush burst into song nearby.

Walter raised his pipe and played, quietly imitating the bird. Backing through the door he felt the fresh air touch his neck like a soft breath. Fronds brushed his elbow. He prayed that George would follow.

The piping seemed to George to come from inside his own head, where the oasis still lingered. He moved towards it and found himself outside with the bird and the stars.

'Zwolloqmiddy,' he whispered, wishing himself and Walter luck because he suddenly felt they both might need it.

Then, after closing the door so that to passers-by the hill looked only a hill again, Big George followed a young outlaw called Walter into the dawn of a summer day in medieval England.

chapter Three
Into the Greenwood

lready in this first light, men and women were leaving the distant village and setting out to work on their strips of the two great open fields surrounding it.

The fields were a patchwork of colours and crops. On the meadow acres the long, waving flowers and grasses showed it would soon be time for haymaking.

But George had no thought for farming. His experience of humans yesterday – to him two hundred earthly years were only yesterday – had made it painfully clear that these people were not necessarily going to be friendly towards him. They might be small but they could be dangerous, so he knew he had better be careful.

He noticed that Walter was also looking

anxiously at the peasants, and keeping out of sight.

But on this open ground it was impossible for George to stay hidden for long, and when the sun rose up above the horizon the workers saw an enormous, shambling figure, silhouetted against it haloed in golden light.

''Tis an angel!' cried one.

'It's the devil!' yelled another.

'It's big – it's bigger than big – and it's coming to get us!' they all howled together. They dropped their tools and fled back to their homes.

'You're not exactly good news, are you?' said Walter, seeing George properly for the first time. He examined the wiry, blue-green hair and beard, the giraffe neck and the unbelievable bulk of this grolyhoomp. 'I thought you'd be an ally in a scrape, but you'll probably get me into the scrape in the first place just by being there. Still, I asked you to come, so I'll have to make the best of it, won't I?'

Walter peered across a mile of wasteland to the dark line of a forest. It seemed to be empty.

'We'd better get you into those trees as quickly as possible,' he said. 'But mind where you put your feet, George. Try not to leave a trail that a blind man could follow.' To show what he meant he tiptoed forward, and George, who thought this was an interesting new way of walking, followed suit.

'That's it,' said Walter encouragingly. 'Tiptoe.'
'Dd-i-i-bb-doo-o.'
In this way they crossed the wasteland, two
figures, forty and four feet high, hunched and
hobbling in the morning sun. All the time George
was looking around for Tilly, the miller's yellow-
haired daughter. But she was nowhere to be seen,
and neither was her father's mill. In fact, the entire
countryside seemed different.
To be sure, its prominent features were still there

– that far-off line of hills, and the shining river looping around the village – but the details were different. This wasteland, those fields, the houses and the people's clothing were all subtly changed.

Seeing this, George knew somehow that Tilly had gone too. The discovery made him sad, for he would have loved to see her again.

But he was also intrigued by the changes and eager to experience this new world, because after the barren landscape of his dream, it seemed more than ever like a magic land. It teemed with colour and life. George was astonished to see the great abundance of flowers growing, the insects crawling below them, the animals scurrying through them, and the birds flying over them in the bright air. The richness of it all was bewildering.

'Coney,' Walter said, as a terrified rabbit skittered away between George's feet.

'C-c-ooohh-n-eee.'

And 'Sparrow,' Walter laughed, when a brown bundle of feathers hitched a lift for half a furlong on George's head. 'That's a bird.'

'B-r-r-i-i-ddd.'

Once they were inside the forest, Walter was a lot happier. He asked George to walk with his knees bent so his head wouldn't show above the trees, and although George found it hard to bend and tiptoe at the same time, he did his best, because he wanted to please his new friend.

Once George had discovered how to move without making a noise, he found he could hear the sounds the forest made and see its life without frightening it away.

He loved the music made by singing birds and rustling leaves, and the sight of some animals feeding quietly in a glade stopped him in his tracks.

'Those are the King's deer,' Walter whispered, 'and this is the King's forest. If we touch them, we're for it – although later we may have to kill one, to eat.'

Walter was determined to walk all day, to put as much distance between himself and Sir Neville's men as possible. By noon, George found he couldn't stand up if he tried. His knees were locked.

They passed an area where the forest had been cleared to make a cultivated field, an orchard and a garden. Smoke billowed through the open door of a small thatched hovel in the middle of them.

Keeping out of sight, George peeped inside the cottage and saw a woman tending a pot over a fire that was burning on the earth floor. She coughed in the smoke. Outside, a man milked a cow under an apple tree and in the garden a girl was spinning wool. George examined her through the trees, but she wasn't Tilly.

The smell of food made them both hungry.

Walter wondered if grolyhoomps could cook. Somehow he doubted it. He couldn't either, for although skinning and cutting up an animal was a skill pages were supposed to learn, he'd always avoided it because it made him feel sick. Likewise on hunting expeditions with Sir Neville he had always made sure he missed his quarry – although since he was skilled with bow and arrow he was sure he could hit his target if he wanted to.

Walter had to admit that there were many useful skills outside his experience, which he'd never needed until now.

He didn't know how to light a fire with nothing but sticks, for instance, and he wasn't very good at finding his way in a forest.

In fact, he was fairly sure they were already lost.

So it seemed certain that if ever they managed to get some meat they would have to eat it raw. But he did not mention this to George.

At five o'clock in the afternoon George rolled over, felling saplings and groaning and rubbing his legs.

Walter, who had been scouting ahead, ran back in alarm, but when he saw George he burst out laughing.

'You only have cramp, George,' he snorted, 'but you've frightened every animal for miles. Now we couldn't catch one if we tried.'

'Cccc-rrr-aaammmppp. Eeeeyii-yyyooo!' George moaned.

At sunset they camped in a clearing a short distance away from the track they'd been following.

George leaned his back against an ash tree that was smaller than himself and watched the red ball of the sun dip behind the trees. Dark birds winged across it like omens.

Walter, meanwhile, was trying to make a fire by rubbing sticks together on a bed of dry leaves, and getting nowhere. When he saw the grolyhoomp grinning at him, he flushed and offered the sticks to George.

'Here, you try,' he said.

Imitating Walter, George rubbed the sticks between his hands and pulped them into dust, burning his fingers in the process. 'Owww!' he said.

Walter shook his head. 'You're no better than me, George. So what are we going to do?'

Just then, a delicious smell of wood smoke and roasting meat came wafting through the trees.

George's stomach lurched.

Immediately, Walter was moving, beckoning

George to follow. He tiptoed until Walter signalled him to stop, and together they peered into another clearing where two savage-looking men were roasting venison on a spit over a fire.

'Poachers,' Walter hissed – too loudly, for at once the men were on their feet, the taller holding out a knife and the other drawing his sword. They glared towards the undergrowth that was shielding George and Walter.

'Come yowt thur,' spoke the knifeman, softly but clearly, while the swordsman flicked his eyes all round the clearing. 'Come you out and show thyzelf.'

Motioning to George to stay where he was, Walter walked boldly forward. He faced the men, erect and proud.

'Why, 'tiz a boy, just!' the swordsman laughed. 'Only a boy. Kill him.'

His companion grinned evilly, pointed his knife at Walter, and slowly pressed it against his throat.

chapter four
The Bargain

Walter winced, but stood his ground.

'George,' he called, very carefully to avoid impaling himself on the blade, 'it's time to show yourself.'

George thought so too. So he stood up.

And up.

And further up.

He stood straight for the first time in two hundred years, sighed with relief, then stepped forward into the clearing and planted a boot as big as a shed in front of the knifeman.

Gurgling, 'Zave my zoul vrom zider!' the man was instantly and copiously sick.

George brought his other foot forward and held it over the head of the swordsman, who thought the sky was falling down on him.

37

He fell to pieces. 'Dunna!' he cried. 'Dunna do uz in!' He screeched like a baby, let go his sword, fell to his knees, wet himself, struggled back up again, and ran.

'Noo noo, dunna leave uz!' screamed his sickly companion, and dropping his weapon at Walter's feet he too left the clearing so fast he made more smoke than Walter and George ever had with their two sticks.

Much later, when they had both eaten their fill, and it was night and the embers of the fire were glowing red, Walter looked up at George's shining face and said, 'Sir, I think we should talk.'

'Tt-o-o-rr-kk,' said George, smiling.

'That's right,' Walter said seriously, 'although I could be speaking French or Latin for all you would know. Yet, I think you understand me even so. That's a mystery. You are a mystery. But there's something we must sort out. It's a matter of honour.'

For a moment George looked thoughtful, then he suddenly leaned down low to Walter and with glinting eyes said softly, 'Sordout. Onner.'

'That is correct,' Walter nodded. 'Honour. You see, when a man of honour receives a favour, he must return it. You're helping me, so I must help you. I have nothing worth giving you except knowledge, but what I know I'll happily share with you. I can teach you about people, George, and the world.'

Walter looked at the size of his pupil and marvelled that he had the cheek to make such a suggestion.

George looked at the size of his teacher, and grinned. 'Ffnishhnoddle,' he said. 'Go ahead.'

'Does that mean we have a bargain?' asked Walter.

'Bb-rraa-gen.'

'Not quite. Listen carefully. Bar-gain. Got it?'

'Bb-arrr-gin. Godditt.'

'Good. Now listen.' Walter pointed above their heads. 'That's a tree, see?'

George stared at his mouth, watching the word take shape. 'Tsadd-rrr-eeeezee,' he mimicked.

'It's an oak.'

'Ooh-kkk.'

'Oak tree.'

'Ohkdree.' George's arm speared the branches and a wood pigeon clattered away squawking. 'Bb-rrr-i-dd,' he added.

'That's right! A bird in an oak tree!'

'Sryt. Abbrriddinnannohkdree.'

'Well done,' said Walter, feeling suddenly sleepy as the day's events began to catch up with him. 'That's really brill . . .' He lost the word in a yawn. 'I'll teach you more in the mornnn . . .' His head drooped.

George closed his eyes too, and listened to the night sounds – the rustlings above his head, the patterings in the undergrowth and the screeches,

barks and whimpers all around.

Clouds covered the moon and the darkness was intense. He still wasn't used to the dark, and it worried him.

For comfort, George reached into the pocket of his tunic and closed his fingers over a small, hard object – the spoon Tilly had held up to his face so that he could see himself. She had given it to him to keep, even though it had been her greatest treasure.

He took it out, held it close to his glowing face

and fingered the cool, smooth surface. It was tiny and fragile, as Tilly herself had been, and holding the spoon George felt he was holding his friend in his hand.

Holding her memory.

Now other faces crowded the darkness.

All the people he had met in this strange world pressed in on him. Behind them, huge shapes hovered and gigantic shadows walked, drawn by the piping fingers of his dream.

George found them all baffling.

But he knew he must look forward, and above all he must learn. The boy would teach him.

Taking a deep breath, George put the spoon back in his pocket. The faces vanished and he felt better, as if a film had been removed from his eyes.

Now he could give this new world some proper attention. He smiled. It had been a surprising earthly day. No doubt tomorrow would be equally astounding.

He was right.

chapter Five
The Girl in the Pillory

George must have closed his eyes again because the next thing he knew the boy was poking him with a stick.

'I'm hungry again,' Walter said urgently, 'and you must be famished. We could maybe find some berries to eat, but I hate berries, and anyway, I can't see berries satisfying a grolyhoomp. So we must hunt and catch ourselves some real food. But we mustn't be seen. Because if we're caught—'

He drew his finger across his throat.

That was a gesture George understood perfectly.

'Come with me,' Walter whispered, 'but come quietly.'

They tiptoed as if they were burglars, with the top of George's head rising above the trees now and again like a blue-green hairy mushroom.

It was early. Mist floated about the undergrowth, hiding all the birds, deer, wild boar, hares and squirrels Walter sought.

Optimistically, he fitted an arrow to his bow. He was looking for a quarry – any quarry. He had no idea what he would do with it when he caught it. The thought of skinning a bloody carcass nauseated him – but he had decided not to worry about that until the time came.

If it ever came, which seemed unlikely, since behind him the grolyhoomp's boots were cracking sticks like fireworks.

Suddenly, Walter sensed something. He held up his hand and George froze, crouching, on his toes.

A shape moved noiselessly through the trees.

Gesturing to George to stay still, Walter crept after it. Within seconds he had been swallowed by the mist and George was alone in the forest.

He didn't move. He waited.

And waited.

While he waited insects crawled inside his beard and bit his eyes. Cramp gripped his legs. The mist wrapped itself around him like a wet blanket. Still he waited.

Then George heard a cry.

In the mist it was hard to tell where the cry came from – it could have been anywhere. But George was sure of two things: it was a girl's voice, like Tilly's, and she was in trouble.

Walter heard it too.

He had disguised himself with branches in an attempt to look like a harmless bush, and now he was stalking the deer along the narrowest of tracks. It was a noble hart with high antlers, and Walter was excited.

The animal paused between two oak trees, lifted its head and sniffed the air.

With his heart hammering in his chest, Walter raised his bow, pulled back the drawstring, closed his left eye and aimed.

Three things happened.

The first was that, as Walter took aim, his attention was caught by a paper pinned to a tree in front of him. On it was a drawing of himself.

His blood ran cold.

Below the likeness bold letters announced:

WANTED
— DEAD OR ALIVE —
WALTER
SON OF THE OUTLAW
ROBERT OF SWYRE
REWARD

Walter gulped. Everybody would hunt him now.

The second thing to happen was the girl's cry. It came from not far ahead and it set the hart bolting, making a kill impossible.

The third thing was as surprising as the others. As Walter turned to go back to George, he fell into a hole.

At first he thought it was a mantrap and he cried out in fear, but it turned out to be just a hole.

It was a very deep hole, though, so deep he couldn't get out.

The girl was making so much noise now that her enemies heard neither Walter's shout nor George blundering through the trees looking for him.

She was tied to a log in the middle of a grassy sward, where three tracks met in the forest.

On a platform facing her stood the jury of twelve men who had decided her fate. Seated on their right were the two justices who had just passed sentence on her, and on their left the verderer, a weasel of a man dressed entirely in green, stood up to proclaim it.

The girl did not care to hear him proclaim it, so she was yelling her head off.

'Stop her caterwauling,' ordered one of the justices, a fat man with folded cheeks and a twitching left eye.

The verderer, law keeper of the King's forest, marched up to the girl and raised his hand.

'Dunna yous touch me!' she cried. 'I en't goin' to let yous hit me, so dunna try!'

Laughing, the verderer clapped his hand over her mouth.

She bit it.

Deep among the trees George found Walter, reached down, curled a finger into a hook and fished him out like a tickled trout.

As he did so they heard the shouting change from a girl's temper to a man's agony. Intrigued, they crept forward to see what was going on.

This is what they saw.

They saw the cross-tracks in the clearing and three areas of grass between them.

One held a low wooden frame with two holes in it close to the ground. 'Those are stocks,' Walter whispered. 'They hold prisoners by the legs.'

In the second grassy area there stood a higher, T-shaped frame with three holes in it – a large hole in the middle and smaller ones at each side. 'That's the pillory,' Walter explained. 'I wouldn't be shut in that for anything.'

'Pp-ill-ooo-rr-eee,' George whispered. 'Sshoottt.'

In the third and largest area they saw fourteen men on a platform, a girl tied to a log and a man clothed in green sucking his hand and dancing.

All the men looked shocked and furious, but none of them was remotely as angry as the girl.

She was livid.

'I told 'im, didn' I?' she was shouting. 'I said I en't gonna let nobody come near, now that's ri', isn' it? An' he did, he did!'

She lunged again at the verderer. The ropes held her back, but even so he jumped out of the way as if she were a sword coming to slice him.

She was a ragamuffin, filthy-faced, tousle-headed, shoeless, wearing a dirty, torn blue dress. Around her neck, an ancient rabbit's foot, worn bare with rubbing, hung on a frayed string. She looked about ten years old.

The twitchy-eyed justice scowled at her. 'Verderer, stop licking yourself and proclaim the sentence,' he snapped.

'I will, yer honner, right away.'

Tucking his injured hand under his arm, the verderer gazed up and down the cross-tracks and around the trees beyond them, then shouted in a voice that scattered birds, 'Oyez! Oyez! Whereas the girl Joanne of . . .'

He looked questioningly at the girl. 'Of where?' he demanded.

'Nowhere,' she hissed. 'I told yous.'

'Have it your own way,' the justice sighed. 'Carry on.'

The verderer pumped himself up again.

'Oyez! Oyez! Whereas Joanne of Nowhere has by this Forest Court been found guilty of the felony of coney-catching in the King's forest, and furthermore of stealing a valuable blue shift from my own washing line – how dare she be so impudent as to thieve from the King's verderer? – and furthermore of abusing the King's officers, she is hereby sentenced to stand for three days and three nights in the pillory in this place, with neither food nor water, there to be seen and scorned by all who pass her. May she repent of her sins or else rot. Oyez. Oyez.'

For a moment, the girl's mouth trembled, but she bit her lip to control herself. And this time, when the two biggest jurymen came to untie her, she offered no resistance. She didn't help them by walking, though, so they had to drag her to the pillory with her feet trailing in the grass.

George and Walter watched as the wooden frame was opened to allow the girl's neck and wrists into the holes, then screwed down tight again.

Now she was helpless, a prisoner with her head and hands forced forward, prey to the gaze of jury, justices – and, unknown to her, a boy and a grolyhoomp.

The fat justice approached her, his left eye jumping.

'Have you anything to say for yourself, Joanne of Nowhere?' he asked.

Joanne of Nowhere spat.

The justice frowned. 'Let pelting commence.'

One by one, the jurymen walked past her at a few yards' distance. In turn, they drew from the folds of their clothing rotten eggs and stale vegetables and mouldy cheeses and threw them at her with great force.

Last of all, came the verderer. He walked right up

to her and pressed a raw egg into her hair. Then he hung the carcasses of two dead rabbits, their feet tied together, around her neck.

Not once did the girl cry out. Her head and hands streamed filth, and the skin of her face was raw, but she didn't cry out. She wouldn't give them the satisfaction.

'*Now*, have you anything to say?' asked the justice.

Joanne of Nowhere glared at him. 'Yiss,' she said grimly. 'I hate yous. I hate yous all. All ri'?'

The justice walked away, shaking his head. His

colleague, who had been silent as death until now, stood up and said, 'This court is now ended. Disperse.'

One by one, the men left the clearing and wended their ways along the forest tracks, going back to their ordinary lives.

The girl was left in the pillory, quite alone, and now at last a tear rolled down her cheek.

Walter looked at George, who would have moved much earlier if the boy had not stayed him with his arm, and shook his head to stay him again.

Then he walked out of the trees into the clearing.

The girl watched Walter suspiciously. She followed him with her eyes as he turned this way and that, tormenting her but coming ever closer. Then swiftly he bent to pick up a lump of turnip, threw it at her and missed.

She snarled at him like an angry cat.

Walter threw another, and missed again.

This time the girl laughed, mocking him.

George had seen enough. If this was a custom of these people, he didn't like it. He rose to his full height and stepped forward.

Joanne of Nowhere nearly fainted.

From her bent position what she saw was a tree with legs walking towards her. She craned her neck to see the branches but the pillory prevented her from seeing past George's waist.

'What's *that*?' she gasped.

'A grolyhoomp,' Walter said.

'What's a grolyhoomp when it's at home?'

'That is,' said Walter. 'Although I don't know whether he's home or not. He seems a little lost.'

'Could he get me out of this? I en't happy with it.'

'No,' said Walter. 'You must take your punishment. Besides, we have other things to do.'

He gazed along all three tracks, chose the least worn and set off down it. 'Come on, George,' he shouted, 'leave the girl there. She's nobody from nowhere.'

George watched Walter vanish into the trees, then splayed out his legs, reached down his long neck and looked at the girl upside-down between his feet.

He liked what he saw, even though she was such a mess. He liked the glint of courage and downright stubbornness in her eyes, and he liked the way she refused to show fear.

He smiled at her.

What Joanne saw she could hardly believe. The grolyhoomp's nose looked as big as the pillory, and each tooth in his enormous grin seemed the size of a door.

'Grolyhoomp,' George said, his humming voice vibrating right through to her toes. 'Hello.'

'Same to you, mister.'

George reached out a hand and lifted the pillory out of the ground with the girl hanging from it. Then he set off with long strides after Walter.

Joanne of Nowhere did not cry out.

She couldn't. She was too busy choking.

chapter Six
Joanne of Nowhere

Walter was waiting for George a little way along the track. When he saw the girl his face fell. 'What did you bring her for, George? Now *you've* committed a crime, so there'll be people after you, too. *And* she'll be jumping with fleas, *and* she'll be dead soon by the look of her.'

The girl's face was purple.

'Glug,' she said in a very queer voice.

George hurriedly set down the pillory and with great gentleness broke it open and set her free. Joanne of Nowhere staggered about, coughing and spluttering. She tried to say thank you, but all that came out was 'aks'.

Walter was furious. Although he had been impressed by her courage in the pillory, he couldn't stand the sight of her now. He was training to be a knight, a nobleman, and she was an offence to his sight.

He pushed her away roughly.

'You're free,' he told her, 'so clear off. Go home.' Then to George he said, 'Come on, let's go and find my father,' and marched away along the track.

George followed on tiptoe.

Two hours later, when they paused to drink at a stream, Walter noticed a movement back the way they had come.

It happened again – a flick of foliage such as a small animal makes when stepping carefully.

He fitted an arrow to his bowstring and crept towards the place, his mouth watering at the prospect of coney or squirrel for lunch.

But what he saw when he parted the bracken was Joanne of Nowhere sitting on the track, picking at the sores on her feet.

Walter shook the bracken violently. 'Go away!' he yelled. The girl squealed and jumped and fled away down the track like the startled rabbit he had hoped she would be.

An hour later she was following them again, keeping her distance but not trying to hide any more, her dress a blue blur in the greenwood. Big George kept stopping to look back at her but, every time, she stopped, too.

Frustrated by such erratic progress, Walter approached her again.

This time the girl stood her ground and scowled at him.

'What do you want?' he demanded.

She pointed at George.

Walter frowned. 'You can't have him. He's not for sale. Who are you, anyway? You'd better answer me properly or I'll stick an arrow in you.'

The girl frowned and bit her lip, but seemed to make up her mind to cooperate.

'Joanne,' she said. 'Jo, really.'

'How old are you?'

'Dunno.'

'Where are you from?'

'Nowhere.'

'Don't say nowhere. Everybody is from some-where.'

'Well I en't,' she cried, her eyes blazing again. 'Leastways, not for a long time I en't. My da was a serf to the Maggot but he died of a fever, and then my ma died of it too, and the Maggot took our house and everything. I was given to another fam'ly, but they beat me so I run away. I bin in the woods ever since, anywhere and nowhere. You tell me to go home, but this is my home.'

All the time she was speaking, she was feverishly fingering the rabbit's foot at her throat.

Walter thought hard. The girl was an outlaw, fleeing from Sir Neville de Magott. That made two of them – three counting George, because you couldn't imagine a grolyhoomp belonging any-where either.

'So, what are you after?' he snapped. 'What do you *really* want?'

Joanne of Nowhere gripped the rabbit's foot tightly. A light entered her eyes. 'I want to be free,' she said fiercely. 'And I'm gunna be free, all ri'? I'm my own person. Nobody owns me. You try to stop me, I'll tell *him*.' She looked at George and smiled to herself, as if already he was her friend.

In the Year of Our Lord 1305 most country people were serfs, or villeins as they were often called. That meant a lord owned them, lock, stock and

barrel. Everything they had was his – they possessed nothing themselves, not even the clothes they stood up in.

It was in the lord's power to make his serfs free men or women if he chose, but that hardly ever happened.

However, there was another way a serf could gain freedom. This was a custom which allowed runaways to stay free if they could escape to a town and remain inside its walls for a year and a day without being challenged or caught.

Such a feat was difficult at the best of times, and next to impossible for a girl with no means. But Jo told Walter that was what she intended to do.

'So why haven't you gone to a town already?' he wanted to know.

''Cos I been hungry, all ri'?' Jo answered him belligerently. 'I'm always hungry. I gets hungry every day. So I have to stay where I knows I can catch food. Besides . . .' she dropped her eyes in embarrassment, '. . . I en't sure where a town is. And if I en't sure where it is, how can I find it?'

Walter laughed at her ignorance. 'Is that why you're following us? Are you hoping we're heading for a town?'

'Maybe. Are yous?'

'No, we're not.'

'But you might be sometime, ri'?'

'It's possible.'

'Well then, I shall go too. But I'm following him, not yous. I'm going with that grolyhoomp. So don't yous try and stop me.'

Walter could hardly believe a beggar girl would dare to speak to him like this. 'Or else what?' he challenged her.

Nowhere Jo jutted her chin, bared her teeth and turned her fingers into claws. She had very long and very dirty nails.

'I'll fight yous,' she said. 'I can fight all ri'. You want to see?'

Walter decided he did not.

'Suit yourself,' he said, and returned to George.

As they progressed, Jo gradually moved nearer, until finally she was walking alongside George, keeping as close as she dared to his enormous plunging feet and peeking up at his face to see if he showed any objection.

George had no objection. He looked down at her and smiled and said, 'Grolyhoomp.'

'Same to you, mister.'

'His name is George,' said Walter coldly.

Jo grinned. 'Mister George.'

'Dibdoo.' George jabbed a finger. 'Dibdoo.'

'Dibdoo?' Jo viewed with alarm the wagging digit swaying above her head like a gigantic pendulum.

'What's he say?' she squeaked.

'We're supposed to be walking on tiptoe so we won't be heard.'

'Oh. Ri'. Dibdoo. All ri'.'

Giggling, Jo sprang silently forward on the balls of her feet, left right, left right, and then they were all doing it, springing dibdoo side by side through the forest, and it seemed such an extraordinary thing to do that they laughed, and George began to sing because he was happy.

His singing was a thrumming that made the trees tremble.

It was a crooning that shook the ground.

It travelled so far and so fast that for miles and miles all the animals cocked their heads at the same time and listened, and villeins working in the fields and woods dropped their tools and scratched their heads and marvelled.

They thought it was an earthquake. But it wasn't.

It was a Georgequake.

After a while Jo said, 'En't yous hungry?'

'We're starving,' replied Walter.

'So why don't yous catch some food?'

Walter looked away.

'If yous had a coney,' Jo asked sharply, 'could yous light a fire to cook it?'

Walter said nothing.

'Yous might be a gent,' she said, nudging him, 'and he might be a grolyhoomp, but you're both useless. Wait here. Dunna leave me.'

She dibdoo'd away and was soon lost among the trees and bracken.

When they had finished eating charred coney, and Jo had doused the fire and covered the ashes with

dust, she looked Walter in the eye and said, 'It's lucky for yous two I decided to come along, en't it? 'Cos I can find my way in the forest. I can sow and reap. I can cook. I can catch birds, coneys, squirrels, badgers. I en't afraid of anything. I en't even afraid of eatin' snails, long as I bakes 'em first. And I can fish with my bare hands, and light fires the same way. I can steal and not get caught – well, mostly. I bet you can do none o' those things, ri'? I dunno about the grolyhoomp, but how would you ask him? So it's lucky for yous I turned up. *En't* it?'

She glared at them. Walter smiled lamely.

Seeing the look of stubborn determination lighting her eyes, George felt a sudden jolt of surprise. He'd seen that look before, in another person's eyes, and loved it.

He reached out to touch Jo's hair. 'Till-ll-y,' he murmured.

Now it was Jo's turn to be surprised, and not just because the touch of that great hand was gentle as a swan's feather.

'You sayin' Tilly?' she asked him.

George nodded. 'Till-ll-y.'

'Well, let me tell you something, all ri'? One of my ancestors was called Tilly. Tilly Miller. She was my great-great-great-great-great-grand-mother. More or less.'

'Who wants to know that?' Walter sneered.

Jo ignored him. 'I know about her, see, because she's famous in our fam'ly. My da told me a story once about how she found a champion who saved her from a fate worse than death. This is her lucky rabbit's foot. Da gave it to me for luck just before he died.'

Suddenly, she rubbed the rabbit's foot furiously with her thumb and forefinger. She stared at George – at Walter – at George again. Her eyes were full of a wild surmise.

'Don't be stupid,' said Walter incredulously. 'If there's any truth in the story, which is unlikely, it

must have happened – what, two hundred years ago? You can't be suggesting . . .' He looked at George and laughed.

Jo shrugged. 'I know it's silly and I en't suggesting anythin'. I'm just saying, all ri'? But it makes you think.'

She kissed her lucky charm, and moved her lips in a little prayer, and crossed her fingers.

As George watched her, and saw Walter stabbing his sword into the earth, lost in thoughts of his father, he felt a surge of affection for them both. He knew they were troubled – he *felt* it – although he had no idea what their troubles might be. He wanted to help them, but he didn't know how. He decided that the best thing to do for the time being was to stay with them and see what turned up.

What turned up was the toughest man in the world.

chapter Seven
The Toughest Man in the world

The man was an ox.

He was big as an ox, built like an ox and he looked like an ox. He could have pulled a plough with each hand. The muscles on his arms bulged like cannonballs. His sun-browned face was battered as a boxer's after a thousand fights – his nose was flattened so much the tip touched his lip, and his ears were like puffy cabbages on the sides of his shaved head.

He looked a hard and heavy man, yet he tripped silently out of the trees in his short yellow smock and pointed shoes like a ballet dancer on dibdoo, and he surprised them all.

One minute they were resting and he wasn't

there, and the next he was in the glade with them, dappled by leafy sunlight and flailing a cudgel round his head as if he would knock their off heads.

'C'mon then, c'mon then, c'mon then, c'mon then,' he sniffed. 'C'mon an' get it. Who's first?'

Walter drew his sword. He stood firm, feet apart, ready to defend and strike. 'Try me, sir,' he said quietly.

Jo hissed and raised her claws. Her mouth tightened. Her eyes blazed. 'Yous c'mon *here*,' she spat. 'See what yous get.'

George, who was so big the Ox hadn't noticed him, lay still and waited to see what would happen.

Still flailing his cudgel, the Ox stuck out his chin, flipped his bushy red eyebrows and jumped up and down on the spot. Twice. 'C'mon, then' he grunted. 'Don't mess wid me now. Nobody messes wid Peter Bullfinch. I can wrestle bulls. I can box bears. I'm the toughest man in the world – ask anybody at the fairs. So, which of you wants this across his ear first?'

Walter pointed his sword at the Ox's throat. 'I am Walter of Swyre, a knight's son,' he said proudly. 'When I become a knight I shall bow to no man. I shall not bow to you now. I can wrestle and cudgel and ride and fight. I shall fight you.'

'So shall I, you fat Bullyfinch,' Jo purred in a voice full of menace.

They began to circle round him.

The Ox was delighted. He jumped in the air and spun on his points. He grinned. Then he lunged forward and stabbed his stave at Walter, who backed away quickly.

While the Ox was distracted by Walter, Jo darted

forward, jumped on to his back and raked her nails across his neck.

She was down and out of reach before he knew she'd been there.

Then the pain hit him.

The Ox roared with surprise and anger. Blood oozed from the scratches.

'C'mon then, c'mon, try that again,' he sniffed. 'Don't mess wid me.'

George was filled with admiration for this boy and girl. The Ox was so much bigger and tougher than them, yet they were bold and unafraid.

He was ready to go to their aid when Walter suddenly lowered his sword.

Jo gasped.

The Ox gaped. 'You messin' wid me, boy?'

'No, sir,' said Walter politely. 'I would just like to know what you want from us. Because we have nothing.'

Peter Bullfinch blinked. He had never been called 'sir' before. Nobody had ever spoken to him so politely. It confused him. All kinds of thoughts and emotions struggled on his face as he looked at Walter's sword and Jo's claws and felt the blood trickle down his neck.

'I wants that thur,' he growled, pointing, 'for my roof tree.'

Walter side-stepped quickly over to Jo. 'This dimwit thinks George's leg is a fallen tree,' he whispered. 'He wants to build his house with him! Let's see where we can take this.'

Jo nodded. 'He looks as if he's had a hundred fights too many. His poor head!'

Walter faced Peter Bullfinch again. 'Do you understand what a deal is, sir?' he asked politely.

The Ox nodded. His small eyes narrowed. 'A deal is a deal,' he said. 'Don't mess wid me.'

'Well,' said Walter, 'the deal is this. If you can lift that tree above your head, you can have it.'

A look of perfect happiness flooded the Ox's crooked face.

He flexed his arms.

The cannonballs swelled and hardened.

He rose on his toes, tripped lightly over to George, dropped his cudgel, set his legs apart, lowered his torso and gripped George's thigh like a balletic weightlifter.

'Watch this,' he grunted.

George slanted an eye towards Walter, who shook his head imperceptibly. So George lay still, his leg straight and hard as an oak tree.

Peter Bullfinch heaved.

Nothing happened.

'You watching me? You ready? Ooooooh!'

He strained and tugged, but still nothing happened. George did not even blink.

The Ox wiped sweat from his brow. He sniffed. He glanced shiftily at Jo and Walter, who were trying to keep their faces straight, then turned his attention once more to his 'roof tree'.

'C'mon then,' he said, hoping for third-time lucky. 'C'mon, c'mon, c'mon, c'mon, tree. Don't mess wid me, tree. Nobody messes wid Peter Bullfinch. Aaaahhhhh-hhh! Ooooaahhhh-hhh!'

His face contorted and scarlet, the veins standing out like ropes, the Ox hauled with all his might and screamed with the effort he was making. And just when it looked as if he must burst like an overstretched bubble, Walter gave a nod and George kicked his leg in the air.

His knee caught the Ox a crunching blow under the jaw and helped him perform four and a half cartwheels through the leafy glade before landing on his head.

George lowered his leg again.

Jo shrieked helplessly.

Walter choked.

The Ox got up and wandered round in circles. 'I lifted a tree!' he gurgled, to nobody in particular because all he could see were shapes swinging round him in a red mist. 'Nobody messes wid Peter Bullfinch! Now that tree is mine!'

But when he was finally able to stand still and see more clearly, he spotted his cudgel in Walter's hand. 'Thass mine,' he blinked. 'Giz.'

Walter smiled amiably. 'Here's another deal, Mr Bullfinch. If I can make that tree walk, it's mine and I get to keep the cudgel. How's that?'

The Ox tapped the side of his nose wisely. 'You're messin' wid me again,' he sniggered. 'Nobody can make a tree walk.'

'Is it a deal?'

'Or are yous a coward?' purred Jo.

'Deal,' said the Ox sharply. 'C'mon then, c'mon then, make that tree walk.'

Walter crossed to George's leg and waved his arms at it. 'Abracadabra,' he cried in a wailing voice. 'Walk, tree.'

He winked at George and gave a little lift of his head.

Jo prayed that George would understand.

He did.

He flexed his leg.

He raised his knee and drew his foot backwards.

Peter Bullfinch, the toughest man in the world, whimpered. 'Tha's not possible,' he moaned. 'C'mon, stop messin' wid me.' His eyes popped as George's knee rose higher and higher.

Then George flexed his other leg.

'There's two trees!' the Ox yelped, his voice squealing into falsetto. 'No, three!' as George raised his right arm. 'No, four! There's four trees!'

And just as a poacher called Simpkin Sampkins had done two hundred years before when he thought he saw a walking wood, so now Peter Bullfinch fell to his knees and closed his eyes and prayed properly for the first time in his life.

When he opened them again, he saw not just four trees but another one even bigger, and this tree was sitting up, actually sitting up, and it had a face on a pole which leaned down over him and spoke words.

Well, it made noises.

'Grolyhoomp,' it said, in a voice that hummed like the lowest drone of the deepest bagpipe in the world. 'Zwolloqmiddy.'

When Peter Bullfinch, the toughest man in the world, heard a tree play the bagpipes, he fainted clean away.

chapter Eight
George Builds a House

For more than a year the Ox had been fighting his greatest battle: how to wrestle good land from wasteland.

When he regained consciousness, the bewildered man took Walter, Jo and George to see what he called his 'paradise' – a place where many years ago the forest had given way to marsh and heath and where now, with the Ox's help, that wasteland was being turned into a farm.

In this open space the sun shone unimpeded. The air rang with the songs of different birds to those in the forest. It was here that Peter Bullfinch, a runaway himself, had ploughed and sown, a pioneer setting himself the task of controlling nature.

Day after day, year after year, he had sniffed and

shaken his battered head and grunted, 'C'mon, c'mon, don't mess wid me, ground.'

The results of his labours were a strip of green corn, a patch of grass, a square of straggly vegetables, eight small apple trees and a lot of weeds. Half a dozen sheep were tethered to posts, along with one cow. A couple of pigs snuffled about.

It really did look like a rough little paradise, and Peter Bullfinch was as proud of it as if it had been a kingdom.

'Tha's all mine,' he crowed, waving his arm expansively as they emerged from the trees.

All the livestock, he said, were prizes he'd won by wrestling and boxing at fairs. He would fight for a ram next, and then there would be lambs, and he would have a real farm.

He grinned happily and bounded towards a heap of timbers perched untidily beside the grass, with a tiny heap of rags on top.

'Mudder!' the Ox shouted, 'look who's come to help us!'

He scooped up the rags into his wrestler's arms and bounded back holding them high, as lightly as if they truly had been only rags or feathers.

But they weren't feathers and they weren't quite rags, they were clothes.

Inside them was a hunched little widow woman.

Two black eyes shone like coals deep inside her nut brown face. They glanced sharply at Jo, then at Walter. When they reached Big George they didn't blink, they just stared. She looked about a hundred years old, though probably she was less than sixty.

'Meet my liddle mudder,' Peter Bullfinch said proudly.

'What's that?' asked the widow woman, stabbing a crooked finger towards George.

'Tha's a grolyhoomp, Ma,' Peter Bullfinch whispered. 'Be polite.'

The Ox was totally in awe of George. He nodded towards a tree trunk dangling from George's hand and murmured, 'See that, Ma? He's going to help us wid the house.'

George looked at her. 'Grolyhoomp,' he smiled.

'Humph,' replied the widow woman. She looked as if she'd seen just about everything during her life, and nothing on earth could surprise her now.

The Ox had tried to build one house already, only to have it destroyed by a reckless hunt when it was half complete.

He described how the huntsmen had galloped headlong out of the forest on the trail of a white stag, and had deliberately ridden through the ropes which were holding the house skeleton steady. They had laughed as it tumbled about their horses' heels.

The Ox was determined that his new house would be too strong to be knocked down – if only he could get it finished. He had scoured the forest for perfect timbers, and rough-carved them to the exact shape and size. His brothers were coming to help raise it. The final task had been to find the big sturdy tree that would literally be the house's 'roof tree' – resting on cruck timbers at the ends and centre, it would act like the ridge pole of a tent to make the structure stable and support its roof.

When Peter Bullfinch had revived from his faint and told the others what he was trying to do, they had all searched the forest and finally found a fallen oak which would do the job almost as well as George's leg. And George had happily obliged the Ox by carrying it.

The Ox could hardly believe that something as magical as a grolyhoomp would actually help *him*. He was vociferously grateful.

'Sire, I will be your man,' he sniffed. 'I won't never mess wid you. Anything Peter Bullfinch can do for you, well . . .' he winked and rolled his cannonball muscles, 'you only have to whistle. Know what I mean?'

Then he gave a piercing whistle himself and four young men came running out of the trees.

They were dressed in brightly-coloured smocks of red, blue, purple and green. George beamed at them – especially at the ones in blue and green – and they gazed at him dumbstruck.

The Ox whispered urgently to them, then danced forward. 'Meet my liddle brudders,' he said, with a clumsy attempt at a bow.

Walter returned the bow, Jo tried a curtsey which didn't come off, and George said, 'Ffing-gothrackywok,' meaning, 'How do you do?'

It seemed the Ox's entire family were runaways.

By God's good grace they were still free – though now speechless.

'I've told them not to mess wid him,' Peter Bullfinch told Walter confidentially, 'and not to tell nobody about him neither. Tha's right, isn' it?'

'Dead ri',' said Jo sternly.

'Or else,' said Walter, pointedly gripping the hilt of his sword.

'Can we build the house now?' one of the brothers asked, nodding impatiently at the tree in George's hand.

Thinking they wanted the tree straightaway, George lobbed it casually towards them. They escaped with their lives by a hair's breadth.

Several hectic hours later Ma Bullfinch was stirring a pot over a fire, watched eagerly by the pigs. It bubbled and steamed invitingly.

George, his mouth watering freely at the smell, straddled the new house frame like a colossus. To Walter's frantic signals and the brothers' shouts and the Ox's yelped, 'C'mon now, c'mon now, c'mon, c'mon, c'mon *now*!' he gently lowered the roof tree towards the waiting notches on the three massive crucks.

Jo was running here, there and everywhere, squinting at angles and measuring dimensions with her keen eyes and screaming the results at Walter who, with as much dignity as he could muster – which was very little, because he was extremely excited – conveyed them to George.

George had very little idea of what he was doing or why he was doing it. In fact, ever since he arrived on Earth without bearings or memory, the things he did, good or bad, had happened more or less by accident. But he desperately *wanted* to understand, and he was beginning to feel that one day he might get the hang of some things about this place.

For now, though, helping Walter and Jo get whatever it was they wanted seemed enough of a task. Trying to think beyond it only made his head ache.

But, suddenly, as George stood holding a tree above the heads of yelping midgets, the dream flashed into his mind again.

There was that cold sun.

There were those distant dry mountains.

There again were the fingers playing on the stem of a pipe. But this time the focus stretched to include the hands beyond the fingers – soft hands that moved with extraordinary grace. And for the first time he could hear clearly the sounds they made, a strange and haunting music that disturbed him through and through.

It was so vivid it made George dizzy.

When the midgets saw the roof tree sway and twitch above them, they cried out in alarm. That woke George from his dream.

He blinked, remembered what he'd been doing, and steadied himself. Once more, he followed the movements of Walter's hands, and slowly, slowly, he lowered the roof tree.

George's arm was steady now, and his aim true. And Peter Bullfinch's work was true. The tree fitted snugly into the crucks and the crucks held its weight without breaking or bending or even creaking.

Then ropes were fastened securely to supporting stakes – and the midgets went wild.

The Ox clapped his hands for joy and pirouetted all the way round his skeleton house.

His brothers cheered and held each other's arms and danced.

Ma Bullfinch stirred the pot twice as fast and sang a very weird song in a very cracked voice.

Jo jumped and waved her arms and shouted, 'Yous bleedin' brilliant, Georgie!' and, as a mark of respect, Walter faced the grolyhoomp, drew his sword, pressed the flat of the blade to his forehead and bent his knee.

George laughed. 'Clyyyngissgwodriyn,' he hummed. 'Will that do?'

Now there came the news they had all been waiting for, as little Ma Bullfinch gave a wheeze and a cough and shouted, 'Food!'

That was only the third actual word she'd spoken since they arrived, but it would have been very hard to find a better one.

'C'mon now, c'mon now, don't mess wid Ma's dinner,' cried Peter Bullfinch, who was delighted with the way things were going. 'Who's gunna get it first?'

He raced his brothers to the pot, and Jo and Walter chased after them. But just as George was going to follow, the day blew up like a firework.

A roe deer burst out of the forest. It streaked through the skeleton house, darted under the roof tree, lunged between George's legs and fled through the tiny orchard on to the wide wasteland.

Behind it, with horns blaring, hooves clattering and hounds snapping, a hunt came charging. And for the second time in a week it headed straight for the Ox's half-finished house.

But this time there was a difference.

This time Big George was there.

chapter Nine
what freedom is

I t seemed to George that the day blew apart in an explosion of noise.

First the deer streaked between his feet.

Next a yelping orchestra of hounds of all shapes and sizes poured out of the trees. And after them whirled hunters on snorting horses, men and women in bright array, riding with bows and arrows and spears and unsheathed swords – and two heralds making even more hullaballoo with their horns.

George didn't like the look of the two leading riders. The first leered most unpleasantly and the second slavered freely through bulbous lips. They looked rather nasty. But there was no time for a close examination because they were galloping towards Peter Bullfinch's house.

The entire hunt seemed to be making for the house.

George was at the house.

And this time he did know what he was doing.

To a forty-foot high grolyhoomp they looked like a gang of very noisy dwarves, but George could see that to his new friends they were a disaster.

He saw the Ox race to the front of his home, open wide his arms to protect it and cry like a baby, 'Mudder, they're messin' wid us again!'

He heard the tiny widow woman chirrup like an anguished bird.

He saw her other sons leave their lunch and scatter.

And as for Walter and Jo . . .

Walter knew he was in trouble when he spotted Sir Neville de Magott's coat of arms – a hawk's left foot sticking out of a pudding – emblazoned on a flag held high by one of the heralds. And when he saw that the leading riders were the Maggot himself and his treacherous new steward Jeremiah Wormscrode – the very people who were hunting him as if *he* was a helpless deer – he jumped for cover behind the remains of the pile of timbers and lay flat on the ground with his hands over his head.

And when Nowhere Jo saw the very man *she* was running away from, the man who 'owned' her and

had taken away her home, she spat like an outraged
kitten and threw herself down beside Walter.

George experienced their shock like an electric
flash in his own mind and moved just as quickly.
With astonishing speed for one so big, he crashed
down a protective foot in front of the house frame
and the babbling Peter. At the same time he opened
his lungs, sucked in enough air to empty the
atmosphere, lowered his head and blew it out with
all his might at the charging hunt.

The hounds didn't like that at all.

One moment, they were yelping with joy at the
prospect of tearing a deer to pieces, and the next

they were yowling with fright because they were flying through the air like wingless birds.

The horses didn't like it any better.

The rush of air hit them full on, stopped them in their tracks, and threw them off balance. Whinnying with terror, they reared and tried to bolt.

The riders didn't like that, nor did they like the tornado. They fought to stay in their saddles. They struggled to control their mounts. They battled against panic.

But when one second you're revelling in the thrill of a chase and the next you're flung into a nightmare of flying dogs and howling horses, it jolts you a little. And at that moment the Maggot, the Wormscrode and the others had so much trouble staying seated, they were quite happy to let their horses turn tail on both the freak wind and the Ox, and the house they thought they'd destroyed the week before.

So it was that in the heat of the moment not one of them noticed what caused the hurricane. No one saw Big George.

By the time dusk fell, the house frame was complete and standing sturdily by itself, and Peter Bullfinch was so happy he gave a party.

He built up the fire, and Ma Bullfinch made a broth with vegetables Peter had grown on the land he had wrestled from the wasteland. There was milk from his cow, and a barrel of cider pressed from his own apple harvest. He was so proud he wanted to cry, and when they had all eaten their fill and he had poured more cider, he proposed a toast with tears in his eyes.

'Let's drink to my house,' he sniffed. 'Let's drink to my mudder and my brudders. Let's drink to my friends. And c'mon, let's drink to grolyhoomps!'

At this, his face crumpled so far that his nose crept right inside his bottom lip. But still he hadn't finished. With great dignity, he raised his mug to George and burped, 'Sire, Peter Bullfinch is your man. Any time you need him . . .'

He couldn't go on. He sat down and sobbed.

George's response was to pick up the cider barrel and drain it.

Afterwards, they entertained each other.

The Ox and his brothers performed a tipsy, jumping dance called a saltarello, which ended when they all fell down.

Ma Bullfinch let rip with a peculiar, wailing chant in a voice so hideously cracked nobody could make head or tail of it. But they all applauded and she smiled with toothless pleasure.

Next, Walter stood up in front of the fire, and with a little piping and a lot of acting he told a story he'd once heard a minstrel sing, about a fearless knight who spent his life searching for a magic goblet, only to die the moment he found it.

It was such a miserable story it made everybody depressed, so it was up to Nowhere Jo to cheer them up again.

Jo didn't know how to do it. She was no good at this sort of thing, she said. She was so shy and scared she wanted to run away, but there was nowhere to run to except the forest, and to her surprise she found she didn't want to go back there by herself. She liked it here.

So she said, 'I'll try to do something, all ri'? But it won't be any good.' Then, very nervously, she began a slow, clumsy, hand-clapping and foot-stomping dance, to a gurgling tune she made up as she went along.

It was terrible. She knew it was terrible.

She was so sure it was a ghastly failure, she wanted to die.

But, suddenly, the grolyhoomp started to sway his great head, and clap and hum along with her, and tap his enormous boot, and that gave her more confidence.

Then Walter did the same, and that made

everybody else want to join in, and now Jo found she was getting excited, so she danced faster and faster until she felt she was whirling at a hundred miles an hour, so fast she hardly knew any more which world she was in.

In the end, she too fell down, but her audience clapped and cheered, and even Walter smiled, which made Jo think that at that moment she was happier than she'd been since her ma died. She winked up at George in gratitude, and he winked back.

By now, everybody was looking at George and wondering if grolyhoomps did any entertaining. Could they sing? Could they dance? And if so, would anyone be safe within a mile of those mountainous feet?

Big George answered them in his own way.

It was dark now and starless, and because the fire had burned low, all the light there was came from George's luminous face. It turned their watching faces green, so that it looked as if they were under his spell.

Which, in a way, they must have been, because as George shaped his lips into an O to produce the low bagpipe drone, all their mouths rounded too.

In this way George told them the story of his

dream – of the mountains and the pipe and the fingers, and how these stirred and puzzled him.

Afterwards, he asked if they knew what it meant. But of course he spoke his own language and nobody understood a single word, so they were even more puzzled than he was.

When George tried to explain all over again, the bagpipe drone of his voice was so soothing it sent them into a trance, and long before he had finished, they were all fast asleep.

Jo was woken by rain splashing her face.

It was quite dark and for a moment she couldn't think where she was – she lay on her back, puzzled by the drops and a sound of hissing nearby.

Then she realised that the hissing was raindrops falling onto the glowing embers of the fire, and, in a tumbling rush she remembered the whole amazing day, from waking up a prisoner to falling asleep with a human ox and a snooty boy and a grolyhoomp.

Jo smiled to herself. This was real freedom – wandering at will and having adventures, meeting people and making friends, living for the moment.

She knew it couldn't last. Soon the boy would find his father, the grolyhoomp would head off home – wherever that might be – and she would be caught and returned to the Maggot for some really bad punishment. And that would be the end of that.

Meanwhile, it was raining and a wind was rising.

Walter stirred beside her. 'Are you awake?' he whispered.

'Yiss.'

'It's raining.'

'Yiss.'

'What shall we do?'

'Get wet, unless you've got any ideas.'

Then there came a word like 'Hngusssllossipussoomp', and they felt themselves being lifted and swung gently and laid down again where it was dry and warm. There was a musky smell and they knew they were lying under George. He was better than any house.

'Magic, en't it?' Jo whispered.

'Magic indeed,' said Walter, in the pompous tone that made her want to stick a pin in him.

How different we are, him and me, she thought – and yet, just now we're the same. The law has turned us both into criminals, even though neither of us has done anything wrong. Where's the justice in that? And here we are, sheltering together under the arm of the strangest person either of us has ever seen.

'He's *like* a person, en't he?' Jo whispered. 'George, I mean.'

'He is,' said Walter sleepily. 'But very big.'

'I reckon he's a person, all ri'. But we got to watch out for him, haven't we? I don't trust people.'

'We must honour him.'

'Honner, ri',' said Jo, who hadn't the foggiest notion what the word meant. 'Honner. Yiss, we'll do that.'

She lay still and thought she could hear George's heart beating. 'I like it here,' she said softly.

'So do I,' said Walter. 'Though it would be better without the smell.'

'I think he smells nice.'

'It's not George I'm talking about.'

'I don't smell!'

'Yes you do, you stink, and it's very unpleasant. You're filthy. *And* you have fleas – I've seen you scratching. I expect it's because you live like an animal.'

Jo was outraged. Her cheeks burned and tears scalded her eyes, but they were nothing compared to the fury in her heart. 'I keep myself clean!' she hissed. 'I en't got no fleas and I en't got no smell, all ri'? It was just those men chasin' me into a marsh. That's how they got me – I was sinkin' in mud. They'd never have caught me else.'

'Well, you reek now,' Walter insisted. 'It's disgusting.'

Jo bit her lip and tried to stay silent, but she lost her temper anyway.

'I'll get clean!' she spat. 'Yous watch me, yous stupid knight with your honner! Jus' watch me!'

She scrambled out into the pouring rain. She lifted her face and her arms to it until she was soaked through and streaming. Then she splashed her feet in the puddles and made sure she splashed Walter too, and stamped about, washing her clothes and her body together, all the time cursing the three great banes of her life.

'Drown all damn an' blasted fleas!' she howled. 'Stick all boys in the damn an' blasted pillory! Shove all damn an' blasted lords in the damn an' blasted dungeon!'

Walter kept silent. It seemed best. You have to be careful with wild things, he told himself.

Later, back in her sanctuary, shivering but extraordinarily clean and fresh, Jo heard George quietly going over his latest lesson.

'Damblass,' he muttered softly. 'Damblassimm. Dibdoo.'

By morning the rain was over and gone and the countryside sparkled as freshly as Jo. After Ma Bullfinch had given them breakfast, her son showed them the way they should go through the forest.

'I've been thinking about your da,' the Ox told Walter, 'an' I reckon I seed him three days ago. Meek liddle chap, wouldn't wrestle wid me. He was a Robert.'

The man had been in the company of a band of outlaws who had passed through the Ox's farm on their way to Swineytown, twenty miles away.

The news raised Walter's hopes of finding his father soon, and Jo was delighted by the prospect of going to a town. If she could hide in Swineytown for a year, her troubles might be over.

As they parted, Walter asked Peter Bullfinch not to tell anyone about George. Peter nodded and looked very tough. 'Jus' let anyone try to mess wid my friend,' he growled.

But it isn't easy to keep something as big as a grolyhoomp a secret.

chapter Ten
Some DUCK

Jo decided that if she was going to be a free
person she had better start acting like one.

That meant learning some manners. The ideal
person to teach her was Walter, but she was too
proud to ask him. Besides, she knew he would refuse.

So she watched him instead.

She followed Walter about. She listened to him
speak. And she copied him. George thought it was
a game and followed suit.

It drove Walter crazy.

By the middle of the morning he couldn't stand it
another minute. He turned sharply and caught Jo
mincing along the track behind him. 'What are you
doing?' he snapped.

'Copying yous, Walter, all ri'?' she answered
belligerently. 'The way yous walk an' that.'

'You'll never walk like me. You walk like a donkey.'

'An' yous walk like a fish!' Jo cried, wounded sorely. 'I dunno why I want to be like yous!'

Walter drew himself up to his full height – which still left him an inch shorter than Jo – and said haughtily, 'You can never be like me. I shall be a knight. You'll be a scullery maid, if you're lucky.'

'I thought knights had chivalry,' Jo pouted. 'Respect for ladies, an' that.'

Unwisely, Walter gave a sarcastic laugh and sneered, 'Are you trying to tell me you're a *lady*?'

She flew at him then. In an instant, she was on his back, kicking, scratching, biting. Walter yelled. He reached for Jo's hair and yanked her head forward. Then he hooked an arm round her neck and pressed her throat over his collar-bone, choking her.

'Will you yield?' he asked.

'No I wunna,' Jo spluttered, and dug her fingers into his eyes.

In another minute they might have damaged each other, but George intervened.

He took Jo in his left hand, Walter in his right, pulled them apart and dumped them both on the top of his head.

'Ssschhnikkkerthropppy,' he growled, meaning, 'Behave yourselves.'

Then he set off walking, and that was when they really started to travel.

George had had quite enough of dibdoo for the time being, so he braced himself and forged through the forest as if it was a field of flowers. Walter and Jo had to grasp his thick hair to stop themselves falling off. Then they had to get used to the swaying of his long neck. But when they'd achieved that, they found they could look sideways at the sky and down on the birds.

It was like travelling by galloping giraffe.

Big George set his nose in the direction Peter Bullfinch had pointed, and went for it. Leaves swished and branches crashed as he stirred the forest like an enormous spoon. You can imagine how dangerous it was up there on his head. But it was exhilarating too. Walter and Jo peeked at each other through the grolyhoomp's hair, and when they saw their own excitement in each other's eyes, they laughed out loud, all differences forgotten.

This was an experience like no other, and sharing it made them friends at last.

As they journeyed, they crossed streams and bogs and wastes, passing distant fields and villages whose inhabitants shielded their eyes to look at them and then hurriedly crossed themselves as if they'd seen something magical and frightening.

Suddenly, they arrived at a great river.

Beyond the river a rolling line of hills stood up like a rampart against the sky. Clustering below them were the walls and fortifications of a small town.

That had to be Swineytown. They had almost made it.

But to get there they had to cross the river.

In those days it was easier and cheaper to travel by river than by road, and the water in front of them was busy with boats, some ferrying passengers, others transporting farm produce, logs and coal.

There were barges with oars, barges with sails, rowing boats, sailing boats and wherries. Heavy horses plodded along each bank, hauling flat-bottomed towboats.

To Jo and Walter, who had never seen a river as big as this, it looked bewildering. To George it seemed as if the entire surface of the water was in motion.

He saw he would have to be careful where he put his feet or he would sink a dozen craft. Even so, as he waded in he caused dangerous waves and the nearby boats rocked crazily.

When they saw George enter the river, the steersmen forgot their tillers and the sailors their sails.

Horses bolted and their towboats dived.

Captains collapsed, crews cringed, and craft collided and capsized.

In no time, the swirling river was littered with upturned boats and swimmers desperately fleeing the monster.

The river was deep. After three steps the water was up to George's chest. Two more and it lapped his beard.

'Do yous reckon Georgie can swim?' asked Jo.

'I hope he can, because I can't,' Walter replied faintly.

Jo thought he looked rather blue about the mouth, and gave him a look which said, 'That's one more useless thing about yous, knight or no knight,' but before she could say it, George stepped into a hole and the water came over his head.

If Walter had stayed calm he might have floated. But he didn't stay calm. He panicked.

He yelled.

He punched the water with his fists as if he would beat it into submission.

When that didn't work, he sank.

But when he came up again, spluttering and still thrashing, Jo was ready for him. She swam up close, trod water and whacked him across the face.

That surprised Walter so much that he stopped punching long enough for Jo to cup his head in her arms and turn over on her back and float, cradling him.

'Yous struggle one more time an' I'll scratch your eyes out,' she panted. 'After that I'll push yous down, all ri'?'

Walter kept still.

As for George, when he first went under he was as shocked as Walter. This was another new experience for him. He'd never drowned before.

The dry mountains swam through his mind, and the fingers moved across his water-filled eyes, and the music of the pipe mingled in his ears with the bubbling rush of the river. It was very strange and beautiful, but George knew that it was also dangerous.

Then he too bounced back to the surface. He felt the sun on his face and the water buoying him up, and suddenly he found he was swimming – clumsily and with a great deal of splashing, but swimming.

George loved it. He paddled about like a duck on a pond. The effect on the river was awesome. Huge waves surged in all directions, toppling more boats and turning sobbing swimmers into screaming surfers. Fish were flung into the air, and Jo and Walter rose and sank and rose and sank until they were seasick.

'Don't let go of me!' Walter cried.

Jo frowned. 'Are yous sorry for what yous said about me?'

'Yes!'

'Say it, then.'

'I'm sorry! I'll never insult you again!'

'And I'm a lady, en't I? Tell me I'm a lady.'

Walter ground his teeth. It cost him a lot of effort, but finally he gasped, 'Yes, you are. You're a lady.'

Jo smiled. Lady Joanne – of Somewhere. It had been worth falling in the river just to hear this snooty knight-apprentice say that.

'Georgie!' she shouted. 'Will yous stop messing about and help us, all ri'?'

chapter Eleven
The End of the World

The watchman on the tower could not believe what he was seeing. He shaded his eyes and scanned eastward a second time, towards the distant river.

This is what he thought he saw.

He thought he saw tidal waves sweeping up, down and across it, although he knew the river had no tide.

He thought he saw all the river craft overturn and their passengers dive into the water as if a hurricane had capsized them, although he could feel there was no wind.

He thought he saw a head the size of several bulls forging through the water, although everybody knows there is no head as big as that.

Therefore, since everything the watchman saw

was impossible, he didn't believe his eyes.

Then, it seemed to him that the head reached the near bank and rose up above it like a pomegranate on a pole.

He didn't believe that, either.

'I'm not cut out for this job,' he thought. 'I get visions.'

For comfort, the watchman looked away, left and right along the town walls. They looked solid enough, thank goodness, and free of mirages. He relaxed a little.

Then he glanced down on his home town. All four gates – north, south, east and west – were wide open for market day, and Swineytown's narrow streets of painted houses bustled with stalls, traders, merchants, pedlars and all manner of town and country folk. Bright shop signs above their heads flashed in the sun. Craftsmen worked inside, making shoes, forging metal, stitching leather, while outside drovers herded cattle, sheep, pigs and geese as best they could through the winding lanes.

It was chaos, but it was always chaos and the watchman loved it. It also stank, but that too was normal.

The watchman's name was Martin, of Watery Lane, Swineytown. He was a short man, square-

bodied, square-headed and square-faced, and he was bowed down with worry.

'It's all very well for our burgesses to say every man must take his turn at being a policeman,' he muttered, 'but I'm a citizen, not a soldier. I'm a butcher, not a constable. They shouldn't put a man like me on duty up here. I can't guard the town. I'm a coward. And I see things.'

He stole another uneasy glance eastward, and this time he saw the pomegranate head floating above the wood that stretched from the river to the town.

'My dad's bottom on it but I'm a sick man,' he moaned.

Then he turned his back on the vision and hurried to tell his Swineytown comrades what he thought he had seen, but of course didn't believe.

Thirty minutes later, Walter and Jo left George lying low among the trees and entered the east gate of Swineytown, in search of news, money and food.

Walter intended to earn money as a travelling minstrel. Jo planned to pick up a few tasty things from the produce stalls.

They would both keep their ears open for news of outlaws and Walter's father.

Jo set out to steal, and on a vacant corner just off the town square, Walter turned himself into a one-boy travelling band. He played his three-hole pipe with his right hand, hit his tabor drum with his left and stamped the ground rhythmically with each foot in turn and sometimes both together.

He was good. He had practised hard at his music lessons, and before long the nearby traders were twitching and tapping their feet. While they were thus happily occupied, Jo picked their pockets.

She was good at that.

Coins were thrown into the cap Walter had placed on the ground beside him. That encouraged a hunchbacked hurdy-gurdy player to join him. Then a stick-thin fiddler arrived. Together they played a jolly saltarello and the market folk hooked arms and jumped up and down the street.

That was a sight to see!

But there was more than people jigging.

There was a bear dancing at the end of a chain.

There was a little dog capering in circles.

And outside the town wall there was Big George.

George liked music. He found its rhythms irresistible. When he heard the jumping dance he gave up lying low, looked over the wall to see what was going on, and pranced about.

When the townspeople saw him, they knew they should be frightened, because according to the rumours, George was probably the beginning of the end of the world. But his glowing, blue-green, hairy pomegranate of a face looked so funny jiggling about up there on its long neck that they laughed instead.

Now, when a crowd of people starts to laugh at somebody because they think he looks odd, it can sometimes turn nasty.

It turned nasty now.

Soon, instead of laughing at George the people of Swineytown were mocking him, and instead of dancing they were taunting, and instead of singing they were jeering. Then they began to throw things at George. Eggs, for instance, and overripe turnips.

Jo and Walter were dismayed. Walter bagged his takings and Jo stole a sack to carry hers, but just when they were ready to run to George, matters grew even worse.

The little capering dog caught the crowd's change of mood and, suddenly, instead of dancing with the bear, he began baiting it.

Other dogs, hearing the rumpus, came yapping and joined in.

The bear's master tried to keep them at bay, but there were too many of them. Then the bear herself became worried, because here were all these dogs jumping at her, snarling and biting, but she couldn't fight back because she was chained to a wall.

She didn't like that.

Neither did Jo, who screamed, nor Walter.

Neither did George.

Three things happened almost together.

First, some people joined the dogs and started baiting the bear as well as the grolyhoomp.

That caused the bear to yank her chain right out of the wall and begin lashing out to defend herself.

And George jumped over the town wall.

When he landed inside, he flattened fourteen market stalls and scattered forty-six pigs, twenty-one cows, thirty-seven sheep and about five hundred geese. Rejoicing in their unexpected freedom they all ran grunting, mooing, baaing and honking through the twisting streets of Swineytown at what seemed about ninety miles an hour.

At first, the folk thought George had come to help them fight the bear, so they cheered him.

But when they realised it was the other way round – which was quite soon because George started protecting the bear by flicking its attackers with his fingers, left and right up the street – he became Public Enemy Number One.

It was pandemonium. The noise was eardrum-shattering, especially when, on top of everything else, George began chuntering 'grolyhoomp' and 'dammblassimm'.

A worried little man with a square head ran into the square. He nudged Jo and muttered, 'This is a proper horse's bottom, isn't it? G-god preserve me from giant pomegranates. But none of it is real, you know. It's just me, seeing things. I'm going to lie down for a bit and then everything will be all right.'

He backed away, wistful and wincing, into the doorway of a butcher's shop, and disappeared.

Then, out of the blue, a fourth thing happened.

Swineytown was invaded.

The first anybody knew of this was when two fat trumpeters staggered into the square and blew a strangled fanfare, which frightened the birds. Behind them, a red-cheeked town crier came puffing and bellowing, 'Oyez! Muster-at-arms! Muster-at-arms! Brigands ahorse! Oyez!'

The result of his announcement was immediate, universal, heart-stopping panic.

Even the dogs took fright and ran away.

The townspeople forgot about the bear.

They forgot about Big George.

They had only two thoughts in their heads – how to preserve their property and their lives. In that order.

George, Jo, Walter and the bear were amazed. They had never seen anything disappear so fast. One minute the streets were stuffed with produce and livestock and the next it was flying into attics, tumbling into cellars and stampeding along dark alleyways.

Windows closed, doors banged shut, and the square and the streets were empty. It was like a conjuring trick.

Swineytown became a ghost town.

George and his friends gazed around in the silence, bewildered and quite alone.

But they weren't alone for long. Somebody was about, somewhere. They heard the sound of tramping feet.

It grew louder and marching into the square there came the most ragged troop of troops you ever saw.

You wouldn't call them soldiers.

They couldn't even pretend to be soldiers.

They were citizens of Swineytown – a ramshackle brigade of shopkeepers, street sweepers, cordwainers, manure pickers and heaven knows what else. Between them they carried some bows and arrows and a few clubs and staves. They all looked very, very frightened.

When they saw Big George they quailed.

'He won't hurt you,' Walter told them. 'He's a grolyhoomp.'

They didn't seem to find that very reassuring.

'He's a friend, all ri'?' said Jo. 'En't yous, Georgie?'

'Dammblassimm,' George said.

The recruits rolled their eyes, but eventually focused on the butcher's shop from which Citizen Martin was emerging, hastily arranging his tunic

and carrying a sword three sizes too big for him.

When he reached the troop he cried, 'Attenshun! Hands up who has the keys to the town gates!'

Nobody moved.

Citizen Martin cleared his throat. 'Hands up who *shut* the gates!'

Still, nobody moved. The troops looked shiftily at each other.

As the implication sank in, Martin's eyes opened very wide. *Nobody* had shut the gates.

His hair stood on end.

Then he looked George straight in the eye, as if grolyhoomping pomegranates were the least of his problems, cupped his hands to his ears – and heard what he dreaded to hear.

George heard it too, and the troops heard it and Jo and Walter heard it and the bear heard it.

They all heard galloping hooves entering the town.

chapter Twelve
Three and a Bear

I n the Year of Our Lord 1305 gangs of brigands, often in the pay of powerful lords, roamed the countryside, plundering manor houses, churches, villages and even towns.

The gang approaching Swineytown numbered fifty leather-jacketed men armed with bows, swords, spears, flails, hooks, knives, crowbars and pickaxes. Thundering along on their half-wild horses they were a terrifying sight.

It was rumoured that they were being paid by Jeremiah Wormscrode, steward to Sir Neville de Magott, to punish Swineytown because its citizens had refused to pay him protection money.

Walter could believe that.

Jo could believe that.

Whatever their motive, the brigands rode

headlong through the open west gate and began to lay the town waste, smashing, looting, burning – and terrorising anyone they came across. Every troop of citizens sent to stop them had fled at the first sight of their slashing swords, and now only Citizen Martin's militia, shaking in their pointed shoes, stood in their way.

When Martin heard the hooves enter Watery Lane he closed his eyes and whimpered. In a few seconds they would mow him down, and his friends with him.

He closed his eyes.

'Lord,' he prayed frantically, 'I am a simple man and no doubt unworthy of favours, but would you be so kind as to send me a miracle, please?'

He begged so hard it hurt, then opened his eyes expecting to see spears and flails and pickaxes come sweeping round the corner into the square.

Instead, he saw Big George, and Martin the Swineytown butcher knew that his prayer had been answered before he'd even asked it.

The grolyhoomp was his miracle.

What happened next was another miracle: the brigands failed to arrive. They never emerged from Watery Lane.

This was how it came about.

Walter and Jo, realising they were in even more

danger from Jeremiah Wormscrode's villains than the citizens of Swineytown, stepped forward to join Martin's militia and fight with them side by side.

That stirred Big George.

When he saw their courage he decided to help.

He stepped over their heads and planted his boot in the entrance to Watery Lane and blocked it.

The lane was just wide enough for horsemen to ride up it two abreast. That suited George perfectly. As the thieves and murderers came jangling and clattering he dipped down like a heron after fish and snatched them up a pair at a time – right hand, left hand, right hand, left hand – and tossed them over his shoulder, over the walls and out of the town.

Each brace of brigands saw the Hands of Justice swoop down from the sky. Each felt themselves collected and crunched, then flung and flying, and they all knew without the shadow of a doubt that at last they were getting their just desserts.

Twenty-four pairs of villains soared like that. The twenty-fifth pair had time to turn around and ride like the wind the other way.

Unfortunately for them, they weren't fast enough.

George reached down and snatched them up. Like a man throwing a discus he swung his arm wide and flung them high and far, far and high, spinning them into a huge looping arc that carried them to the very middle of the river, where they sank three rowing boats and a wherry.

Watching these last villains leave his beloved town so spectacularly made little square Martin smile for the first time that day.

'Martin,' he told himself, 'you may be a simple man, and you may be a coward, but you have amazing visions.'

So Big George was transformed from End of the World and Public Enemy Number One to the Saviour of Swineytown inside a few exciting minutes.

'These midgets are very changeable,' he observed, as citizens tumbled from their houses and ran rings round his legs. 'But I suppose it makes life interesting.'

Walter was still no closer to finding his father. But that night they had a piece of luck.

As afternoon moved into evening, the towns-people brought them food by the cartload and fêted them merrily. There was dancing. George capered a jig and Walter even measured some elegant steps with Jo, who managed not to fall over and, for a few minutes, felt almost a lady.

At sundown the gates were locked. Bells sounded a curfew to warn everybody to go home, because there were no street lights and it was dangerous to be out after dark.

One by one, the citizens returned to their homes, and soon Walter, Jo and George were left alone again.

They decided to spend the night in the square, because that was the only space big enough for George to lie down in.

It was very smelly, since an open drain ran through it, but Walter and Jo were used to stink and George accepted it as just one more peculiar custom of this constantly surprising world.

They lay side by side on the ground and watched dusk turn to darkness. The only light now came from George's face and the dim tallow candles flickering inside the windows of the houses. Soon even those were snuffed out.

There were noises – owls, and cats, and rats that skittered past their feet and plopped into the drain. And there was another, quite different sound – the chink of a dragging chain.

The bear was still around.

At a loss without her master, who had fled from the town when the tumult was at its height, she was creeping close to the people who had befriended her.

Walter wasn't sure he liked that. He grabbed a handful of pebbles and threw them at the noise. 'Scat!' he shouted.

'No!' cried Jo. 'Let her come.'

'Why?'

'Because I want her, all ri'?'

Jo fumbled round the square until she heard the bear's breathing, then felt for the chain and gave it a tug.

The bear came willingly.

'I'll chase it while you're asleep,' Walter warned her.

'Yous can say goodbye to your eyes, then.'

'Zwifnnbwww,' said George. 'Let the bear come.'

Even in the dark George had felt Jo's longing, and he realised that behind the tough exterior that was her defence against a dangerous world, there hid a lonely girl who wanted a friend above all else.

Now, once again, they lay quiet.

Jo ruffled the bear's dirty fur and sighed contentedly. 'Now we're four outlaws, en't we?' she whispered.

'I'm leader,' Walter said arrogantly.

'No you en't. Nobody's leader. We're all equal.'

'*You're* my equal?' gasped Walter, trembling with indignation.

'Yiss, I am.'

'And the bear, I suppose? The bear is my equal, too?'

'Yiss.'

'And the grolyhoomp?'

'The grolyhoomp most of all. He's more equal than any of us.'

Walter knew she was right.

While his friends bickered, George – who was

used to one day lasting nine hundred earthly years – was trying to come to terms with a world where night seemed to fall with every blink of an eye.

And he was listening to the stars.

Why did it always seem as if they were speaking to him? What were they saying? He lay on his back in the little walled town, watching galaxies spin overhead, and he heard their song like wind lyres.

'Gardey-loo! Gardey-loo!' cried a woman's voice, as she emptied a chamber pot out of a window. The splash echoed round the square, and a surprised and sodden cat ran scampering down Watery Lane.

Then a timid voice whispered, 'Who g-goes there?', and a candle lantern wavered into view, shaking nervously in the hand of the Swineytown nightwatchman.

He stopped at the edge of the pitch-black square. 'Does *anybody* go there?' he croaked. 'Show yourselves if you do.' He raised the lantern but all it illuminated was his own face – the haunted face of Citizen Martin carrying out his last duty of the day.

'Grolyhoomp,' George said.

Martin nearly dropped his lantern. He peered towards a ghostly green glimmer in the middle of the square. From where he was standing it looked like the biggest glow-worm in creation.

'Is that you, my miracle?' he breathed. 'Are you still there?'

Jo said, 'We're all here. Why don't yous come and join us?'

Martin did – and changed the course of their quest.

Sitting down beside them, he ventured his opinion that life was a pig's bottom. He might be only a simple man but he knew which side his bread was buttered, and that was his bedside. He'd be relieved to find himself there alive and well when his spell of guard duty was over, because it would be a lot more than the previous nightwatchman had managed.

'Why, what happened to him?' Walter asked sleepily.

'Master Wormscrode's spies cut his throat, boy.'

'Why did they do that?'

Martin explained that only yesterday morning a handful of outlaws had arrived in Swineytown, bringing with them a gentleman who asked for the town's protection. It was granted, and the outlaws left without harming anybody, but just before sundown a trio of thoroughly nasty-looking men had slipped into town and concealed themselves until dark.

During the night they came out of hiding,

kidnapped the gentleman and escaped with him over the town wall.

The nightwatchman must have disturbed them. He would never disturb anybody else again.

It was Martin's opinion that this afternoon's raid was a revenge attack upon Swiney for harbouring the gentleman.

It was typical of Jeremiah Wormscrode, who was a bad man to cross.

'What was the gentleman's name?' asked Walter, wide awake now.

'Robert,' Martin answered. 'His name was Robert. Poor man, I wouldn't give a snail's bottom for his chances now.'

chapter Thirteen
Trial by combat

They left Swineytown as soon as its gates were opened in the morning.

Walter's heart was heavy, for he knew he was returning to what was for him the most dangerous place in the world – Sir Neville de Magott's castle.

It was the worst possible place for Jo, too.

She had lain awake most of the night, wondering what she should do. The thought of leaving the town on which all her hopes of freedom rested, only hours after setting foot in it, horrified her. Why, even to think about it would have been impossible for her a week ago.

But Jo was changing.

It was when she saw the gates opening that she finally made up her mind. There and then she cast all doubts aside, collected the bear's chain and led her out of town.

Walter was astounded.

'You know what will happen if you're caught,' he said, 'so why take the risk?'

Jo shrugged. 'Because it's like family, all ri'?'

'What do you mean?'

'Georgie an' yous an' the bear – you're all there is for me. I en't got nobody else. Anyhow, who's gunna hold your head up when yous fall in a river again?'

There was no answer to that.

It seemed that their quest was going to end where it began, and that thought cast a gloom over Walter and Jo as they headed back towards Magotty Castle.

George felt their anxiety as if it was his own. He was finding that the longer he was in their company, the more he was becoming involved with their destiny. So he stayed close by them and walked dibdoo so he wouldn't give them away.

For their part, Jo and Walter kept watch for hunters who might be tempted to attack a grolyhoomp from the cover of the trees, thinking him the biggest and best game they had even seen.

In this way they guarded each other and hid from everybody else.

On the second day they met a caravan lumbering through the forest. George held the bear's muzzle to keep her quiet, while Walter and Jo watched the passing cavalcade with growing dismay.

It was like a circus.

A dozen wagons swayed along the uneven track, laden with the belongings of several knights and their ladies and household retinues. They had dogs and donkeys and goats with them, and pilgrims and other travellers had tagged themselves on the end, deeming it wise to band together for safety and company in the dangerous forest.

The bright colours of their clothes, the painted wagons and the horses' flashing harness made such a show that George's heart leaped to see them. But they threw Walter into deep gloom.

'They're heading for Magotty Castle for the midsummer festival and tournament,' he said. 'I'd forgotten about it. There will be cavalcades like this all over the forest, and that means the castle and all the land around it will be full to bursting. How can I rescue my father with all those people everywhere?'

He had vaguely hoped to find out where his dad was being held prisoner, and somehow sneak him out when nobody was looking. That plan was now in ruins.

'Don't worry, there'll be a way,' Jo said confidently, to cheer him. 'We'll just have to find it, all ri'?'

Walter nodded, but there were tears in his eyes.

Sure enough, when they reached the edge of the forest and looked out towards the hill on which Magotty Castle stood, they saw an amazing sight.

All the land around the base of the hill was crammed with rainbow-coloured pavilions. It looked like the encampment of a great army the night before a battle, except that this camp was thronged with people singing, dancing, shouting, eating, drinking and playing games.

Over it all loomed the whitewashed walls, painted roof and fluttering banners of Magotty Castle, glinting majestically on its green hill like a palace in a fairy tale.

George was entranced. 'Zzynnymmroggleth-wingerotygon!' he breathed. 'Will you take a look at that, now!'

Walter winced. It didn't look entrancing to him, it looked impossible. All he saw was crowded tents and watchmen pacing the castle battlements, and he knew he could never slip past all those without being noticed.

The alternative – to push boldly through the

middle of it all as though he had every right to be there – was too terrifying to think about. So Walter didn't think about it. He did it.

Telling Jo, George and the bear to wait for him under cover of the trees, he stepped out into bright sunshine and a world of midsummer madness.

Then, taking a deep breath to still his thudding heart, Walter walked steadily forward, into the lions' den.

Inside the fairy castle the fairy king was strutting round and round his great hall, congratulating himself.

'What an amazing man I am!' he chortled. 'What intellect I possess! What brilliance! What power of thought! Who else would even dream of staging a public execution to round off a midsummer festival, eh, Wormscrode? It's genius, that's what it is. I'm surprised there's room for my mind in my head – eh, what?'

'To be sure, sire,' sniggered the toady scurrying behind him, 'you have the brain of the century. And I'm the man to tell you so, to be sure.'

Sir Neville de Magott leered stiffly at his new steward. He was a strange-looking man, tall, thin and rigid – picture a cardboard rectangle with a head and you've got him. But the oddest thing about him was his leer.

Sir Neville leered all the time. He never stopped. He leered when he smiled, when he frowned and when he was furious. He leered at breakfast, lunch and dinner. He woke up leering and went to sleep leering into his pillow. He even leered in his dreams.

This gave an odd twist to his face, a sideways expression that was downright unpleasant. It was particularly unpleasant just now.

Jeremiah Wormscrode, with his cringing manner, drooling mouth and thin, trailing moustache that looked like a slug on a wet cushion, was no pin-up either.

Jeremiah had risen in the world by aping the moods of his masters. When they smiled, he smiled. When they were angry, he was angry too. When they cried, he cried, and if they made a joke, he roared his head off. That lulled them into thinking they had the perfect servant, at which point Jeremiah betrayed them and took over their position.

He had done that to the trusting, honourable Robert of Swyre, and now here he was in the Great Hall as Sir Neville's right-hand man, while Robert was down in the dungeon.

So it was that when Walter was catapulted into the hall by the castle guards, he was greeted by the two people he most dreaded to meet.

The Maggot was delighted to see him.

'Look who's here, Wormscrode,' he crowed. 'Come to see his dad, I expect.'

'I have, sir,' said Walter, trying hard to be brave, 'and also to plead for mercy. I beg you to spare the life of Robert of Swyre and grant him a pardon.'

'Beg pardon?'

Sir Neville's leer assumed a new character,

outraged and menacing. 'You're asking me to be merciful to a traitor? And to yourself, too, I suppose – you'll be wanting *two* pardons, forsooth. You've got a hope.'

The Maggot jerked about dramatically and waved stiff arms as if he'd been starched from head to foot. 'I'll tell you what you *will* get, Walter of Swyre,' he snorted, 'you'll get a double beheading. At sundown on Midsummer Night, as the climax to the jousting, you and your dad can say hello to the axe. How does that sound? He-he-he, another smart idea, eh, Wormscrode?'

'He-he-he, to be sure, sire,' Jeremiah simpered.

Walter felt his face turn pale and his legs tremble. But he stood his ground, kept his head and thought fast – faster even than the Maggot.

'You mentioned jousting, sir,' he said carefully. 'Would you agree to include in it a trial by combat for my father's life?'

'Trial by combat?' Sir Neville squeaked.

'Trial by combat?' squealed Jeremiah. 'Whose trial, boy? Whose combat?'

Walter was inspired. Very politely, he reminded Sir Neville of an ancient custom which allowed a man accused of a crime to try to prove his innocence by challenging his accuser to a duel.

Looking hard at Jeremiah Wormscrode, he

added, 'If my lord will permit, I will take part in the tournament and fight for my father's life. If I win it, he is innocent and goes free. How does that sound?'

For a moment, the Maggot was speechless. Then he roared with laughter and slapped his wooden knees.

The Wormscrode smiled half-heartedly.

'By gad, you've got a nerve, boy,' Sir Neville chortled. 'You're hardly big enough to get on a horse, let alone do battle from it, yet you think you can joust with my best knights at the tourney *and win*?'

'I will fight them for my father's life,' Walter doggedly repeated. He was standing very straight now, and though his face was pale, his eyes were shining.

'What a lark,' said the Maggot gleefully. 'Two entertainments for the price of one! We'll have a battle between a puny David and a cartload of Goliaths – and almost certainly a death when he gets his block knocked off – and we'll *still* have our execution at the end! That can't be bad, eh, Wormscrode?'

'Sire,' protested Jeremiah, 'you cannot be serious—'

Sir Neville slapped him soundly about the ears. 'Don't you *sire* me,' he said, leering harder and

wider than ever. 'I'm the genius around here. What I say, goes. But . . .' here he hesitated and frowned '. . . if I am the genius, why didn't I have that idea? Why didn't *you*, you idiot? Why'd you leave it to a boy? Where's the use in a steward without an intelligent thought in his head? And what are you grinning at? You're always grinning, Wormscrode, I've noticed.'

He battered Jeremiah's ears all the way up the great hall and back again.

When he returned, breathless with the exertion, the Maggot told Walter, 'You have two days to prepare yourself, boy. Tomorrow is Midsummer Eve and the tourney is the day after. That isn't long, so you'd better get practising. We want a good show. And hear this – when you ride into the lists you'll be entering a knockdown tournament. You must win every round, so that by the end you're the only one left sitting on a horse. Otherwise, you die and your father dies. Have you got that?'

Walter blinked. 'Yes, my lord.'

'Very well. Go and get yourself kitted out. Wormscrode, fix him up with a horse and armour and a shield and a lance and anything else he needs. And fix yourself up while you're about it, because if by some miracle this boy gets past the others, you'll be his last obstacle. That's fair, since you were his father's accuser.'

When he heard this Jeremiah Wormscrode gave such a triumphantly evil leer of his own, you would think he'd been practising it all his treacherous life, just for this moment.

'Dismiss,' said the Maggot to both of them. 'And may the bravest man win.'

Walter was brave enough now to dare one last request. Unfortunately, it was one too many.

'Please, sir, may I see my father?'

Sir Neville de Magott shook his creaking head like the pendulum of a rusty clock. 'You may not,' he tocked. 'But you *will* see him, boy. And he will see you. On Midsummer Day I promise he'll have the best seat at the tourney, to watch you die.'

chapter fourteen
Bring on the Dancing Knights

'Ymmylllochmidjoo?' asked Big George, meaning, 'What's that, Jo?'

From their shelter among the trees, George, Jo and the bear had seen the midsummer gathering grow ever bigger as they watched anxiously for Walter's return. Now, Jo squinted along George's pointing finger and saw, through a tiny gap among the pavilions, some peasants raising a rough wooden structure at the foot of castle hill.

Two long lines of board enclosed a strip of green like a race track. Beyond them, a bank of seating rose high in the air.

'Those are the lists, Georgie,' Jo explained.

'Ll-iss-tss?'

'For the jousting, all ri'?'

'Jjowwwsstngg.'

'That's the word. But oh, Georgie, I wish we didn't have to hide all the time, don't yous? I wish we could just go out there, ri', and enjoy the fair, and walk about and not be afraid. Just be free.'

'Fff-rr-eeee.'

'It's good to belong to somebody, like your family – but without bein' *owned*, ri'? The law says I'm the Maggot's property, and I can't stand that. Georgie, what d'yous think is going to happen to me? And what's going to happen to yous? If yous was to go out there they'd use yous for target practice. On top of that yous can't even speak sense – well, not so anybody can understand, anyway.'

She looked at him with troubled eyes. George gave her a wide, gentle smile. 'Grolyhoompjoo,' he said softly.

Jo grinned. 'That's your answer to everything, en't it? Well, maybe it's not a bad one. Hello then, what's this?'

She pointed at a mysterious object lumbering through the tents towards them. It looked like a mobile scrap heap.

As it came closer they heard clanking sounds and saw underneath the scrap a bony, dejected-looking grey horse, and behind it all a red-faced boy who

kept prodding the horse with a warped lance to keep it moving.

The boy was Walter, the nag his fiery steed, and the bits of rusty tin and mesh were his armour for the tournament. These, and the bent and splintered lance, were all that Sir Neville's miserable, mean, sly steward had allowed him.

'How can I possibly joust some of the best knights in the kingdom with this lot?' Walter groaned, as he told them the Maggot's edict. 'I'll never survive the first round, let alone win the tourney and save my dad's life. They plan to execute him as the climax to the festival!'

'Why did yous volunteer?' asked Jo, looking puzzled.

Walter sighed. 'Because I couldn't think of anything else. And because I was good at jousting in my knight accomplishment classes. But that was kid's stuff, played for fun. This will be the real thing, and deadly serious.'

Jo looked at his pale, grave face and in her mind's eye saw him hobbling into the lists. 'Don't worry,' she said brightly, 'there probably won't even be a contest. Because one look at yous an' those real knights will fall off their horses laughing.'

All day long a constant stream of cavalcades like the one they had met in the forest toiled up the hill to the castle, bringing new knights and their families to the festival.

Among them Walter saw the dreaded black eagle banner of Sir Ribrub de Crackling and his son

Ralph. Sir Ribrub, the Dark Knight, was last year's jousting champion and a favourite to win again – which meant that if Walter survived the early rounds he would almost certainly come up against him in the lists.

That was a most unpleasant prospect.

As well as the great knights who owned vast estates, many knights who had no land at all had also been drawn to the tourney in the hope of winning a big prize. Most of them were poor and shabby and looked, like Peter Bullfinch, rather beaten about the edges.

It so happened that the poorest, shabbiest and most beaten knight in the land was at that moment being beaten again in a faded green pavilion not a hundred feet from where George and his friends were hiding.

His name was Sir Harry le Frit, and his assailant was his sister Gwendolyn.

'Get out of my sight, you big booby!' Gwendolyn bellowed in a deep roar that was anything but ladylike. 'Go out there and fight for us!'

The pavilion doorflap billowed open and a tin scarecrow hurtled out and fell flat on his back. A helmet followed.

Inside the pavilion the voice ranted, 'Find

another idiot to practise with – heaven knows you need it!'

'Yes, Gwenny dear, I will, right away, dear,' the scarecrow muttered, collecting the helmet and struggling to his feet with a lot of creaking and grinding.

Once upright, he looked directly towards the trees and spotted Walter sorting his scrap. He clanked over.

When he saw Walter he said, 'That was my sister Gwen. Isn't she sweet? She wants me to win the tourney.' At that his face fell and his pale blue eyes looked as though they could weep. 'But I've never won anything in my life and I don't see how I'm going to start now. One look at a lance and I'll be flat on my back, as usual.'

'Same here,' said Walter.

'The trouble is,' the scarecrow continued, 'I don't like hurting people – though I've noticed they don't mind hurting me. Gwen says if there was a booby prize for the tallest and most incompetent knight, I'd win it every time.'

'If there was a prize for the smallest and most stupid of knights, I'm sure I'd win it,' said Walter sympathetically.

The scarecrow smiled, bowed and held out a thin, mailed fist. 'Sir Harry le Frit, at your service.'

'Walter of Swyre, at yours, sir,' said Walter, shaking the fist.

'Jo of Nowhere,' said Jo, shaking it also.

'I'm not really a *sir* at all,' their new friend admitted, 'or even a *le*. I just call myself that because it sounds imposing. It doesn't make a groat of difference, though. I still get beaten.'

Sir Harry le Frit put on his helmet, tried to look fierce – and noticed George.

His breathing accelerated inside his helmet. Steam seeped through the slits in his visor.

'Wh-wh-wh-whatever is *that*?' he panted.

'*That*,' said Jo and Walter together, very firmly, 'is our secret. Now he's yours, too.'

Within a few minutes they had negotiated a deal whereby, in return for George not sitting on him, Sir Harry would keep his mouth shut. He would also help Walter prepare for the tourney by giving him the benefit of his long – though each time short lived – experience.

'If you remember that nothing I do ever works,' he said brightly, 'and therefore do the opposite of whatever I tell you, you can't go wrong.'

While Walter was trying to work this out, Jo finally lost patience with hiding. Announcing that, 'There's no point in being free if you can't do what you want,' she followed Walter's example and stepped boldly out of the trees into the excitement of the midsummer festival, disguised as a roving entertainer, with her cap jammed down across her eyes and a bear dancing behind her at the end of a rope.

An hour later she was arrested.

But what an hour that was!

The bear danced and Jo jigged, and as they spun a corkscrew trail through the bright pavilions, people clapped and threw money.

They bumped continually into other entertainers – strolling players, musicians, acrobats and jugglers, all making a loud noise to draw attention to themselves. They passed stalls selling ale and trinkets and pies. They dodged gamblers playing games with dice and drunks rolling about singing.

Jo felt dizzy with the excitement of it all.

Then, right in the middle of the pavilions they came upon a wrestling ring. Inside it there danced a man as big as an ox, who flexed his cannonball muscles and sniffed as he pirouetted on his toes and heaved all comers over the ropes into oblivion.

'C'mon now, c'mon now, c'mon now,' Peter Bullfinch challenged the onlookers, 'who's next?'

Jo sent in the bear.

'Don't mess wid me!' the Ox cried, sticking up his fists, but when he saw Jo he laughed and jumped down and tossed her into the air. 'Jo!' he cried happily, 'my liddle friend! What you doin' here?'

When she explained, the Ox tutted and his battered face looked thoughtful, but then he grinned and said, 'Tell Walter not to worry. The strongest man in the world will come to the tourney.'

Jo moved on through the fair, wondering what a dancing wrestler could do against armoured knights on horseback.

She was still thinking about it when she turned a corner and found herself staring into the thick-lipped, slavering face of Jeremiah Wormscrode.

'You and that bear,' he slurped, 'are under arrest.'

When Jo was brought before Sir Neville de Magott, an enormous banquet was taking place in the castle's Great Hall.

Sir Neville sat with his chief guests at a high table on a platform at one end of the room, leering down at the knights seated at the tables below.

The hall was noisy, crowded and smelly. Every table buckled under the weight of food – soup and bread and fish and fowl and roasted swans and peacocks.

Servants scurried about to replenish sauces and jugs of wine.

Everybody ate with their fingers and used thick slices of stale bread called trenchers for plates. As they ate, acrobats entertained them, dogs crunched bones on the floor and Sir Neville's falcon watched everything with a bright and supercilious eye.

It watched Jo as Jeremiah Wormscrode dragged her up to the high table.

At the time, Sir Neville was helping himself to a peacock's wing and watching an acrobat perform a fire-eating triple somersault, so he gave them only a cursory grimace.

'What's up, Wormscrode?' he growled.

The steward cringed, and the trailing slug of his moustache slithered round his mouth. 'This, sire, is Joanne, a criminal,' he drooled. 'She's a runaway. Her parents are dead and she is your property, but she fled to deny you her service. I have brought her to you for punishment.'

'What do you suggest?' asked Sir Neville – rather vaguely, because he was more interested in waiting for the acrobat to burn his mouth off.

'I recommend the severest penalty, sire.'

The Wormscrode would have said more, but Jo shook him off and stormed up to the Maggot and said, 'Can I say something, your sirship, all ri'?'

Sir Neville was astonished. He looked at her now for the first time – irritably, as you might scowl at an annoying fly before swatting it to kingdom come.

'What?' he snapped.

Jo took a deep breath and repeated the words Walter had spoken only hours earlier. 'I claim trial by combat, an' I challenge this nasty man to a duel, 'cos he's my accuser. That's my right, en't it, your sirship?'

She poked her tongue out at Jeremiah, who spluttered and turned purple. His slug of a moustache squirmed. 'How dare you!' he slavered.

But Sir Neville cooed with delight. 'By gad, Wormscrode, here's another one with a nerve!' he snorted.

'You wouldn't agree, sire – would you?' Jeremiah squealed.

'Wouldn't I just! A chit of a girl against a fully grown weed – what a comical contest! We'll squeeze it in tomorrow between the jousting and the beheading. You've got a busy afternoon ahead of you. But what entertainment, eh, begad!'

Jo cleared her throat and crossed her fingers. 'There's just one more thing, all ri', your sirship,' she said. 'Since I'm only small I can choose a champion to fight for me, can't I?'

157

Sir Neville frowned. 'Well, that's in the rules, so I suppose you can. But who'd fight for *you*? You're nobody.'

'Mebbe I am,' Jo said humbly, 'an' mebbe I come from nowhere, but I got a champion anyhow. I'll bring him tomorrow. He's called Georgie.'

Chapter Fifteen
Midsummer Madness

There is always something strange about Midsummer Eve. Magic floats on the air.

It was floating on the long midsummer evening of the Year of Our Lord 1305. The result was a kind of madness that affected everybody.

For some – like Peter Bullfinch, sprawled behind the wrestling ring soused in wine – it brought an enchantment which made even fairies seem possible.

For others – like Walter, Jo, Sir Harry le Frit and Robert of Swyre – it brought an anxiety about the morrow which caused the hours to hang like weights around their necks.

Everybody, happy or sad, felt the madness in some way.

But nobody felt it more than Big George.

He sat just inside the forest rim, looking out at a real live fairy tale.

As his eyes roved round the scene he saw that every pavilion and castle turret boasted a glittering pennant that fluttered and made the cheerful chuckling sound that falling water makes.

He saw the people's bright clothes catch the glow of the evening sun like coloured fires, and he saw the sunlight flash and dazzle on the armour of knights practising for the tourney.

At the same time, George heard interesting sounds everywhere: the clash of the knights' lances hitting the quintain, the happy shouts of children, dogs barking. He heard men and women calling and singing, and from inside the distant castle walls the ceaseless noise of blacksmiths forging and hammering new armour for the morrow.

On top of all this, he heard noises of merriment where jugglers, conjurors and tumblers were growing ever more daring as the heady wine took hold.

'Ooothmadderwoggglyy,' George whispered, awe-struck. It was magic.

Near at hand, though, something both solemn and comical was going on.

Walter and Sir Harry le Frit were practising

jousts. Jolting up and down on their nags, and hardly able to stay upright because of the weight of their armour, they tilted at one another – urging their horses into a gallop and desperately trying to unseat each other with their enormous lances.

They missed every time.

Jo ached with laughing, although she knew that really this was very serious because it could be a matter of life or death for both of them.

Especially for Walter.

'Walter expects to die tomorrer, you know, Georgie,' she said softly. 'He probably will too, because he'll fight clean even if everybody else fights dirty. Walter really believes in this chivalry stuff, see. He believes in courage an' truth an' gentleness an' honner and all the things knights are supposed to have. That's good, but it en't fair if the others don't play by the same rules. There en't nothin' gentle about gettin' your head knocked off, is there?'

Then she winked. 'Mind, yous can fight as dirty as yous like for me, so long as yous win, all ri'?'

They watched Walter and Sir Harry wearily lower their lances again, and charge again, and miss again, and fall from their horses with a juddering crash. They lay still on the ground, bruised and battered and exhausted.

'*We've* got to fight dirty for Walter tomorrer,' Jo whispered, 'yous an' me, and never mind what he wants. I dunno how, though. We'll have to make it up as we go along.'

She looked anxiously at George then, and prodded his arm. 'Georgie, are yous listenin' to me?'

George smiled. He didn't know what Jo meant, and he had no idea that he was supposed to fight for her tomorrow.

But he liked the sound of it.

It was all part of the magic and madness of this wonderful Midsummer Eve.

chapter Sixteen
The Jousting Favour

Walter couldn't sleep. In the end he gave up trying and got up quietly. It was still very early. No one else was awake. A mist blanketed the pavilion field, hiding the lists and promising heat later on. It would be too hot inside his armour – although probably he wouldn't be inside it for long.

Walter sighed. He was extraordinarily nervous. His hands shook. He felt like crying, but that would be neither a manly nor a knightly thing to do, so he tried not to do it. Besides, it would shame his father.

The thought of his father almost broke him.

Today, they would see each other at last, briefly, before Death visited them both. Walter clenched his fists. He must put on a good show, to make his father proud and give him one thing at least to smile about.

But as he checked his equipment to make sure it was all in order, the handle of his lance below the fist guard dropped off.

Walter really could have cried then. He had just learned how to compensate for the lance's warp, but now it had given up the ghost altogether. That must have happened when he and Sir Harry fell off their horses last night.

It was clear that the Wormscrode had not only given him a worn-out horse and crumbling armour, but also a useless weapon.

Walter took a long, deep, shuddering breath. He would show him. Walter of Swyre would show everybody what a real squire could do. He wasn't sure how, but he'd do it.

He looked up then and saw Big George watching him.

George took the broken lance from his hand. He examined it carefully, then smiled.

'Goddit,' he said.

'What do you mean, 'goddit'?' Walter cried. 'It's too short now. My opponent's lance will have me off my horse before mine gets anywhere near him. I've no chance now.'

George took no notice. He chuntered to himself,

as if he was thinking out loud. Then he winked and
put a finger against his nose and whispered
conspiratorially, 'Dibdoo, Walllttterrrr.'

Walter gaped at him. 'Dibdoo?'

George nodded. 'Dibdoo.'

When Jo woke, her first thoughts were also about what the day might bring. Would she be back in the pillory by nightfall – or in the rat-infested dungeon beneath Castle Magott? Would Walter be alive? Would his father still have a head on his shoulders? And as for that amazing, wonderful grolyhoomp – what would happen to him?

It was all too frightening to think about, so Jo strolled across the dewy grass to Walter and George, looked out over the misty encampment and said, rather shyly, 'What are yous two goin' to do for favours?'

'Favours?' said Walter, surprised.

'Ffayyyvoos?' George repeated.

'Yous know very well, Walter,' said Jo, 'that knights allus fight for the honour of a lady. An' they carry her favour, as a token of her love. That's ri', en't it?'

'Well, yes, I suppose so,' said Walter uncertainly, 'but—'

Jo blushed. 'Then I reckon yous got to have favours like everybody else. It en't fair otherwise. Now I know I en't much like a real lady, an' prob'ly never will be, but I'm the only one yous got. So I'm gunna give each of yous a favour to carry, cos you're my knights, all ri'? The trouble is, I en't got much. So here goes . . .'

Before Walter could protest, Jo had torn the left sleeve off her dress and knotted it round his broken lance.

Walter felt embarrassed. 'I don't know what to say,' he mumbled.

'Then don't say anythin'. Go out there an' fight for your lady. Yous got to win now, 'cos that's a token. Now you're the Blue Knight.'

'The Blue Knight,' Walter repeated. 'I like that.'

'Ffayyyvoos,' said George.

'You're catching on quick,' Jo grinned. 'All right, Georgie, it's your turn now. This is for yous, 'cos you're my champion – you're gunna fight for me today, all ri'? I'll tell you when. Now bend down.'

She beckoned to him and George leaned down towards her. Then Jo took the ancient rabbit's foot from her neck, rubbed it between her thumb and forefinger for luck, and fastened it to George's tunic, over his heart.

'There, Georgie. Yous got a lady's favour too. It's like Tilly again, ri', only this time it's Jo – Nowhere Jo, eh.'

'Till-yyy.' George fingered the spoon in his pocket. Then he touched the rabbit's foot. 'Jooo.'

Jo grinned. 'Yous got ladies all over the place, yous naughty grolyhoomp. Now then, both of yous, stop wastin' time an' get out there an' fight. An' *win*, all ri'?'

chapter Seventeen
Knightly Ninepins

So began the strangest event in the entire history of knightly tournaments. Before long the sun rose and vanquished the mist. The people woke in their pavilions. Peter Bullfinch opened a bleary eye behind the wrestling ring, squinted at the light, groaned and scratched himself.

Midsummer Day had begun.

By nine o'clock the pavilion field was empty because everybody was crowding the boarded jousting lists to get a good view.

At nine-thirty the ladies, in richly embroidered dresses, climbed the steps to the stand, where they would have a perfect view of their heroes' triumphs and disasters.

At nine-forty-five Sir Neville de Magott arrived with his party and sat in the front row. A burly guard manacled a small, pale-faced man to the seat on his left. Immediately, a long-haired woman with a lovely but lined face pushed determinedly through the crowd and ran round the lists to join the prisoner. The guard tried to stop her but Sir Neville waved him away, and the woman sat beside the man and looked at him with love and fear.

Sir Neville leered at her and the ladies and waved rigid arms at his peasants. They cheered him, because like Citizen Martin of Swineytown they knew which side their bread was buttered, and Sir Neville said to himself, 'How pleasant it is to be popular! What a great man I am! And it all comes naturally! Well, let's not hang about, let the good times roll!'

He clapped his hands and fourteen trumpeters in golden livery marched forward and blew a noisy fanfare. The people cheered again, this time voluntarily because they were excited.

Then a Herald rode into the lists, reined in his horse in front of Sir Neville, unfurled a scroll and shouted, 'Oyez! Oyez! Whereas Sir Neville de Magott of Castle Magott has graciously commanded that a grand tourney shall be fought here this Midsummer Day in the Year of Our Lord 1305, we beg him graciously to give the signal to begin!'

The Herald rolled up his scroll and Sir Neville

leered graciously, rose stiffly to his feet, cranked up
his right arm and dropped it. The people threw
their caps in the air and yelled their heads off as to
their left and right, at each end of the boarded
enclosure, a heavily armoured horseman appeared.

The tournament was starting.

Already, though, there was something strange about it. Instead of growing silent in anticipation, the people began to snigger. Sir Neville frowned with annoyance, but when he gave the horsemen a second glance he tittered himself.

Soon everybody was in stitches – except the manacled man. His pale face flushed scarlet and he hung his head in shame, because he could see that one of those horsemen was his only son.

The other was Sir Harry le Frit.

It was sheer bad luck that Walter and Sir Harry had been drawn against each other in the first round – although it meant that one of them at least would progress to the second round, which was a marvel in itself.

To the onlookers the very appearance of these two contestants was a marvel – a gangling tin scarecrow pitted against a rusty midget with a torn blue sleeve dangling from his chopped off lance. You couldn't choose between them for clownishness.

'Joust!' cried the herald, to prevent the tournament descending into farce before it had even started. 'Charge!'

Walter gulped. He whispered a prayer, lowered his visor and spurred his horse forward.

Sir Harry le Frit gulped. For the first time in his jousting career he had hopes of winning a tilt. 'Watch this, Gwenny,' he squeaked, and spurred his horse into a gallop.

The horses' hooves thundered on the grass. The knights' armour rattled, and inside their helmets their heads rattled too.

Then, as they drew close to one another they raised their shields, lowered their lances and urged their horses even faster.

Walter gritted his teeth, closed his eyes and waited for the crash.

Sir Harry le Frit gritted his teeth, closed his eyes, and waited for the crash.

What happened next was a complete surprise, both to them and everybody else, because just when it seemed that Sir Harry's lance would pierce Walter like a stick in a toffee apple, he disappeared.

Faster than an eye can blink, the longest lance in the world – it might have been a pole, or perhaps a very thin tree – appeared out of nowhere and locked into the broken fist guard of Walter's lance. Faster still it thrust the lance forward, hooked it into Sir Harry le Frit's chainmail jacket and scooped him out of his saddle like the yolk out of an egg.

The crowd blinked, mystified.

Sir Neville de Magott was mystified.

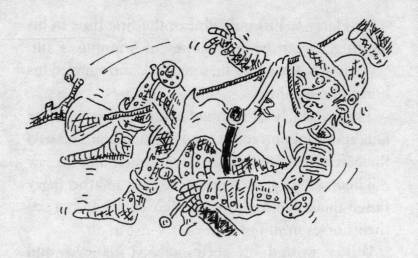

Jeremiah Wormscrode was mystified.

Robert of Swyre was mystified.

Walter, his son, was not just mystified. He was flabbergasted.

But Jo knew exactly what had happened. Lying low beside the grolyhoomp among the empty pavilions, she wriggled her toes with delight. 'Yous done it, Georgie,' she sang, 'yous saved Walter! But let Sir Harry down gently, all ri'?'

The grolyhoomp nodded and raised the thin tree like a fishing rod, swinging his wriggling catch high over the pavilions and dropping it at the forest rim. When Sir Harry le Frit opened his eyes at last he was very surprised to find himself in the arms of a bear.

The tournament went downhill from there – or uphill, depending on whose side you were on.

For Walter it passed in a blur.

He was aware that somehow Sir Harry le Frit had vanished, which meant that he must have won the first round. So he rode up to the stand and saluted Sir Neville and his father and mother, and he saw the love and pride in his parents' eyes and the anger in Jeremiah Wormscrode's.

After that, nothing made any sense at all.

Somehow, Walter's lance returned to his hand in time for him to face his second opponent, Ralph de Crackling. He saw Ralph bearing down on him, imagined the hatred in the piggy eyes behind the black visor, saw the black lance point at his heart. He spurred his own horse forward and lowered his lance.

Walter thought he must have shut his eyes again, because the next thing he knew there was an almighty clang and then a crash as Ralph hit the ground screaming.

Among the empty pavilions Nowhere Jo lowered her catapult. 'Two down, four to go, Georgie,' she grinned. 'It's fun, this, en't it?'

Knights went down like ninepins.

The third knight, a red-haired giant with a scarlet

shield, hardly knew what hit him, because at the moment he charged, Jo begged George to use the extraordinary talent she'd heard at the Ox's house party.

'Sing, Georgie!' she cried. 'Throw them bagpipes at 'im, loud as you like! Put 'im off 'is stride! Knock 'im down with music!'

To show what she meant she directed at the scarlet knight a piercing hoot, which sped through the air like an arrow of sound. George caught on immediately and fired a humming roar that made everybody in the lists throw themselves down and hold their ears to stop their heads bursting.

The Scarlet Knight couldn't do that. His helmet was in the way. Besides, his horse was already on the move – his joust had started.

But the sound was directed at *him*, and he took its full force. The thrumming noise flew into his helmet like a swarm of bees. The bees buzzed round and round his head, making him reel. They flew into his ears and fluttered crazily in there, whining and stinging.

The Scarlet Knight thought he was going mad. He cried out, dropped his lance and feverishly tried to undo his helmet. It wouldn't come off. It was stuck. He roared in frustration and beat the helmet with his mailed fists to dislodge the bees from his ears. He was doing that, knocking himself senseless, when Walter reached him.

All Walter had to do was tilt the knight out of his saddle, but as he drew close he crossed the sound path himself and the noise burst into his helmet, too, rattling his brain and making him so dizzy he almost missed.

Almost, but not quite. Wildly he swung his lance and clipped the knight's shoulder just as the Scarlet Knight dealt himself a knockout blow to the jaw.

The Scarlet Knight toppled from his horse and fell to the ground unconscious. George stopped singing, Jo clapped her hands in glee and the people looked up and saw Walter holding his lance high in triumph.

They were still wondering what had happened when Peter Bullfinch, as he had promised, entered the lists like a tornado. Using the famous whirling technique which so bewildered his wrestling opponents, he flailed his cannonball arms, lifted the Green Knight, Walter's next opponent, clean off his horse, and spun back out of the lists like a disappearing top. The knight hit the ground with a bone-shattering crash and stayed there. The next thing the crowd saw was Walter waving his lance in the air again.

Four down, two to go. Nobody had ever seen anything like it.

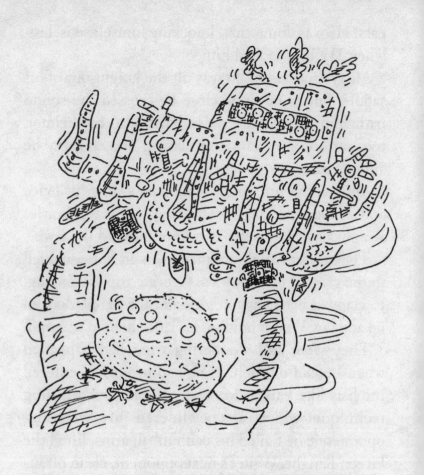

After each peculiar victory Walter rode up to the stand and saluted his smiling parents. The onlookers weren't laughing at him now. They were cheering.

Sir Neville leered viciously and ordered his steward to get on his horse and be prepared to bring this nonsense to an end.

But now Walter had to face his greatest

challenge. His next opponent was to be Sir Ribrub de Crackling, the Dark Knight and the reigning jousting champion.

Sir Ribrub wasn't going to take any nonsense from a renegade boy. He stormed into the lists in a fury, slammed down his visor and set off immediately towards the little upstart.

But the little upstart wasn't ready.

The midsummer sun was beating down, and inside Walter's armour the temperature felt like a thousand degrees. His skin prickled. Sweat streamed through his hair and into his eyes as he cantered wearily back into the lists and lowered his lance.

Only then did he realise his foe was already charging at him full tilt. And only then did he realise who it was.

The shock all but unseated Walter. He slipped sideways in his saddle. Dizzily, he tried to pull himself upright again, but it was all he could do to hang on and not fall. Upside-down, he watched Sir Ribrub's lance hurtle towards him, fast as a javelin, with death on its tip.

For Jo and Big George, what happened next was pure inspiration.

'Do somethin', Georgie!' Jo shrieked.

'Ssommthhnnn,' George hummed.

'Now, ri'?'

'Nowwry.'

'*Georgie!*'

Galvanised into action, George grabbed Jo in his fist, thrust her over the heads of the crowd and put her down on the neck of the Dark Knight's horse, facing him.

'How are yous, mister?' said Jo, smiling sweetly as she tore off her right sleeve and stuffed it into Sir Ribrub's visor. 'Nice day, en't it?'

Sir Ribrub de Crackling was not just blinded, he was so surprised he forgot what he was doing. By the time he remembered, he was two miles away and too late. And by then, of course, Jo was long gone – in fact she'd come and gone so quickly she was just a blue blur and nobody else appeared to have noticed her.

Sir Ribrub thought she must have been a fairy.

Five down, one to go.

Walter was still hanging upside-down in his saddle as he saluted the beaming Robert and scowling Maggot and prepared to meet his last opponent – Jeremiah Wormscrode, the cause of all his family's misery. He was so tired he hardly knew where he was any more.

But the Wormscrode knew very well.

He cantered up to the stand on a glistening chocolate-coloured horse and bowed to Sir Neville with a toadying stoop. His fat lips blossomed into a smile. 'Sire,' he drooled, 'your next champion pays you honour.'

Turning to the prisoner, he bowed mockingly and waved the point of his lance within an inch of Robert of Swyre's face.

'The next time you see this,' he snarled, 'it will have your son's head on it.'

Then Jeremiah Wormscrode took up his position in the lists and closed his visor with a snap.

'Time to do one more deed, Georgie,' Jo whispered urgently. 'Only I've run out of ideas, so it's up to you, all ri'? Walter is up against his worst enemy now. Can you think of anythin' to save 'im?'

George scratched his head. He looked puzzled. Then his eyes gleamed and his beard parted in a slow, enormous grin.

'Ssavve Walterrr,' he said, nodding and smacking his lips.

Smacking his lips is how Big George did it.

You know how, if you suck in your breath really sharply, you can drawn up something light from a table, like a feather or a fly?

That is what George did now.

It was a great trick, so great that nobody knew what happened – except Jeremiah, and even he was confused.

One second he was crowing and cantering and sighting along his lance at an upstart boy, with every intention of skewering him to kingdom come, and the next he felt himself hurtling through the air and landing in a wiry bush in attractive shades of blue and green.

He was trying to slide out of it when he looked down and noticed that he was a long, long way from the ground. So, gurgling with fright and slavering spit by the bucketful, he grabbed the wires and hung on.

As he dangled he looked up into two deep, dark, hairy tunnels.

These seemed to be sucking at him too, because every odd second he was drawn up towards them and every even second he was pushed down again. He felt like a puppet bobbing on a string.

It was a nightmare. He didn't know which was the more terrifying, the tunnels or the drop. But he did know that he couldn't hang on for much longer, because the weight of his armour was pulling him down.

Jeremiah Wormscrode felt the wire slipping

through his fingers. He whimpered. Then, just when he was sure things couldn't get any worse, they did.

An abyss opened up in front of his face.

It was dark, hot and humid, like staring into the mouth of a volcano. Then, like a volcano erupting, the abyss belched out an extraordinary roar which sounded – unless he was very much mistaken – like 'grolyhoomp'.

But Jeremiah Wormscrode had no time to consider this because now he was flying again, in reverse this time, blown instead of sucked.

He soared above the pavilions, planed down over the peasants' heads, missed his horse by a mile and landed slap in the lap of Sir Neville de Magott.

chapter Eighteen
The Seventh Knight

S ir Neville wasn't himself after that.

But Jeremiah was worse – he was gibbering.
Tears of terror drenched his cheeks. He threw
himself on the ground, clutched Sir Neville's knees
and wailed, 'Forgive me, sire, for I have sinned! I've
been to the jaws of hell and back but I know that
can only be the beginning of my punishment! Oh,
sire, I confess! I confess!'

'Confess to what?' gasped Sir Neville, trying to
pull his body back into shape.

'Why, sire, to everything!'

'*Everything?*'

'Everything! Because everything I have ever done
has been wicked! Let me confess, sire, please!'

'Oh, very well, if you must,' said Sir Neville –
rather absently, because he was seeing if he knew

what day of the week it was, to judge whether he needed to pull his head into shape as well. 'Confess away.'

That is precisely what Jeremiah Wormscrode did. He owned up to every lie, theft, fraud, betrayal, assault, kidnap and murder he had committed since the day he was born. It took hours and became very boring.

Sir Neville was amazed that one man could get through so many misdeeds in a single lifetime. 'Let me get this straight, Wormscrode,' he yawned, as soon as he could get a word in. 'Are you saying you're a crook?'

'That sums it up nicely, sire.'

'And Robert of Swyre is innocent?'

'Absolutely.'

'Well, I'll be blowed,' Sir Neville said.

While the Wormscrode was confessing his sins, Walter too was trying to pull himself together.

He had finally fallen right out of his saddle and was lying sprawled on the grass, too bruised and tired to get up.

Then Peter Bullfinch, singing 'C'mon now, c'mon now, what's the madder wid you?' hauled him to his feet and propelled him towards the stand. 'Don't mess wid me, Walter,' the Ox whispered. 'You go up to that Maggot and claim your prize.'

Staggering the last few steps on his own Walter ignored the weeping Jeremiah, clanked up to Sir Neville, swayed, removed his helmet, bowed and croaked, 'Sir, as victor in this tournament and trial by combat, I claim my father's freedom.'

'Do you, by jove?' said Sir Neville.

'Freedom, yiss!' a girl's voice shouted from somewhere among the empty pavilions. 'Give 'im freedom, all ri'?'

And an extraordinary humming voice, which vibrated the air like the drone from a thousand bagpipers, echoed 'Ffreeem! Ffreeeeeemm!'

Now the people took up the cry. 'Robert of Swyre is innocent!' they shouted. 'Make him Steward again and execute the Wormscrode instead!'

'I say,' cried Sir Neville, 'that's a good idea!'

Jeremiah Wormscrode took the hint at record speed. He leaped the lists and was streaking through the pavilions before anyone could stop him.

Only Jo, standing on George's head, saw what happened next. Only she knew that, quick though the steward was, the grolyhoomp's boot was even quicker, and that was why Jeremiah Wormscrode turned into a human rocket that whooshed out of the pavilions and crashed deep inside the forest.

When he arrived there the bear, who was very hungry, grunted for joy and began chasing him.

She may be chasing him still.

Then Jo watched the burly guard loosen the manacles from Robert of Swyre. A lump lodged in her throat when she saw that pale, gentle man step forward to embrace his son, and she knew from the way they clasped each other that both were weeping.

Now the crowd took up a new cry.

'Honour the boy!' they shouted. 'Honour the new champion!'

Jo leaped recklessly from George's head and raced towards the lists. 'Yiss, yous do that, yous old Maggot!' she shouted. 'Yous give Walter honner, all ri'?'

Sir Neville looked uncertainly at his people. They were overexcited, jumping up and down like yapping dogs in a hunt. When dogs get like that, he thought, you can't trust them – they'll turn on you and bite if you aren't careful. And these dogs seem determined to have their way, and here's that ragged girl inciting them still further. Better give in for now. Just for now.

So, Sir Neville, being a coward at heart, beckoned Walter to come to him.

Jo reached the stand just in time to see Walter

kneel and Sir Neville, leering like a lunatic, dub
him on the shoulder with his sword and say, 'Arise,
Sir Knight.'

The crowd cheered, the ladies simpered and Jo –

who really was no lady – threw herself at Walter, flung her arms round his neck and kissed him.

Walter was so surprised he fell over again.

When he'd recovered he squinted up at her grinning face and said, 'Will you tell me something, Jo?'

'Anythin'.'

'What's going on?'

'Everythin's goin' on,' she smiled. 'An' it's all good an' it's all because of that grolyhoomp!'

But everything was not good, because like a wicked magician Sir Neville had one last nasty trick up his sleeve.

He whispered to the herald, and the herald marched forward and cried, 'Oyez! Oyez! SILENCE! Sir Neville de Magott wishes to make an announcement!'

When the people had quietened, Sir Neville grimaced and shouted, 'We may be denied an execution but our entertainment isn't over yet. Neither is the tournament. Because, my people, I decree a seventh round! This renegade . . .' Here he clamped an icy hand round Jo's shoulder, 'has chosen trial by combat to prove her innocence. Her champion's adversary was to be that grovelling ninny Wormscrode, but since he's run away we shall have to choose another foe to replace him. What say you?'

'We say *aye*!' the people shouted, as eager as ever to see blood spilt.

'And who better,' leered the Maggot, 'than our new champion?'

'Aye! Aye! Aye!' Caps soared skywards. Feet stamped the ground. 'Let Walter of Swyre be the Seventh Knight! Let him prove he's a true knight – make him fight once more!'

Jo gaped at Walter in dismay.

Walter stared at her in horror.

'Who's your champion, Jo?' he asked in a shaky voice. 'It couldn't be . . . could it?'

Jo nodded. 'Who else?'

Walter's eyes rolled.

'Call your champion, girl,' Sir Neville commanded.

Jo brushed away tears. 'What shall I do?'

'You have no choice,' said Walter, struggling to his feet. 'You must call him.'

'But how you gunna fight a grolyhoomp?'

'I've no idea. Anyway, I don't want to fight George. He's my friend. Perhaps he'll think of something.'

Jo gazed across the pavilion field. There was no sign of Big George – he was keeping well hidden, as they'd agreed. Well, that was futile now.

She took a deep breath. 'Georgie,' she cried, 'show yourself!'

George did.

But it wasn't at all in the way they expected.

chapter Nineteen
champion George

Something was happening to George. He was gripped by a very odd idea. It was while he watched the loving reunion between Walter and his father that it suddenly occurred to him that he might be dreaming.

Because wasn't it only yesterday – or even today – that he had woken up in a strange forest and discovered an extremely small girl called Tilly, and after a most peculiar adventure lost her again?

And wasn't it soon afterwards that his rest had been disturbed by another very small person, the boy whose extraordinary quest was ending here?

It was bewildering, because in the huge timespan of George's life, earthly days seemed to pass in a blink, and yet so many things happened in them it made him dizzy to think about it.

How was anybody to make sense of a conundrum like that, other than to think it was all a dream?

But if he was dreaming he must be sleepwalking.

And if he was sleepwalking, where was his bedroom, and his bed?

That is how it came about that at exactly the moment Jo shouted to him, George stood up to look for his bedroom – and saw in the distance a rounded hill that seemed familiar.

He decided to have a closer look at it.

Whether George understood what was happening in the lists is anybody's guess. Yet what happened now was extraordinarily apt. You might say it worked like a dream. The sight of a forty-foot-high grolyhoomp rising out of their tents like a genie out of a lamp gave the tournament spectators quite a start. They cried out in terror. Many fell to their knees. Others fainted clean away. They all liked excitement, but they'd had that already and this was one thrill too many.

'Help!' yelped Sir Neville, 'is *that* your champion, girl?'

'That's him all ri',' Jo nodded. 'Big, en't he?'

'He certainly is. But what's he doing? Why is he walking away?'

Jo, who had no idea what George was doing, said confidently, 'He's getting hisself ready, I expect.'

But she frowned and glanced at Walter, who shrugged helplessly.

'Georgie!' Jo cried. 'Come back!'

Walter shook his lance and shouted, 'Come on now, grolyhoomp, come and fight! Don't mess with me, now!'

When George finally stopped he was so far out of the lists he seemed to have shrunk almost to human size. There he waited while Walter, helped by Peter Bullfinch and Sir Harry le Frit, who had just arrived back from the forest, hauled himself up on to the despairing heap of bones that was his horse, dropped his visor like the clang of fate, and rode out for one last joust.

At last, he was ready. The Seventh Knight faced Jo's distant champion. And Big George faced him.

Sir Neville raised his arm.

The chief trumpeter raised his trumpet.

The people held their breath.

The herald drew his breath in.

Any second now.

Jo closed her eyes, pictured the rabbit's foot on George's chest and frantically rubbed it in her mind for luck. When she opened them again she had the strangest impression that events were happening in slow motion, like a dream . . .

She saw Sir Neville's arm fall like a lazy feather.

She heard a long, lingering trumpet note, and the drawn-out cry of 'Oye-e-e-ez!' from the herald.

She saw Walter spur his nag forward and she saw George start to run.

But even in slow motion George was running amazingly fast. He zoomed out of the distance at a hundred miles an hour, growing larger and faster with every pounding step.

The people cowered.

The leer froze on Sir Neville de Magott's face.

Walter's horse whinnied with terror and reared up on its hind legs, pawing the air with its hooves as if warding off an evil spirit.

And Big George, thundering forward, gave out the most amazing war cry anyone anywhere has ever heard.

'Zzzunkerrsmitkinnfuongerrumpterrighttsniggleoo opstengrollsmoglewwwtroggly!' he roared at the top of his voice – which, more or less, is grolyhoomp-speak for 'I spy with my little eye, something beginning with B!'

Nobody knew that, of course.

All Walter knew was that his horse was

performing a two-hooved dance and the ground was shaking and George was bearing down on him like doom on legs. There were only a hundred yards between them now.

Seventy-five.

Fifty.

The way his horse was prancing it was impossible for Walter to use his lance. So he screamed instead.

'Aaaaahh!' he shouted.

'Aaaaaaaaaaaaaaaaaaahhhhaaaaa!' replied George, tipping the Seventh Knight an enormous wink as he thundered past at about a thousand miles a minute.

After that, George paid no more attention to Walter or Jo or the other midgets than if they had been the figments of a dream.

With his great loping strides he was far away from them in no time at all, a diminishing figure racing towards the afternoon sun and a curious hump-backed hill.

Then, suddenly, he vanished.

chapter Twenty
Arise, Sir Grolyhoomp

Believing that Walter had chased away a giant which had threatened all their lives, the people paraded him on their shoulders like a hero, up and down the lists for the next hour.

But Walter's victory was Jo's defeat. She had lost her trial by combat.

Sir Neville called her over to him for sentencing.

'From now on,' he growled, contriving a leer so grotesque Jo thought his face was dividing in two, 'you will be the property of my steward Robert of Swyre, to dwell in his house and do his bidding until your life's end. Do you understand?'

Jo nodded dumbly. Choking back a sob, she looked wildly for an escape route but found none.

She was back where she had started.

'Come to your new master, girl.'

Robert of Swyre was beckoning to her. His wife Mary held his hand and their son Walter stood beside them like a battered tin soldier, grinning broadly – smirking at Jo's misery, no doubt.

Jo wasn't having that, so with dark eyes blazing she marched up to Walter and cried, 'I en't gunna do no bidding from yous, all ri'? I en't your serf. Yous don't own me!'

Walter smiled infuriatingly. 'I never said I did.'

'Nobody owns you, Joanne,' said Walter's father, in a voice that was at once warm, soft, calm and astonishing.

'*What?*' she gasped.

Robert of Swyre smiled. 'You saved my son's life. That means you helped save mine too. In return, I can do no less than give you what you most desire. From this moment you are a free person.'

Jo couldn't speak. She stared at him like an idiot.

'Go on, father,' said Walter.

Robert of Swyre let go of his wife's hand and gently but firmly took Jo's in his strong fist. 'I believe you like to be called Joanne of Nowhere. Is that so?'

'Well, I . . . yiss . . . I suppose I do,' Jo babbled. 'But that's because—'

'From now on, would you do us the honour of becoming Joanne of Swyre, and living with us in our home?'

Jo felt dizzy. This couldn't be happening. 'Living with yous as what?' she whispered.

'As family, Jo. As our daughter and Walter's sister. Well, what do you say?'

Jo's eyes filled with tears. The lump was in her throat again. She felt stupid. But truly there were no words, no words. She looked helplessly at Walter.

Walter beamed.

'She says all ri',' he said.

Next morning, very early, Walter and Jo tiptoed

from the sleeping house and started to run. They were on a mission, Walter said.

'What sort of mission? Where's we going?' Jo asked him, but Walter said it was a secret, which was infuriating but exciting too.

He led her through the fields with their chequered crops, past the jutting forest rim and across a great wasteland towards that distant, curiously rounded hill. When they drew near Jo saw that it was clad in bushes and low trees, and covered by an enormous briar rose.

At its foot Walter put a finger to his lips and whispered, 'We have to climb. No talking now.'

It was very steep. As they pulled themselves up Jo saw that Walter was searching for something.

Higher they went, and higher. For a moment, Walter seemed anxious, but then he grunted, 'Over there', and headed towards a bush whose roots were raised slightly from the ground. He peeled away the turf beneath it and uncovered a hole.

Jo shivered. 'We en't going down there, are we?'

Walter nodded, lowered himself into the hole and disappeared.

Muttering a prayer, Jo followed – and dropped like a stone on to something that was neither hard nor soft but rose and fell like waves on a beach.

She had expected it to be dark, but an eerie green

glow to her right made her heart miss a beat. She'd seen that light before, coming from Big George's face!

'What's he doing?' she breathed.

Walter, sitting beside her on what she now realised was George's chest, whispered, 'He's sleeping. This is how I found him. I woke him up and asked him to help me. Well he's done that, so now he's come back to rest again. I thought that was probably what had happened, but I had to make sure he was all right.'

'What happens now?'

'Nothing. We have to let him sleep.'

Jo gave a little shriek. 'I don't want to leave him here!'

Walter frowned. 'He doesn't belong out there, Jo. I mean, have you ever seen a grolyhoomp out in the open before?'

Jo shook her head sadly. 'He belonged to us, though, didn't he?'

'Maybe, for a short time. But I wouldn't like to trust him to anyone else. He's too important.'

In her heart Jo knew Walter was right, but she didn't give up easily. 'Before we go I want to whisper somethin' to him, all ri'? It's a secret.'

'Very well. But be quick. I don't want anyone seeing us leave.'

Walter moved away and Jo, wiping her eyes, climbed up to George's face and leaned towards his ear.

'Georgie,' she breathed, 'can yous hear me?'

There was no response. He was asleep all right.

So Jo did what she was determined to do. Holding her arm stiff she reached out her hand and touched Big George's shoulder as if her finger was the tip of a sword.

'I knight yous, Georgie,' she whispered, ''cos yous deserves it, all ri'? So, arise, Sir Grolyhoomp!'

George slumbered on.

Jo looked at him for a long while, then returned to Walter. 'What do we do next?' she asked him.

'Close up the hill so nobody can find him.'

'Let's do it then. What yous waitin' for?'

As they climbed back into the world they heard George give an enormous snore. It made them laugh, and laughing made them feel better about leaving him.

As they replaced the roots and then the turf so carefully that afterwards even they couldn't find the entrance again, Jo said hopefully, 'He might come out again tomorrer, mightn't he? After he's slept a bit?'

Walter smiled at her persistence. 'Yes, Jo,' he said gently. 'Perhaps he will. Come on, let's go home.'

After that Jo, Walter, Robert and Mary, all of Swyre, lived very happily together.

Robert became once more the honest steward to Sir Neville de Magott that he had been before. He grew to be his trusted friend, too, and was able to influence him in many good ways – even to relax a little and stop leering quite so crazily.

Walter returned to his studies. In time, he

became one of the greatest knights in the land, and a renowned jousting champion – although never again did he achieve quite such a triumph as the time when a grolyhoomp called George gave him a hand.

And Jo? Well, Jo soon changed her mind about wanting to be a lady. After all the excitement she'd had with Big George, that seemed too tame for words. Instead, she decided that *she* could become a knight too, because, as she told Walter, 'Anythin' yous can do, I can do too, all ri'?'

And Walter had to agree.

So Jo became the first girl ever to go to Knight School.

But that's another story.

afterword

Three things remain to be said.

The first may concern you, and it is this.

Although this story may seem to have happened a very long time ago, it's not so long ago really. Think of it this way. Like Tilly Miller before them, when Jo and Walter grew up they both married and had children of their own. And their children had children, and their children's children had children, on through the generations right up to today – and perhaps to you.

So you see, there's a big possibility that you yourself may be connected to the tale of Big George *and the* Seventh Knight.

The second thing concerns Big George.

He returned to his hill to carry on with his rudely interrupted sleep, but that hill is quite a puzzle. It began life as a dome made to look natural, and as the centuries passed it grew more and more to look like a real hill. But it never was a real hill. It still isn't.

So keep your eyes peeled. If you see a hill that looks like a hill but isn't a hill, you may be getting warm. If it has a wild briar rose growing on it, listen for snores.

The third thing concerns both you and George, and it's this.

Remember that the inhabitants of a star hidden deep inside the constellation of Ursa Middling sleep for exactly nine hundred Earth years. Add 900 to 1103 – the year Big George first fell asleep – and what do you get?

You get shivers running up your spine and your hair standing on end, because you could have a grolyhoomp knocking at your door the day after tomorrow, wanting breakfast.

Be sure to have some ready for him.

Big George and the winter King

contents

Foreword

Whispers from Space

Although Time stands almost still on Halrig, Big George's home star in the far constellation of Ursa Middling, on Earth it flows like a river, drowning year after year.

George sleeps on regardless, snoring like a hundred oinking pigs inside the hill that protects him. And as he sleeps, the Fourteenth Century steals by. Earth grows older but no wiser.

In England people are born, live their lives, and die. Kings and Queens come and go. Not long ago plague visited the countryside so savagely it almost emptied it of people, so that whole towns and villages had to start all over again. On Planet Earth there are always upheavals.

Even so, around Big George's hill the seasons pass serenely by. The wild rose on its summit, planted in George's memory hundreds of years ago by Tilly Miller, still bursts into leaf each spring, flowers in summer and fades in autumn. Then winter freezes the soil so hard you would think nothing could grow in it any more. But next year the rose will bloom again. It always does.

All this time Big George whistles and blows in his sleep and the rabbit's foot pinned to his tunic by Joanne of Nowhere rises and falls, rises and falls.

Here in his bedroom everything seems changeless.

But it is not.

7

Imagine.

Time on Planet Earth has reached December in the Year of Our Lord 1399 – two hundred and ninety-six years since Big George's spacecraft fizzed through our atmosphere and crashed into an English forest, wiping out his memory.

Not far away, in the border region between England and Wales known as the Marchlands, a Welshman called Owain Glyndwr has been making such a nuisance of himself that the newly-crowned English King Henry the Fourth has sent an army from London to teach him a lesson.

It is a very small and ill-equipped army, which only yesterday marched raggedly past Big George's hill. He didn't hear them, of course.

This mysterious borderland, this country of mists and mountains, is a strange and magical place hinged between two countries and really belonging to neither. And on these December nights, hinged between two centuries, the magic seems so strong that people cross their hearts and fingers and believe that anything can happen.

Everybody is nervous. The soldiers, the Welsh, the English and the March people alike all look for omens and signs. They find plenty, though none is quite as magical as the vision which has begun to appear in the night sky: a fiery comet, blazing westward and trailing a ribbon of light. That, the people say, foretells a miracle.

For once they're right: two miracles are going to happen here very soon.

One of them is called George.

chapter one

A Stranger in a very Strange Land

In December 1399 a great freeze gripped the Marchlands between England and Wales. The cold reached into the most unlikely places until finally it pushed its icy fingers right through the clods of Big George's hill and touched the sleeping figure inside.

It painted a silver coating over the message pinned to his chest and the rabbit's foot beside it. It froze his beard, dimmed the green light that glowed in his cheeks and stiffened his boots to stone.

Attacked by the frost from all sides, George shivered in his sleep. Icicles pricked his eyebrows like needles. He tried to brush them away but his fingers wouldn't move.

The effort roused him. He sat up stiffly and sleepily. He blinked into the darkness beyond the range of his cheeks' emerald glow. He flapped his arms and hugged himself. 'Grolyhoomp,' he muttered through lips frozen hard as bricks. 'Snik-backer-wigglo!' – 'Hello! My, but it's cold!'

He yawned and his breath steamed.

Creakily George rose to his feet. He thought it might be less cold outside, so he pressed his shoulder against the hinged wall. It opened slowly, dislodging clods that slithered down his neck like nuggets of ice.

George crawled through, took a look outside – and gasped with surprise.

Although it was night, after the deeper darkness of his bedroom he could make out the shapes of bushes and straggly trees. All were rigid with the frost, which on this December night was a living thing that clamped chilly fingers over George's face and body and made his long locked neck stiffer than ever.

It certainly was not warmer out here, but George hardly felt the cold now. All his attention was given to the sky. It brimmed with stars. Above his head the Milky Way shimmered. To his left and right galaxies stretched to the horizon. And moving westward with an almost visible motion was a most extraordinary comet trailing a white ribbon of light.

George gazed entranced.

And he listened.

It seemed as if the stars spoke to him. The galaxies sang. The Milky Way hummed. The comet whispered, 'Look at me. Watch me. Follow me – follow my tail!'

Watching it, listening to it, something exciting happened to George. Inside his damaged memory he felt a small – a very small – shift ... as if a key was opening, very slightly, a forgotten door.

He had no idea what lay at the other side of the door, but the very fact of it opening at all delighted him beyond measure.

It gave him hope. Because to lose your memory is a strange and terrible thing.

When Big George cracked his head during his landing on Earth, he lost all connection with the things which, until then, had made him real to himself.

He no longer knew who he was.

He did not know where he was.

He did not know where he had come from, or why he was here.

And to add to his misfortunes, when he met the people who lived in this world he couldn't understand a word they said.

Big George, in fact, was as lost as you can possibly be.

But George was not stupid. Far from it. He looked for clues and pointers. He tried to learn the people's language by mimicking the sounds their words made. He looked inside their heads and hearts to understand how they thought and felt. But even so, after two unforgettable adventures, he was still not much further forward.

The problem was it was bedtime on Halrig. George should be asleep now. But he had learned to his cost that if he nodded off around here, when he woke everything would be changed.

He had lost Tilly Miller and Simpkin Sampkins that way and now, crouching outside his hill, sniffing the starlit land, he knew that another change had taken place. Which meant that his new friends Walter of Swyre and Joanne of Nowhere would also have disappeared.

Here people came and went like dust on the wind. That was confusing.

It was also bewildering that among all the people he had met none looked anything like himself. He was a stranger in a very strange land.

Yet now, suddenly and unexpectedly, the comet had spoken to him.

'Follow me,' it had whispered.

George stood up. 'All right,' he said to himself, 'that's what I'll do. I'll follow that star. And while I'm following it I'll learn about this place – I'll look and listen, see and find. That will be an adventure!'

He knew he would have to be careful, though, because up to now nearly everybody he'd met had been unfriendly.

There seemed no one he could trust. Because who can you turn to when there's no one else like you in the world?

Fired with this new purpose, George stood up tall and straight.

Stretching his cramped muscles he unfolded himself until he towered higher than any tree in the forest.

For one last moment he waited, tasting the air and savouring it.

Then, closing his ears to the clanging universe and trusting a comet to guide him, he strode away into the winter night, heading westward.

chapter Two

Follow that Star

As Big George began his journey he eagerly looked for things to learn. What he found first was a puzzle – a puzzle about all the changes that had come over the world since he was last awake.

Then there had been birds, flowers, leaves, sunshine and soft warm air. Now, as a new day slowly dawned and the comet and the glow in his cheeks faded, George saw a grey, bleak land in the grip of bitter winter. The trees were leafless skeletons, black and still. There were no flowers and no colours. Birds were silent. Instead of comforting softness, the air pinched his face like the nails of a bad-tempered child and the ground rang hard as iron under his tramping feet.

Having no experience of winter, because on

Halrig there are no seasons, George thought that Earth had been stricken by a terrible disease, and was dying.

He worried about that a lot, until he heard a distant beating of drums. He ducked down behind a copse, peered warily round it and saw that ahead the flat lands he'd been crossing were giving way to low hills rising to a misty horizon.

And he saw that climbing the nearest hill, and moving westward like himself, was a small army.

A drummer led the way, sounding a rhythmical, hypnotic beat. Behind him an untidy line of soldiers shuffled like a column of weary ants. Half a dozen were on horseback while the rest slogged it on foot.

George's concern was to pass the ramshackle army unseen, so he waited until it was out of sight and then, keeping low, wheeled northward to circle the hill.

But when you're a forty-foot-high grolyhoomp it's hard to be invisible, and even though George crouched as low as he could without actually toppling over, his head and shoulders were for a few moments clearly visible to the drummer, who was a little ahead of the rest.

George forged on, unaware he had been seen but aware that the drummer had missed a beat. If he had turned he would have seen that the tiny man had become a pale and shaking wreck, certain he had seen his first Welsh monster, and convinced that this trip was going to turn out badly.

In that he was quite right.

All that day the monotonous drumming echoed inside George's head. All day he marched westward, through a country ever more disturbed by hills. He saw no one else because the local people, farmers all, were keeping to their hearth-fires. Cultivation was impossible in weather like this.

He heard a few sounds, though: an axe chopping wood, a shepherd calling his sheep, a dog barking – and once, far away, a cockerel crowing like a wailing bagpipe and making the lonely land seem even more lonely.

At least, thought George, the sounds proved that the land wasn't quite dead yet.

In the afternoon he reached a river that gleamed a dull pewter in the fading light. Although it was wide the water was low and George was able to cross it by jumping from island to island, cracking and crunching ice-floes to powder beneath his great boots.

After the river the hills grew higher and closer together with deep narrow valleys between, so that from a distance the country looked as if dozens of whales had beached themselves there.

Dusk was short and swift. The stars pricked out again and in the western sky the comet sailed into view, showing George the way to go.

He adjusted his direction slightly.

When it was almost too dark to see the ground beneath his feet, he reached the summit of the highest hill of all – and noticed two things.

The first, far below, was a ring of light made by the clustering fires and candles of a small village.

The other was even more unexpected: George noticed that high above the village and his own head the comet had stopped moving.

chapter Three

village in the Hills

On that bleak midwinter evening the village of Kingswell – crouched beneath a mountain with a comet hovering above – looked like a scene from a Christmas carol. (Think 'Good King Wenceslas' and you'll be very close.)

A small stone church with a wooden tower was perched on a hump of ground scattered with yew trees. Below it houses, farms and barns huddled together for company.

On another rocky hump a fortified manor reared like a black fist. It was more castle than house, and at this windless hour the flag on its battlements hung limply. All of its windows were dark except one, where a torch weakly flared.

To George on his cold hilltop the lights of Kingswell seemed to twinkle like stars, as if the village was the centre of its own small universe. That was also exactly how its inhabitants thought of it, because if you lived in Kingswell everywhere else was a very long way off.

It could stay there too, the villagers thought, because in their experience the outside world brought nothing but trouble. Why, only a few decades ago had it not sent the plague, whose effects were all too visible in the churchyard? And now there were rumours that the English king was sending soldiers to wreak more havoc on their innocent heads, as punishment for the behaviour of that rebellious Welshman, Owain Glyndwr.

What had Kingswell to do with a Welsh prince? Or an English King? A curse on both their countries, for Kingswell was neither Welsh nor English, look you, and didn't want to be either.

Besides, it had enough troubles of its own already.

Why, had not its lord, Sir Simeon Griphook, become such a weeping baby since his poor wife died that he had completely lost his grip on the village and now seemed to be losing his wits?

And was not his daughter, the motherless Bess, miserably unhappy to see her father and Kingswell sinking under the ruthless sway of Solomon Sneck the Sorcerer?

And was not that sorcerer hungry for more and

more power, until it seemed he would not be satisfied until he had all of Kingswell crushed inside his bony fist?

And did not everybody else have troubles, right down to the lowest of the low – to Huw Evans the pig boy, who was unhappy because he had no power at all and no authority, even over his pigs?

With all that going on, the villagers whispered around their winter fires, they needed an invading army like a hole in the head. Why, they grumbled, crossing themselves superstitiously as they spoke, they would rather be visited by a monster, or a giant!

If those villagers had looked outside at that moment they'd have thought their wish had been granted for, high above them on the mountain, George's face was glowing like a green cheese moon, and his shape – which could have been a man's if it had not possessed a swan's neck and been so utterly huge – reared up gigantically against the stars like their worst nightmare.

And now that nightmare was moving – descending – heading their way!

George, who ever since he landed on Earth had been looking for somewhere to belong, decided to look into Kingswell – and listen and learn and seek and find.

But as he made his way down the mountain by the light of his cheeks he felt anxious, as we all do when we're entering the unknown.

For George, everything and everywhere was unknown.

When he reached the village he heard music. From the dark manor there came the soft twanging of a harp, accompanying a lilting voice which chanted words that were neither song nor speech but something in between.

Walking tiptoe ('dibdoo' he called it), George was able to approach the manor unseen and unheard. But as he neared the lighted window, which had been opened to let out the smoke from the fire inside, he stopped sharply.

Because outside the window, peering inside and listening enthralled to the chanting, there was a boy.

chapter four

The Boy at the window

Huw Evans had a dream.

It came to him every morning when, at first light, he woke on his straw pallet in the cowshed which had served his family for a house since the day his father died.

Lying very still, he dreamed that this was the day when the fabulous Great Hero of Kingswell would return and transform him from a pig boy to something altogether wonderful.

In his dream Huw saw the Hero quite clearly: a massive red-bearded giant who rode full tilt out of the west with the setting sun turning his head to flame. He came for one purpose only – to touch Huw's starving family with magic and change their lives for ever.

Tears of longing scalded his eyelids. 'It *could*

happen!' he told himself. 'It isn't impossible because it happened once before, right here in Kingswell. And anything that has happened once can happen again!'

That was why Huw was trespassing here now, risking discovery, clinging to ivy outside the manor hall window, shivering with cold and eavesdropping on the people who – all except one – despised him.

Inside the hall, by the flickering light from torch and fire, a minstrel was chanting the Legend of the Winter King.

He was an old man, well past eighty, but as he sang he moved nimbly about the hall, stepping lightly between sleeping dogs and the sprawling legs of his audience, who had heard the story many times before but never tired of hearing it again.

'From the western lands in the hour of our need
Rode a King who would answer our prayers indeed
And set our people free...'

He paused and looked round the room to make sure everyone was awake for the climax of his story.

Near the fire the languid frame of Sir Simeon Griphook stiffened with anticipation.

At his knees the small figure of his daughter Bess tensed, her dark curls and eyes shining brightly in the firelight.

Close by, the crouching form of Solomon Sneck stirred, unhooked itself like a straightening question mark, then hunched back again.

Beyond them, away from the fire, the worthy people of Kingswell clustered like ghosts in the shadows, holding their breath.

The minstrel was satisfied. He could end his tale.
'*See the villains flee before him!*
See their blood on his sword and spear!
See the glory of the sun shine round him
Shielding him from hurt and fear..!'
Huw's knuckles tightened round the ivy. Once again in his mind's eye he saw the mysterious Hero who, centuries ago, had visited a village called Simonswell to free it from oppression. After a wonderful victory he had disappeared as quickly as he came, but he left behind a hope that should the need arise again another King, another Giant, would come riding out of the sunset to perform miracles of daring.

In gratitude, and to ensure that the story would never be forgotten, the villagers had done two things.

First, they renamed their village Kingswell.

Second, they established the annual Ceremony of the Winter King, during which a simple soul was crowned King for the season and honoured as the Spirit of Christmas.

The custom was still going strong and the people of Kingswell felt sure that this year it would be more important than it had ever been before. As soon as the minstrel had ended his song their mutterings began.

'We should start praying for that King to come

back before those English soldiers get here!'

'That's only a rumour. There may be no soldiers at all.'

'Even if there are,' said a third man, a swarthy fellow with a squint who scratched his nose incessantly, 'they mayn't find us. We're not easy to find.'

Then they began to worry about the terrifying things that were foretold to happen as the old century died and the new one reared over the horizon.

'We've got all that coming to us, see, as well as the soldiers. Dragons rising from the earth.'

'Griffins diving from the clouds, breathing fire.'

'Black poison flowing across the ground and turning your feet to mush.'

'What are we going to do?'

'What *can* we do?'

'We can pray, that's all. Pray for that King to come, look you.'

Huw was afraid. He was scared by the rumours of ruthless soldiers seeking revenge. He was worried by the superstitious talk because he was sure it would all come true.

And he trembled at the sight of Solomon Sneck the Sorcerer unwinding his lumpy frame again and shouting, in the harsh reedy voice that sounded half sneer and half threat, 'Newt's ears! I could solve all your problems with spells, if only. . . '

He stopped and stared insolently at the lord of the manor.

Sir Simeon Griphook returned his stare with a listless gaze. 'If only what, Solomon?'

The enchanter smiled. 'If only you'd give me the power I seek, my lord. If only you'd say the word.'

Bess Griphook clutched her father's arm. 'Don't listen to him!' she cried. 'Everything he says is a lie!'

Huw heard no more. He saw the malice slide across Solomon Sneck's eyes but then his fingers, numb with cold, slipped out of the ivy and he fell heavily to the ground.

The fall knocked the breath out of him. As he lay there Huw thought despairingly of his mother and sister huddling with the animals for warmth. And in his heart he knew that even though this winter was so bitter, and the loss of his father so great, the Hero of his dream would never come.

'Dreams are useless,' he thought. 'And stupid. Because why would a King come to a cowshed?'

Sighing, the Kingswell pig boy struggled to his feet, turned for home – and in a flash of green light had a *real* vision for the first time in his life.

chapter Five

Grolyhoomp

Huw yelled with fright.

He knew he shouldn't do that because he'd give himself away, but seeing the unbelievable bulk of Big George hiding the stars and lighting the air around with his eerily glowing face, he couldn't help it.

He also felt that praying for a giant to come had been a very bad mistake.

He yelped again when George leaned down over him and grinned. His cry startled a dog, which began to howl, and that disturbed another dog further off, whose barking roused ten more dogs and every cat in Kingswell. In no time there was such a hullabaloo that the guard on the manor battlements woke up and called out in drowsy alarm, 'Who goes there? Show yourself! Who goes there!'

Huw fled. He ran from giant, guard, dragons, griffins, dogs, cats and the cold snake eyes of Solomon Sneck.

But he got nowhere at all because after only two steps he tripped on a rusty chain lying across the manor drawbridge and fell into the moat.

 He was sinking in icy slime when a hand the size of a horse plucked him out and set him dripping on the bank.

Huw coughed up something nasty and croaked,

'Don't kill me, please, I'm needed at home! Don't rob me, because I've got nothing! Don't frighten me, because I'm a coward!'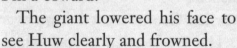

The giant lowered his face to see Huw clearly and frowned.

 Huw, looking a sickly shade of green and feeling even sicker, thought he should give a reason why his life should be spared.

'You see, sir,' he babbled, 'two months ago my father was

chopping trees for Solomon
Sneck – he's our landlord –
when a tree fell on him.
Father died, and because we
were no use to Sneck any more
he turned us out of our house and
made us live in the cowshed.'

Talking about his family's
misfortunes made Huw
want to cry again.

'I look after Solomon
Sneck's pigs, see,' he sniffed,
'but now it's winter they can find
hardly any food. It's the coldest
weather anyone can remember
and *we've* got nothing to eat
either, except what I can beg or
steal and what Bess brings us – Bess
is my friend, though her father would
be mad if he knew she was
friends with a pig boy.

'There's three of us at
home, sir,' he babbled on,
for now Huw had started
he didn't seem able to
stop. 'There's me, my
sister Rachel, who's three,

and my mother Sarah. Mother's going to have another baby soon, so she's hungry all the time. And she's not strong, and I'm frightened for her, sir, very frightened. So don't kill me, please – I'm needed!'

Breathless after the longest speech he had ever made, Huw Evans gazed up at the glowing giant. The giant looked baffled.

Huw cleared his throat.

'Beg pardon, sir,' he said, very slowly and clearly, 'do you understand what I'm saying?'

George lowered his face even closer. Pointing to himself, he opened his mouth and let out a noise that sounded like a beehive.

'Gg-eee-orr-ggge,' he said.

'Pardon?'

'Grolyhoomp.'

'Wh-who are you, sir?'

'Geeorrgge.'

George thought he was getting the hang of the language – people kept saying 'George' to him so it seemed friendly to say it back.

He wanted to be friendly.

Huw peered at the notice on the giant's tunic.

'If found. This is George,' he read. 'He is a grolyhoomp. Signed, Tilly Miller.'

'I'm Huw,' he said.

'Hooooooooo.'

Huw blinked. This must be somebody's idea of a joke. Warily he rose to his feet and backed away inch by inch. Then he turned and ran. After a while he looked round to see if the joke had gone. It hadn't. It was following him.

'Wicle snokrig, flimmernoot,' George buzzed. 'Carry on, boy.'

Suddenly and inexplicably, Huw felt happy. The grolyhoomp's enormous grin made him want to laugh for the first time since his father died. What a wonder he'd found! People whispered about dragons and griffins but *he* had found a grolyhoomp! Wait till Mother and Rachel saw him!

In his excitement Huw ran even faster, with George following dibdoo in his shed-sized boots.

And that is how it happened that Huw the pig boy arrived home with magic at his heels.

When Rachel saw George she screamed. You can understand why. There's big – there's very big – there's colossal – and then in a different league altogether there is Big George. To a three-year-old girl looking anxiously for her brother through the cowshed's low doorway it seemed he was returning with the Devil at his heels.

Rachel's cry brought her mother scurrying, and when Sarah saw George she fainted.

Rachel screamed a second time, Huw ran into the cowshed in dismay, Rachel slammed the door shut – and George was left outside and on his own again.

Half an hour later Sarah Evans was conscious again – but very worried.

'You can't possibly keep him, Huw!' she cried. 'How could we feed him, for a start?'

Huw shrugged. 'Dunno, Ma.'

'He could eat a cow three times a day. Four cows, even.'

'Maybe he doesn't like cows.'

'Bet he likes pigs, though,' Rachel said, peeping through a window at George's enormous bulk. 'We've got pigs, Huwy.'

'They're not my pigs, are they?' Huw protested. 'They're Solomon Sneck's, and if that grolyhoomp so much as touches one Sneck will hang me up for meat myself!'

'Don't say that, Huwy! Don't say that!'

'So what I ask again,' murmured Sarah Evans weakly, 'is what on earth are we going to do with a grolyhoomp!'

If only they'd known, George wasn't hungry. You don't eat while you're asleep, and he was supposed to be asleep.

He was thirsty, though. He would have to have a drink soon.

Shivering with cold, he fingered the spoon in his pocket and the rabbit's foot on his chest and recalled Tilly's smile, Jo's spirit and Walter's courage.

He missed them a lot, and standing in the dark outside a rickety cowshed in another unknown place filled with strangers, he felt the all too familiar loneliness fall over him like a heavy cloak.

He sighed – then shrugged it off. 'No use moping,' he told himself. 'What good does it do? Look, listen, seek, find – that's the thing to do. And maybe when I've done it I'll belong here.'

That's what George was hoping as he stood in the darkness in this remotest of valleys, locked magically in no man's land and no-man's time.

Magic really can happen in a circumstance like that, and George felt it hovering in the air around him like a presence that might show itself at any moment.

He became so sure it was going to happen *now* that he held his breath and waited for it.

And waited, forgetting to breathe again.

And still waited, holding that breath until he thought he would burst.

That is how things were at the cowshed when Bess Griphook, escaping from superstitious talk and the sinister presence of Solomon Sneck, arrived with a basket of food for her friends and met a grolyhoomp for the very first time.

chapter Six

count Your Blessings

WHOOOOOSH!
The sound of Big George releasing the pent-up breath he could hold no longer would have beaten the biggest sneeze of all time by at least a thousand per cent.

It crossed the borderland into England like a hurricane, met the King's soldiers fifty miles away and knocked them down.

It blew Bess back through the gate she'd just come in by – but then George breathed in and sucked her back again.

A lot of girls would have wept in a situation like that, but Bess was no crybaby. Instead of weeping she lay on the ground with her eyes shut and counted her blessings.

'I'm still alive,' she thought. 'That's a top

blessing. I'm ten years old, tall, strong, skilled at music, dancing, horse-riding and embroidery – though I don't like that much. So what am I afraid of? I'm afraid of opening my eyes, that's what.'

Steeling herself, she squinted through trembling eyelids and saw Huw bending over her holding a lantern and looking worried, and behind him – a Thing.

'We heard the noise,' Huw said. 'It sounded as if the cowshed was falling down, so I came running. Are you all right?'

Gingerly Bess moved her arms and legs. 'I think so. But ...' she lowered her voice to a whisper ... 'what's *that*?'

'Ah.' Huw glanced over his shoulder and grinned. 'Bess, meet George.'

'George? That monster is called *George*?'

'Apparently.'

'What is he?'

Huw pointed to the notice. 'A grolyhoomp. That's what it says.'

'What's a grolyhoomp?'

'Dunno.'

Huw gazed apologetically at George. 'I'm sorry,' he said gently. 'I'll have to take Bess inside before she freezes. But I can't fit you in, can I? You'd raise the roof and squash the beasts. Don't go away, though.'

Huw helped Bess to her feet, led her inside and closed the door.

George smiled and kept on smiling. Only it wasn't a smile any more. His cheeks had frozen stiff.

Inside the cowshed cows stamped and pigs grunted and their breath steamed in the smoky light from the fire.

Bess choked on the acrid air. 'How could any man condemn people to live like this?' she wondered. 'And Huw's mother's going to have a baby. That man can do anything!'

It was Sneck Bess had come to talk about.

'He frightens me, Huw. He controls my father by pretending he can speak to my mother in the spirit world. He says she needs his help to reach Heaven – and Father believes him! He'll give that sorcerer anything he wants, so Sneck asks for property and power – he says the only way he can help my mother is by having more and more power himself every day!

'The way things are going he'll have our house soon, and then he'll be Lord of Kingswell and *we'll* live in a stinking cowshed like—'

Bess stopped. 'I'm sorry, I didn't mean that.'

'Yes, you did, child.'

Sarah Evans spoke quietly, glancing into the dark corners of her home where unseen creatures she didn't like to think about scuffled and squeaked.

'Do you think I don't feel as you do about this place? But I remind myself that once a miracle happened in a stable, and then it doesn't seem so bad.'

A spasm crossed her face and she closed her eyes. She was very tired.

Bess turned back to Huw and whispered, 'That man has so much to answer for. He trusts nobody, hates everybody – and he has eyes in the back of his head. He really is a sorcerer!'

'He told us he was when he first arrived here,'

Huw reminded her. 'Nobody knew where he came from but we were pleased to have him because we thought a sorcerer would protect us. Instead he uses his spells against us!'

Bess's dark eyes blazed with anger. 'We have to stop him. But how can we fight magic?'

Huw looked at the dwindling fire, the restless animals and his now-sleeping mother and sister. 'No use asking me, Bess. How could I defeat a sorcerer? I can't even feed my family.'

His gaze reached the window. It should have been black as the night outside, but as he looked it turned green.

George had been trying to warm himself up, blowing his cheeks to loosen them, flapping his arms to de-ice them and banging his feet on the hard ground like a musician clanging cymbals.

As he pranced about the farmyard he looked into a frozen cattle trough and saw a puckered, rumpled, palely shining face gazing back at him. For an instant the face reminded him of other faces – faces from long ago that were now forgotten and lost to him – still lost because that door which had opened a fraction refused to open further. The loneliness returned ten-fold, and for comfort he returned to the cowshed, knelt down and peered through the window.

His eyes met Huw's – and for a moment Huw could have sworn that the grolyhoomp was weeping.

chapter Seven

Sorcerer

In olden times people fully believed in things we don't believe in any more.

For example, they believed that the earth was flat and you could fall off the edge.

They certainly believed in the power of evil spirits, and all along the borderland there was absolute belief in witches, sorcerers and all kinds of magical goings on.

If you believe in something strongly enough, maybe it will happen.

If you really believe in fairies maybe you'll see them.

Look at it this way. Think of the twitching movements you could have sworn you saw in the hedge at the bottom of your garden, when you knew for certain there was no one there. And do you remember seeing curtains twitching in the window of an empty house – or the creaking sounds your own house makes when everybody is in bed?

Little things like that make you nervous and can easily cause you to believe that something supernatural is happening.

So what do you do?

You cross your fingers.

That, a million times stronger, is how the people of Kingswell felt in the dying days of 1399. They knew absolutely and for certain that evil spirits were lurking everywhere, like cats waiting to pounce.

Their fear was so strong that crossing their fingers was not enough. They needed much heavier protection – they needed a magician on their side.

It was just their bad luck that the magician the people of Kingswell got was Solomon Sneck the Sorcerer and Enchanter.

Sneck had once been a soldier in the army of the English King. He had not been a brave soldier, but during a skirmish with the Scots he had managed to save the King's life while actually trying to run away.

As a reward he was given a small piece of land on the Welsh border, next to the land belonging to Sir Simeon Griphook.

The thought of owning property went to Sneck's head and he came to Kingswell with the ambition of grabbing all the land and power there was to be had. He was an impatient man, and since he knew that achieving your ambition by fair means takes a long time, he chose foul.

He chose enchantment.

On the road to Kingswell he did several things he thought would help him on his way.

He changed his name from Simon to Solomon because he thought that made him sound less simple and more wise.

From a conjuror he discovered that the hand can be quicker than the eye.

From a soothsayer he learned hocus-pocus, which is the art of talking rubbish while making it sound perfectly sensible.

From a necromancer he acquired the know-how to recite spells that terrified and potions which smelled disgusting, and the knowledge that the more terrifying and disgusting he was the more people would pay.

He also bought herbs, spices, a cauldron, gunpowder to make flashes (flashes impress the customers, the necromancer told him) and a secret weapon to be used only in an emergency and handled with the greatest possible care.

Finally he stole a cloak and a pointed hat from a jester he met at a fair.

In this way Solomon Sneck came to Kingswell a fully qualified bogus sorcerer – small part conjuror, small part soothsayer, large part charlatan – and the most brazen liar in the country.

The first thing he did, without batting an eyelid, was to tell everybody he had been awarded his property for releasing the King from the spell of a wicked wizard by means of an even stronger spell of his own – and also for helping the Queen talk to her long-dead ancestors.

The people of Kingswell were impressed.

They were even more impressed when they saw Sneck in action.

They watched his frothing cauldron with popping eyes. They gasped at the explosions. They heard with awe the mumbo-jumbo with which he made balms for boils and carbuncles, the 'frogs' eyelashes, newts' ears and the 'smile of an unborn cat gathered precisely one hour before midsummer dawn'.

Sneck made it up as he went along, and like an actor hooked on applause he became addicted to his own performances and grew ever more melodramatic and outrageous.

So did his fees.

And he found that the necromancer had been correct: the more incredible the treatment, and the higher the price, the more the people of Kingswell believed in him.

Nobody believed more than Sir Simeon Griphook.

Bess's father missed his dead wife so much that when Sneck said it was possible to meet her in the spirit world he jumped for joy.

'I would give anything to contact my darling Mary again!' he cried. 'If you can speak to her you shall have whatever you desire!'

'Land,' said Sneck, sneering behind his sleeve at this sentimental fool. 'I desire land.'

He got it.

In séance after séance he pretended to enter the world of the dead and speak to Simeon's beloved Mary. Afterwards, overwhelmed by grief and joy, the tear-stained knight handed over a part of Kingswell.

At this rate the sorcerer would soon have more land than the lord of the manor himself. Eventually he would have it all.

But 'eventually' was not soon enough for the impatient Sneck. He wanted Kingswell, lock, stock and barrel, before the year was out.

There wasn't long to go...

chapter Eight

Séance on a Sunny Afternoon

On the afternoon following Big George's arrival, the weather changed and became less cold. The sun shone and the icicles hanging from the village roofs dripped like tears.

From his place of concealment in a copse behind the manor house (it had been Bess's idea to keep the grolyhoomp hidden as a possible secret weapon against Solomon Sneck) George peered through the winter trees and watched the daily life of Kingswell going on.

He saw Huw driving his pigs back from the forest where they'd been snuffling for acorns.

He saw the villagers at their winter tasks: chopping wood, salting meat, baking bread, making shoes and tools and clothes.

He saw labourers building a stockade against the threat of the approaching army.

He would have liked to help, but Bess said he should lie low. It seemed to George that he was always expected to stay out of sight and he wondered why.

Was he in danger – or dangerous?

Were people afraid of him?

If they were afraid, he thought, it could only be because they didn't know him. George didn't think he was frightening at all.

That was only one of the many puzzles about being on this planet. Another was going on inside the manor.

From the window of an upstairs room a high-pitched whining song reached him, accompanied by a peculiar smell which tickled his nose and made him want to sneeze.

George hoped he wouldn't, because his sneezes always had a devastating effect.

At this point the trees grew close to the manor wall. Gambling that no one would come round the back of the manor and see him, George inched forward, propped himself on an elbow and put an eye to the window.

Inside he saw a small stone chamber almost bare

of furniture. In the middle stood a round table on which incense burned, its smoke spiralling thinly upwards.

Also resting on the table were two pairs of hands.

One belonged to a thin, starved, weeping man whose shoulders shook as tears carved ravines into his tragic face.

The other hands were never still. Eight fingers and two thumbs – each shiny and sinuous as a snake – stroked the table, gripped, loosened and slithered – and then rapped it sharply.

The owner of these extraordinary hands was shrouded in a loose black robe. Only his bent head was bare and George saw waxen skin, hooded eyes and a bulbous mouth. It was from this mouth that the keening song came.

Suddenly the table replied to the knock.

It rocked violently on its legs and leaped under the four hands.

The weeping man howled like a lunatic.

'Father!' came a shout from the shadows under the window, just out of George's view. 'Please don't cry!'

George squinted down and saw Bess. She was sitting on a low bench, leaning forward with her fingers gripped into angry fists.

'Leave him alone!' she shouted at the shrouded man.

His eyes glittered and flicked a warning at her. His voice wailed.

'Beware the world of the spirit, girl. You are causing your mother great anguish. You are hurting her so much that soon she will retreat from us and in her place will come vengeful spirits to destroy you!'

'My mother has already retreated from us,' Bess cried. 'And it isn't spirits who'll destroy us, it's you! I wish you'd never come here – get out of our house!'

Solomon Sneck smiled and George could see that the sorcerer was enjoying Bess's distress. He lowered his head towards her and whispered, 'Your house, girl? Mine, I think, very soon.'

Bess flew at him with fists flying but her father stopped her. He held her close, his eyes beseeching and sorrowful.

'Be still, Daughter,' he pleaded, 'and leave us.'

'But Father—'

'Leave!' Sneck hissed, 'before I turn you into the rat you are!'

With a scream of frustration Bess fled from the house.

Bess was so upset she didn't want to see or speak to anybody. She also needed time to think what she could do about the sorcerer, and a place to think it.

So she ran into the copse behind the manor – and skidded into Big George. She had forgotten he was there.

George looked as bewildered as Bess felt.

'Did you hear that man?' she cried. 'He's going to cast a spell on me! Like he's cast a spell on my father and half the village. I hate him!'

Then, looking curiously at George, Bess added, 'You don't know what I'm saying, do you? Yet I feel that somehow you do!'

'Snool frig y nath,' George answered, smiling. 'Keep talking, I like it.' He was thinking, This girl sounds like Tilly Miller, and she *is* like her in many ways, yet she's quite different too. That was another puzzle.

Bess was thinking, This grolyhoomp sounds Welsh... though he doesn't look it. Maybe if I talk to him slowly he *will* understand me.

And so, speaking as slowly and carefully as if she was talking to an idiot, she told George about her troubles.

'My father means everybody well and thinks well of everybody,' she said, 'but Solomon Sneck means only ill. Father, because he's such a good man, can't see it. He doesn't see how strong Sneck is growing, and he doesn't understand that while he's mourning my mother, Kingswell is slipping into ruin.

'I've tried to rouse him, but he doesn't hear me because his heart is breaking. If something doesn't happen soon to shake him out of his despair, I'm afraid he might die.

'So *I* have to do something myself to stop Solomon Sneck. I don't know what, yet, but I won't let that evil enchanter kill my father, I won't!'

Bess looked defiantly at George. He smiled back encouragingly, enjoying the music of her words and the spirit flashing in her dark eyes, and winked.

That enormous slow blink was inspirational to Bess. As had happened with George himself, inside her brain a door opened and light flooded in. Astonished, she gaped at George with her eyes ballooning.

'George, I don't know how but you've just given me the best idea I've ever had. I'm going to out-magic the magician!'

An hour or so later, when Huw was shepherding his pigs through the churchyard near the grave of 'Lady Mary Griphook, Dear Lamented Wife', Sneck's hooded figure suddenly reared up in front of him.

Huw thought he'd seen a ghost and yelled. The pigs stampeded. A sow lurched into Sneck and knocked him down, and before he could get up two fat porkers trod on him while a third performed a horrid act on his face.

Horrified, Huw tried to help the sorcerer to his feet.

'Keep off me!' Sneck raged, pushing Huw away and hurriedly wiping his face on his cloak. 'If you don't keep those beasts under control I'll throw your family out of the village altogether! Think about that!'

Huw pictured his family hiding in a tree in the frozen forest at night while wolves bayed below and winter spirits howled in the air, and his heart sank.

Then he remembered the grolyhoomp and it rose again.

'You don't scare me any more, Mr Almighty Enchanter,' he muttered. 'A hero has come to Kingswell who will flatten you if you're not careful.'

Sneck wasn't supposed to hear that, but his suspicious ears could catch a bat's sneeze five miles away and trouble ten times further.

'Hero? What hero?' he snorted. 'What a liar you are, Evans. Who'd believe anything a swineherd says?'

But as Sneck went on his way a tiny seed of doubt rooted itself in his head.

'Don't trust that boy not to be telling the truth for once,' it said. 'Keep your eyes peeled, Solomon. These are such strange times that anything could happen.'

The sorcerer looked furtively about, quickened *his* step and crossed his fingers – which goes to prove that even magicians can believe in fairies.

chapter Nine

BOy BESS

That evening the air cooled and George once again lay gathering frost, peeping into the manor – and finding another puzzle as, in the shifting light of fire and tallow lantern, he watched Bess Griphook being transformed.

Sweet-smelling herbs covered the floor of her chamber. More herbs festooned the walls. They were supposed to counter the smells of smoke and unwashed sweat but Bess paid no heed to those anyway – stinks were an everyday part of life in the Year of Our Lord 1399.

Bess had worse things on her mind.

Holding her arms up so her maid could remove her robe she asked, 'Why is it, Syb, that a girl has to become a boy to be taken seriously?'

Fat Sybil chuckled, wobbling her chins. 'Why,

child, that's just the way the world goes, innit? Men be the masters.'

'But that isn't fair.'

'Has always been so.'

'Well, that doesn't make it right. Do I keep my chemise on?'

'You'd better, child. You'll freeze without. And you shall wear a tunic over, and a super-tunic over that to keep out the cold, and also hose and a rabbit-skin hood. Everything of the coarsest stuff because you're only a poor boy seeking work.'

Bess wrinkled her nose. 'Rabbit skin! I prefer ermine and silk.'

'That's because you're a lord's daughter and live differently from the rest of us. 'Twill do you good to join the real world for a bit.'

Sybil collected Bess's new garments from a three-legged stool in a corner. A mouse sleeping under it skittered away, disturbing the hood that had once been a rabbit.

'One of these days I'll catch that mouse and pull his tail right off!' Chuckling, Sybil bustled back to Bess and began to dress her.

Sybil Stack was a jolly woman with big red cheeks, big chins and big ambitions. She saw herself not as Bess's maid but as her friend – which was true – and also as Sir Simeon's future wife, which was not.

But beneath her bluster and high hopes she was

soft-hearted, generous and utterly loyal to her young mistress.

On went the tunic, accompanied by Sybil's prattling stream of talk. 'You watch that enchanter now, girl. Don't want him enchanting you, and I wouldn't trust him as far as I could spit a goose. And as for that father of yours, a good shaking would stir him better than a spoon. Here, put a toe in this.'

Bess stared, revolted by a rag in Sybil's hand that looked more like a long-dead serpent than something to wear next to your skin. 'What is it?' she gasped.

'What's it look like? It's hose, my girl, hose!'

'It's horrible. It'll make me squirm, I know it.'

But on went the hose, slithering up Bess's legs and tickling as it went.

When the dressing was complete, down to a filthy pair of hide working boots, Bess was unrecognisable. She strutted around the chamber, scowling at the coarse cloth scratching her flesh and trying to walk like a boy.

She produced an ungainly swagger.

'Sneck won't like that,' Sybil tutted. '*He's* the swaggerer round here.'

Bess frowned. 'I'll get it right soon. I'll practise walking like Huw.'

'He drags his feet.'

'Then I'll drag my feet. I'll do anything it takes.'

She drooped and shuffled, copying the way Huw slouched after his pigs.

Watching her, a tear sprang into Sybil's eye. 'Oh, come here, child!' she cried, enfolding Bess in her ample arms. 'You're a brave girl but this is a foolish and dangerous thing you're set on. If that sorcerer sees through your disguise goodness knows what he'll do. Why, you could end up in his cauldron yourself!'

Bess shuddered. 'Don't say that, Syb. I promise I'll be careful. And now there's one last thing you must do for me.'

Sybil wiped her nose on her sleeve. 'Anything, child. What is it?'

'Cut off my hair.'

chapter Ten

The Grolyhoomp Song

Bess's transformation was a puzzle too many for Big George to take in – the last straw that broke his patience. Because it's all very well saying you will look and learn and seek and find, but when you don't understand the results it makes your head spin.

George's head was spinning all right.

He was also bored with hiding and keeping still. If you think about it, turning into an icicle must be the most boring thing in the world.

George wanted action for a change.

So he stretched his numb legs, flexed his iced-up arms and took a stiff aching step away from Griphook Manor.

And another.

George craved excitement, although if he'd

known the kind of excitement coming his way
he might not have been so keen.

But just now the very fact of moving made good
things happen inside him. Sensation returned
to his body. His feet and fingers began to
belong to him again and his blood
pumped purposefully through his veins.

With power surging through his body like
water released from a dam, George felt like
singing.

So he sang.

He sang to the moon, the stars and the hanging comet. He sang to the village and the hills.

When George sang softly he created a humming sound that reverberated inside your ears. When he let rip he produced a noise that was truly awful.

Imagine a cat's miaow, thunder and a grating door all going full pelt at once. Magnify that noise a thousand times and you're coming close to the sound of Big George singing.

Anyone out in the hills that night would have thought the world was ending.

Anyone out in the hills that night with eyes to see would also have thought they saw a gigantic pale-green lantern swinging through the mountains.

Unfortunately the only person there could not even see something as big as Big George's shining face.

His name was Biffin.

Blind Biffin.

Blind Biffin liked being out at night because he moved through darkness better than people with sight, and that pleased him. His stick was his antenna and his hearing was doubly acute – he had the sharpest ears in the Marches, sharper even than those of Solomon Sneck.

This meant that although Biffin could not see George, he heard him so clearly it sounded as if the world was being torn apart about two yards in front of him.

Biffin stopped walking.

Anxiously he waved his stick about, probing it along the frozen ground – *tap-tap, tap-tap*.

Blind Biffin was in his own way also a magician.

Sightless since birth, he would have liked to have been a builder and create amazing structures. Since he couldn't do that he taught himself to make amazing structures of sound – he learned music and became a magician with a harp.

Biffin's music made happy people sad and sad people happy. His tunes gave rest to the weary and peace to the tormented. They could lead you into battle and even to the grave, sending you to Heaven with a smile on your face.

People said that while Solomon Sneck's magic cured the body, Biffin's soothed the soul.

That gained him entry to every house and manor in the Marches but even so he liked the outdoors best. That was why he was here now among the borderland hills, hearing the world end.

Tap-tap, went his stick.

He took a wary step forward.

Tap-tap.

The fearful roaring noise stopped.

But the silence was worse because in it Biffin heard other sounds that were even more frightening.

He heard a footfall like a muted earthquake and breathing like a gigantic bellows.

Trembling and holding his own breath, he took another step.

Tap-tap. Tap-tap.

For months, doom-mongers had been prophesying that as the century closed unearthly monsters would appear. Biffin had scoffed then, but he believed them now.

'Th-there's a lovely monster, isn't it?' he stuttered in a lilting trembling voice. 'D-don't eat me. I'm all bones, see. Welsh bones they are, too, and they taste really horrible. You'd prefer English, look you.'

Biffin swallowed and waited for developments.

There were no developments.

There was only silence, broken by the breathing. That was slow, heavy, close and very worrying.

George had heard Biffin's stick through his singing.

Tap-tap. Tap-tap.

He had thought the hills were deserted, but at this sharp sound he shut up and stood still. He peered into the darkness ahead.

Tap-tap. Tap…

Into the range of his face glow there arrived a short bearded man wearing a long mantle of sheep's wool. The man approached George carefully, prodding a white stick.

His eyes were also white, and sightless.

The man spoke, and George thought it would be polite to reply.

'Sloop riksy friddly,' he said. 'Who are you?'

Biffin got the fright of his life.

The words reached him from an impossible height, breath blew over him like a warm wind. More than at any other time in his life he wished he could see.

He waved his stick again – *tap-tap, tap-tap* – and stepping forward jabbed it into Big George's foot.

'Oo-er,' he said.

Biffin touched George's boot with his fingers and tried to make his way round it. It took a long time – impossibly long. The boot was immensely high, too, with laces thick as hawsers.

'I don't believe this, look you,' he mumbled. 'This is a boot to terrify God.'

Biffin waited for the monster to do something.

George waited for Biffin to do something.

Neither did anything.

The weather grew colder.

And colder.

They both waited so long they froze solid and stood motionless like two icy statues on the frosty mountainside.

That is exactly what they looked like next morning when Huw the pig boy came wandering up the valley, with his pigs and half the population of Kingswell trailing behind him, looking for a missing grolyhoomp.

chapter Eleven

It's a wonder

Solomon Sneck was greedy, vain and mean. He was, in fact, the greediest, vainest and meanest man in the Marchlands and quite possibly in the whole world.

So when an odd-looking boy knocked on his door and offered to work for him for nothing but the pleasure of watching a great wizard perform wonders, Sneck's usual suspicion melted away in the warmth of adoration.

And when the boy said he came from a far distant town where Sneck's reputation was legendary, the enchanter's hooded eyes gleamed and his chest swelled with pride. So did his head.

My fame has travelled far and wide already! he thought happily. If I take on an assistant I'll be able to perform twice the magic twice as fast and my fame will travel twice as far! Or is that four times? And then taking over Kingswell will be just the beginning. There'll be no stopping me. Beetles' trotters and tail ends!

Sneck preened himself like a peacock and stared at the boy. There was something odd about him, but he couldn't put his finger on what it was. The boy's head was shaven, he looked uncomfortable in his clothes and he kept scratching – but what of that? Scratching was normal, it came with your fleas.

Sneck shook away his doubts. It's my vivid imagination, he decided. This boy is a worshipper and it's wonderful to be worshipped. Being worshipped gives you a lovely glow.

'What's your name?' he asked sharply.

The boy looked startled. 'My name?'

'You have a name?'

'Er – yes, of course. It's – ah – Richard. Yes, that's it! Dick!'

Sneck smiled indulgently, still basking in the sunshine of his long-distance fame. 'Well, Dick, if I allow you to work for me there will be four rules which you will obey as if your life depended on it – which it probably will. Do as I ask, don't get in my way, don't tell anybody my secrets – and call me sir. Understand?'

'Yes, sir.'

'Break any rule and you're toast. Clear?'

The boy grimaced. 'Clear – sir!'

'Very well. Follow me. I have a magic surgery in an hour. You can assist me.'

Sneck strode away along a bare passage.

Bess – now Richard – blinked nervously and followed. She passed doors to the left and right – all closed – behind which creatures rustled and scuttled.

At the end of the passage Sneck entered a small

room piled high with dried, wrinkled plants. He selected four and slapped them down on a table.

'Here's your first lesson. This plant is called lungwort. I use it for ailments of the chest.'

The others followed, one by one.

'Feverfew – for headaches and childbirth. Marjoram to make poultices for bruising and swellings. This last one is lemon balm, to cure fevers and colds. You got that, boy?'

'Got it,' said Bess, memorising the herbs and their uses. There seemed nothing there to cure sadness.

'Got it?' Sneck glared at her. '*Got it*?'

'Oh! Ah! Got it – sir!'

'That's better. Don't forget. Now grind them up.' He pushed a mortar and pestle across the table. 'Then grind these. And these. And these…'

As he spoke he opened cupboards and produced jars full of dried worms, toads, eels and lizards. Dozens of dead eyes stared up at Bess. She shuddered.

'Something the matter?'

'No, sir.'

'Then get on with it. I'll be back soon. Remember the four rules, if you want to live. If you don't, I'll enjoy your decease.'

Laughing at his own joke, Solomon Sneck left Bess to complete part one of her attempt to beat a sorcerer at his own game.

While Bess was learning to be a sorcerer's apprentice, Huw Evans and the villagers were trying their hardest to thaw out a frozen musician and a gigantic sign of the times.

Huw said George might be the new saviour of Kingswell and the villagers agreed.

'Were we not told there would be monsters?' they cried, chafing George's legs with their hands. 'And have we not seen the travelling star and heard rumours of wild beasts coming out of the forest to kneel down before it? Those are marvels indeed, but this – this is a true *wonder*, look you. But even wonders are useless if they are lifeless. So let us warm it up!'

George's hands were massaged, his face was slapped and his ears pulled. Children clambered over his rigid body and jumped up and down on it.

Huw pummelled the grolyhoomp's feet and the pigs snorted into his nose.

Slowly the colour of George's skin changed from blue to pink.

His fingers twitched.

When they saw this the people retreated in fright

and their children shinned down George's body like startled monkeys.

Blind Biffin, getting the same treatment, moaned and moved slightly.

'We're not too late!' they all cried. 'Praise the Lord for miracles!'

They didn't know it, but the miracles had only just begun.

Big George and Blind Biffin felt sensation returning to their bodies and it was agony.

'Ooowwwww!' George yelled.

'Ooooohh!' screeched Biffin.

'Aaaggghhhhh!' the villagers cried in terror, backing even further away.

Only Huw did not retreat.

He drove his pigs up close to George – so close that the people gasped and waited for them to be eaten.

'George,' Huw said gently, 'you've given us a fright.'

'Grolyhoomp, Hoooooo-oo,' George whispered. ''Hal-sligrracker-bluwan-ikdedd.' (Meaning, 'I'm getting cheesed off with feeling cold!')

Watching George shivering and hearing his teeth chattering like a gigantic woodpecker drilling a tree, Huw understood.

'The grolyhoomp needs a coat,' he said. 'And a hat. And gloves. And a scarf. We'll have to make them for him.'

The villagers measured the grolyhoomp's height and girth in their minds. Then they pictured their tiny spinning wheels. The clack of their jaws dropping could be heard in Kingswell.

Like the villagers, Bess too was afraid of the task ahead.

She was afraid of forgetting a rule and becoming toast.

She was afraid of wrongly mixing a potion and poisoning somebody – though she wouldn't have minded if that person had been Solomon Sneck.

Most of all she was afraid of being recognised and having her cover broken.

She needn't have worried.

Sneck's magic surgery took place in a barn beside his house. Three fires had been lit there – not for his clients' comfort, the sorcerer was far too mean to care about that, but for effect. Thick black acrid smoke hung in the air like a pungent fog, gathering under the roof timbers and swirling about the floor. It gave the place a lurid eerie atmosphere which contributed immensely to the impression that black and powerful magic was taking place.

That smoke put the fear of the Devil into Sneck's customers, but it aided Bess by hiding her.

She stood with streaming eyes where the smoke was thickest, watching her friends and fellow villagers being fleeced by a crooked enchanter, seeing them hand over money they couldn't afford and receiving in return mumbo-jumbo and a useless poultice made from everyday herbs laced with beetles' glands and pigs' earholes.

Solomon Sneck, though, was in his element. He revelled in hocus-pocus and Bess had to give him credit for being a great showman. His performance, timed to perfection, was calculated to inspire and terrify in equal measure and to send his customers away quaking in their shoes but believing in him absolutely.

For two hours Bess watched him wheedle and bully and entrance. She saw him smear a boy's blistered tongue with – so he said – the saliva of a five-legged hare, tie the so-called intestines of an adder round the neck of an ugly girl who wanted to be pretty, and rub slugstain and nutbalm on the feet of a man with a headache.

She listened to his chants with complete bafflement, hoping that sooner or later something that made sense would turn up.

It did not.

Finally, when the surgery was over, the sweating sorcerer ordered Bess to clear up the mess.

'Those idiots believe everything I tell them,' he chortled. 'What fools they are. And Griphook is the biggest fool of all. Well, his end is near!'

He flicked an eel's head on to a fire, where it exploded in a scatter of sparks. Then he threw back his head, tossed one of his own potions down his throat, and with a rippling choking laugh that chilled his assistant's heart, fell fast asleep.

chapter Twelve

George in the Dark

By mistake Solomon Sneck drank enough potion to make him sleep for twenty four hours. For that reason he did not hear the din of the grolyhoomp's return.

But Bess did.

She ran from the barn and saw a crowd come lurching down the street, circling George like children dancing round a maypole. In front a man played a pipe and a woman whirled like a top, hysterical with excitement.

People hurried from their houses to see what was happening and join in the fun.

'So much for keeping George a secret,' Bess thought, not knowing that Huw had set up a search party to look for him. She watched George now, beaming with happiness and stepping on tiptoe to avoid crushing anyone.

'Dibdoo,' he chuntered. 'Dibdoooo!'

Everybody cheered.

There was not a man, woman or child there who did not believe that the grolyhoomp was a wonder conjured up by the spirits of this enchanted time. They fully expected others to follow, although they had to admit that this one was enough to be going on with.

'George!' Bess shouted. 'Over here!'

Having watched her turn into a boy George recognised Bess at once. He reached over the heads of the people and gathered her out of the barn door as if she weighed no more than a hayseed. Then out of the crowd he gathered Huw, wide-eyed with astonishment at the effectiveness of Bess's transformation, and held them both close to his grinning face.

'Noodlinsies,' he said happily. 'Friends.'

Looking so nearly into George's eyes, Bess and Huw felt his delight sweep through them like a wave. It was intoxicating. 'Noodlinsies,' they repeated, laughing. 'Noodlinsies!'

The word seemed a charm to ward off Solomon Sneck's evil spells.

The procession halted in the village square.

Here Blind Biffin stepped forward.

'There's work to be done,' he shouted, waving his stick for emphasis. 'Who will spin? And who will weave? Today we must work faster than we have ever worked in our lives, because before this night the Stranger must have his coat. So be off with you!'

Awed but excited by the enormity of the task ahead, the villagers hurried into their houses and began the greatest clothing exercise Kingswell had ever seen.

Years later minstrels would sing the story of this day:

'Into their houses the people ran
And the weavers wove and the spinners span
To make a coat that was not for any man.'

While in the village square three extraordinary figures – a swineherd, a giant and a girl pretending to be a boy – stood among rioting pigs and shouted 'Noodlinsies! Noodlinsies!' to each other at the tops of their voices.

The noise of George's shout shook Kingswell Manor, momentarily rousing its lord from his grief.

Shut away in the dark empty hall, Sir Simeon Griphook parted a curtain and saw a blue and green head rising above the roofs of the houses.

He blinked and looked again.

The head was still there, its mouth opening and closing like a fish.

Sir Simeon closed the curtain and sat down quickly. 'My grief is turning me mad,' he shuddered. 'I'll have to stop it.'

But stopping grieving seemed like betraying his dead wife's memory – and that sad thought made him cry all over again.

By dusk that afternoon George had his new coat – and also mittens, socks and a hood with a scarf attached that was twenty yards long and covered every inch of his giraffe neck. Since everything was made with wool shorn from the villagers' own flock George looked like a forty-foot-high Kingswell sheep.

But he felt warm for the first time since he had woken up shivering inside his hill.

Evening drew on. Big George sat in the square, thinking hard while cats rubbed against him and a little white dog with a black face lifted a leg against his boot. He took no notice.

Inside their houses the villagers were all in bed, sleeping the sound, well-deserved sleep of the exhausted.

Bess had returned to her father, who was too miserable to notice her changed appearance.

Huw was back with his family in their lowly byre.

George was alone, thinking and looking about him.

Outside the village the whale-backed hills rose blackly in the light of the rising moon. The comet hung motionless overhead, now pointing its tail at Kingswell like a bright finger.

It was very, very peaceful, and the peace entered George's heart.

He heaved a sigh. 'I should like to belong here,' he said to himself. 'Here or somewhere near. Though anywhere would do, if it would be my home.'

He thought he was learning many things. Some were to do with size, because everything here was so *small*, others with the weather, which was different each time he woke up, but most were to do with the people.

The people were like the weather, changeable. One minute they were singing, the next fighting. One moment happy and the next in tears. With them you never knew what was coming next, so it was always a puzzle.

This whole world was a puzzle when he thought about it – it seemed to George as if life on Earth must be in some sort of code, so that to understand it you needed a key to unlock the code first.

'Well,' he told himself, 'one day I may find that key. But for now I only know what I've seen and what I feel. And what I feel most of all is loneliness.'

Once more he fingered Tilly's mirror-spoon and Jo's lucky rabbit's foot, and smiling he remembered the courage of Walter of Swyre, who although only a boy had fought the greatest knights in the land for his father's sake.

Children, thought George, are the very best thing about this place. I should like to belong to the children.

That was the moment when George decided to do whatever was necessary to help Bess and Huw in their hour of need. Because somehow he felt that they needed him as much as he needed them.

'That's what noodlinsies are for,' he muttered sleepily. 'For help. Help…'

As he dozed, George's mind wandered over the things he'd seen. He wondered idly what had become of the soldiers he'd passed on his way here, but the thought drifted away from him like a feather on a breeze.

Actually, at that moment the King of England's

expeditionary force was camped in a field fifty miles away, on the edge of a frozen bog.

The King had ordered them to live off the country they passed through, but the further west they travelled the harder this became, for the weather grew steadily sharper and the people steadily poorer. By now the soldiers were half starved, behind time and very irritable.

'I'm getting a bad feeling about this expedition, Sergeant!' bellowed their Captain, a thick-necked, thick-bodied, thick-headed man called Witless who was always shouting. He was struggling to read an inaccurate map by the light of a flickering candle. 'I have no idea where we are!' he yelled. 'And the stupid yokels who live here keep directing us the wrong way!'

'I don't think they're stupid, sir,' answered his Sergeant, a stooped man with the voice and face of a sick cow and a very apt name. 'I think they do it on purpose.'

'Well, Sergeant Moo, if their purpose is to delay us they've succeeded completely. We're days behind schedule!'

That was the soldiers' worry. Big George knew nothing of it.

He was falling asleep.

chapter Thirteen

S O S

The next day two events combined to make the inhabitants of Kingswell very unhappy.

The first was that Solomon Sneck the Sorcerer discovered their grolyhoomp and took him away from them.

Sneck found the dozing George when he stumbled sleepily from his house in the early dawn in search of mouse tails and cat lice, and walked slap into George's beard in the middle of the village square. The beard did not feel like mouse tails, it felt like walking into a hedge. And even half asleep Sneck knew there wasn't a hedge in Kingswell square, unless one had sprung up in the night, which was unlikely.

He woke up at once, gaped at the monster in dismay and demanded an explanation from the villagers. When he heard the story of how this grolyhoomp had been discovered frozen in the mountains, he demanded that George be concealed immediately in the woods. His excuse was that a grolyhoomp should be a secret weapon – which, if you remember, had been Bess's idea first. There wasn't, he said, much point in having a secret weapon if your enemy could spot it a mile off.

Sneck's real reason was that having a grolyhoomp about the place could interfere with his plan to take over Kingswell. He wanted George out of the way while he found a way to get rid of him – and there was a good chance that the wolves and bears of the forest would save him the trouble.

The second event was the breathless arrival at noon of a Welsh spy, racing home to tell Owain Glyndwr that the English army was already in the Marchlands and would soon reach Wales.

For an hour the spy paused at Kingswell to refresh himself and his horse. While there he terrified the villagers with a dark tale of what was coming to them.

'Hundreds of soldiers there are, look you,' he cried, swallowing piecrust and swilling beer at the same time. 'Thousands. There's death on the march, isn't it? There's blood lust. I have seen it myself in their eyes, look you!'

He told of swordsmen, pikemen, archers and horsemen laying waste the countryside as they came. 'Looting, isn't it? Murdering. Burning. And your village is right in their path – they will walk all over you and wipe their shoes on you. Run for your lives! Run today!'

'We are not cowards,' said Blind Biffin, who was shaking nevertheless. 'Besides, where would we go? We have nowhere else.'

Before the spy resumed his journey, Solomon Sneck took him to one side.

They spoke in whispers, but Biffin was nearby and their words dripped into his sharp ears like water into a bucket.

'The soldiers are coming for Owain Glyndwr,' Sneck hissed. 'If you hand him over they'll go away.'

The spy was amazed. 'You mean *betray* our leader?'

'For money. He'd be worth a lot, wouldn't he?'

'You mean *sell* our saviour? Surrender him to certain death?'

'It's a good idea, isn't it,' Sneck purred. 'I've just had it. It would work well here too, so if you don't mind I'll keep it for myself. We'll sell *our* saviour! SOS! Holy molespit, what a wonderful, perfect plan! It will make all my dreams come true!'

When the spy went on his way Biffin told Huw and Bess what he had overheard.

'He means to sell George, doesn't he?' cried Bess. 'We must save him!'

'Isn't he big enough to save himself?' asked Biffin.

Bess and Huw were not at all sure he was. Because it seemed to them that George was a complete innocent.

chapter Fourteen

cockatrice

During the night the weather changed again. A thaw set in. Clouds covered moon, stars and comet. Fog hid the ground. Rain began to fall.

Big George, hiding in Kingswell Wood, felt the damp hardly at all, because although water dripped steadily through the bare branches above him, it slid off his oily wool coat like water from a duck's back. But it was more than a little spooky.

Mist drifted over the ground and through it the black tree trunks crowded like spectres. And that ghostly sight brought other ghosts to George's mind – ghosts of things he had seen but hardly understood.

His head was dizzy with images of horses and flags and castles and pavilions, green mountains and yellow fields, brown rivers and blue skies. His pent-up store of impressions clustered round him in the darkness like living things.

Among them he saw an untidy boy who lived with pigs, a girl who cut off her hair, a charlatan in a pointed hat who boiled newts' eye strings for a hobby, and a village clouded with anxiety.

'Have to help them,' George whispered to the night. 'But who can help me?'

The rain fell all night and ran down George's cheeks like tears.

At dawn it stopped and a weak sun peered through the clouds like an invalid poking his head out of doors.

By then the icy earth had thawed to squishy mud, the trees of the wood stood like reeds in a swamp and the people of Kingswell squelched about their houses like herons treading water.

Perhaps it was this sudden change in the weather which unbalanced Solomon Sneck, or maybe it was just his impatience. Whatever the reason, one thing is plain – this was the day the enchanter made a very big mistake.

This was the day the sorcerer grew too big for his boots.

Sneck was in a great hurry to do two things: kill the grolyhoomp and impress his new assistant –

both at the same time.

He had found that he enjoyed Richard's admiration even more than he'd expected. Adoration and praise were addictive, and he drooled with delight to see the awe in his patients' eyes when they saw his cauldron bubbling, and swelled like a balloon with satisfaction at their burbling gratitude when he presented them with a toad's gill to lash their skins at nightfall.

And to have an assistant hanging upon his words as if they were gospel was like entering paradise.

'I'll teach that boy,' he told himself smugly as he dressed that morning. 'I'll show him he's working for a god. And I'll teach that grolyhoomp a lesson he'll never forget!'

Sneck squeezed his heavy body into a tight-fitting tunic, put on his best conical hat and waited impatiently for Richard to arrive.

Bess was late, because that morning it had taken her even longer than usual to persuade her weeping father to get out of bed. So she had to run to the sorcerer's house with her coarse clothes scratching and her tom hose drooping round her ankles.

As soon as she arrived, Sneck snatched up a sack and dragged her along the passage leading to a number of rustling rooms.

At the second door he hesitated. Bess heard a frantic scuffling inside.

'Rats,' the sorcerer commented casually, 'Kingswell size.'

At the next room he stopped again, put his ear to the door and listened. There was no sound here.

Sneck ran his fingers nervously through his hair.

'Prepare to be impressed, Dick.'

Carefully he unbolted the door and slipped inside.

'Quick now – hurry, boy!'

Bess followed him in…

… and screamed. She couldn't help herself.

This room was full of bats.

They hung from beams like bunches of

grapes. They pinged desperately against a barred window. When the door opened and Bess entered they plunged at her head like a flock of starlings.

She ducked out of the way, only to find that she was crouching among frogs and toads that jumped and croaked in a whirlpool around her ankles.

She screamed again.

'Impressed, Richard, are you?' Sneck gloated. 'Well let me tell you, you haven't seen anything yet – and it will be better for you if you don't. So close your eyes. *Now!*'

Solomon Sneck had decided that the appearance of a grolyhoomp to interfere with his plans was surely the emergency when his most secret and dangerous weapon should be used.

But it *was* dangerous!

He thrust the sack at Bess, dived like a swimmer into a heap of straw in a corner and emerged clutching something that squirmed in his hand.

'Don't look, boy!' he cried, keeping his own eyes tightly shut. 'This is the one useful exotic creature that crooked necromancer sold me. Everything else I use is everyday Marchlands stuff, cunningly tweaked with spells and potions.

'But this … this is seriously scary. It's so frightening it terrifies me! This, boy, is a cockatrice. One glance into its eyes and you're either dead or put in a trance that could last for ever. Open the sack now, Richard. *Open it!*'

Very frightened, Bess held out the sack.

Nothing happened.

She squeezed open her eyelids the smallest fraction – and wished she hadn't.

Because what she saw was Solomon Sneck stumbling around and groping for the sack with a wriggling crested snake gripped tightly in his hands.

It seemed to sense that Bess was looking and faster than lightning swung its head towards her. Its eyes, glittering with coloured lights, flashed like kaleidoscope.

They took Bess by surprise and before she could shut her own eyes tight the lights struck her.

Fortunately it was only a glancing blow diverted by her closing eyelids, but even that was like a spear piercing her brain. She staggered and would have fallen if Sneck had not thrust the creature into the sack and caught her.

'I warned you!' he snapped. 'Heed everything I

say from now on, do you hear? I told you, my word is law!'

Bess nodded dizzily.

'Now follow me, and bolt the door behind you!'

Bess stumbled out after him, feeling more than half hypnotised.

By the time they reached the grolyhoomp in the acorn wood they were caked in mud.

The sack in Sneck's hand was ominously still.

When George saw Bess he sat up and grinned.

'Bbb-ee…' he began.

She ran forward to forestall him, shouting 'Richard! I'm Richard!'

George looked surprised for a moment, but then he smiled again. These people were always playing funny games.

'Rrrr-iiiii-chchchch-aaa-rrrrr-ddddd!' he burbled.

Bess sighed with relief. 'Call me Dick,' she suggested. 'It's easier.'

Sneck shouldered between them.

'That's enough idle chat,' he snarled. 'We have work to do. Here, boy, hold this.'

He pushed the sack into his assistant's hand.

Bess gasped, feeling the cockatrice's unexpectedly heavy weight. A sudden movement almost dragged the sack from her hands. Thinking it was preparing to strike her again, she turned her head away.

Impatiently Sneck indicated to George that he was to lie down. Interested, George complied and waited to see what would happen.

What happened was an extraordinary performance as the sorcerer prepared himself for his task.

'Pay attention, boy. You're going to see a master at the height of his powers,' he boasted. 'Watch and tremble.'

Like a weightlifter girding his body for the snatch, Sneck set himself up for action.

He cracked his knuckles, flexed his arms, dipped his knees and, holding his jaw with both hands, jerked it from side to side.

His neck creaked.

To warm up he performed nineteen press-ups and twenty-six sit-ups, then attempted a high kick and fell over.

'Laugh, boy, and I'll turn you into a pancake,' he growled. 'Now give me back the sack.'

Eagerly Bess complied, although she was worried about the next bit. She watched anxiously as Sneck strode towards George, holding the sack in the air.

Furrowing his brow in concentration, the sorcerer began an incantation.

'Hocus-pocus flummery floo
What happens next will be the death of you.
Cockatrice eyes and cockatrice stare
Will send you to Hell and keep you there!'

His voice rose to a shriek as he whirled the sack and sent the cockatrice flying out. It writhed in the air and landed on George's chest.

Bess screamed, 'Don't look at it, George! Close your eyes!'

She was too late.

George and the cockatrice gaped at each other.

Solomon Sneck gaped too – in furious disbelief at Bess.

'Break my spell, would you, boy?' he screamed. 'You've just sentenced yourself to death!'

Sneck's arms rose. The skin tightened on his cheeks. His fingers pointed like pokers, then hooked into claws. Bess hurriedly backed away but Sneck was quicker: his claws gripped her arms . . . her shoulders . . . then fastened on her throat. She quailed at the murderous light in his eyes as she felt his thumbs sink savagely into the soft skin and begin to choke her.

But before Bess lost consciousness Solomon Sneck saw, out of the corner of his eye, that something unexpected was happening to his delightful pet...

When the cockatrice looked at him, George was surprised by the lights it unleashed like arrows from its eyes.

Those arrows hurt.

He didn't like that, so he blinked and bounced the arrows back like boomerangs.

Nothing like that had ever happened to the cockatrice before and it was too amazed to protect itself. Its own glance coming back sent it cross-eyed and rigid as a plank.

George picked it up.

'I think this is yours,' he said – in Halrigian, of course. Casually he dropped the cockatrice into Sneck's unprepared arms.

The fall loosened its crossed eyes and a kaleidoscopic blazing glare hit the sorcerer like a bolt of lightning.

Sneck's horrified stare turned instantly rigid. As the cockatrice flopped to the ground and slithered off into the forest, the would-be King of Kingswell slipped into a helpless trance.

An hour later Solomon Sneck was still entranced, staring at nothing with his arms raised, his fingers pointing like pokers and the skin stretched tight as a drum across his cheeks.

At his feet lay an empty sack and all around him black skeletal trees stood to attention like ghostly prison guards.

The enchanted enchanter was quite alone, because by then Bess, George and the cockatrice were long gone.

Chapter Fifteen

It's a Knock-out

Unfortunately, Solomon Sneck did not remain entranced for ever as he had threatened Bess. Sneck's cockatrice was a mere shadow of the real thing – he'd been fooled there too by the crooked necromancer. That was lucky for him, because after six hours the trance began to wear off.

By then Sneck was soaked to the skin, chilled to the marrow, sneezing continuously and angrier than he had ever been in his life.

His first thought as he emerged from oblivion was the memory of his assistant's betrayal.

His second was to vow the most spectacular revenge the Marchlands had ever seen.

His third was deciding what form that might take.

Unfortunately for Bess the sorcerer was inspired,

and the idea he dreamed up was so nasty and devious it made him laugh in the middle of his cold.

'Hatchooo!' he spluttered as he slopped into Kingswell. 'Hoosheee!' Although he was utterly filthy he didn't bother to clean himself up. He went straight to Kingswell Manor – and bumped into George in the courtyard.

George was practising how to cross your eyes on purpose to avoid the glance of a malignant cockatrice. It was part of his research.

'Just you wait,' Sneck growled as he scuttled between George's feet, 'I'll have you for breakfast.'

Some breakfast.

Without waiting to be announced the sorcerer splashed straight into the Great Hall, where he found Sir Simeon Griphook sitting at the long table with his head in his hands and his daughter crouching on a stool beside him.

Bess's buxom maid Sybil moved protectively beside them as Sneck entered.

It was lucky for Bess that she had been standing at the window watching George when Sneck entered the courtyard. She was already wearing her proper clothes and that gave her time to throw a purple snood over her shorn hair.

Sneck burst into the hall shouting with rage.

'I'll get rid of him!' he cried. 'I'll crown him in

glory then nail him to the English flag! I'll sell him for silver and the soldiers can tear him apart a piece at a time!'

Sir Simeon wailed.

Bess jumped up. 'Have you no respect?' she demanded. 'Can't you see you're upsetting my father?'

'Mind your own business,' Sneck snapped.

'My father *is* my business!'

Sybil, unable to keep silent, waded into the argument like a wrestler entering a fighting ring. She took a deep breath, which swelled her massive figure to twice its normal size. She looked terrifying.

The sorcerer was impressed.

'What are you talking about?' Sybil roared.

Sneck backed away from her. 'I've just told you!'

'We didn't understand. Tell us again slowly. And with respect, if you please.'

Slowly, grimacing with frustration but with so much apparent respect for Sir Simeon that the unhappy knight stopped weeping in amazement, Solomon Sneck explained his plan to crown his assistant Richard as Winter King at Kingswell's Midwinter Feast.

Richard, he said, would be feted and honoured, but afterwards he would be surrendered as ransom to the advancing English army in return for their promise to leave Kingswell in peace.

'I think I can guarantee English cooperation,' he added smugly.

Bess was surprised. 'How can you?'

'That's my secret.'

Sir Simeon cheered up enormously as at last he

saw a way out for his people, and his mind began to work positively for the first time in months.

'Why would the army leave us in peace?' he asked. 'King Henry wants Owain Glyndwr, not an innocent boy.'

'We'll tell them he's Glyndwr's son,' Sneck said triumphantly. 'They'll think they can catch their enemy through him!'

Bess shuddered.

'Father,' she cried beseechingly, 'don't agree!'

That was *Bess's* big mistake, because her cry clicked a switch in the enchanter's brain.

He remembered how Richard had cried out to the grolyhoomp and thought, 'That's funny. The two voices sound the same.'

He looked narrowly at Bess and mentally superimposed his assistant's face on top of it.

The fit was perfect.

Sneck gasped. 'I must have been blind!' he told himself. 'Why, the cunning little vixen! But no matter – I'll crown her Winter Queen and the soldiers can have her as Glyndwr's *daughter*!'

His mouth twitched into a smile.

'Well, Sir Simeon? What do you think of my plan?'

The knight stared at his daughter, seeing her properly at last. 'I'll think about it,' he said, 'and let you know in the morning.'

After supper Bess tossed a cloak over her shoulders and slipped out of the manor to tell Huw about Sneck's plan.

In the courtyard she looked for George but couldn't see him. She hurried across the drawbridge.

That was as far as she got.

A figure blacker than the night loomed over her. She cried out but a cloth was thrust swiftly and roughly into her mouth. Then she was bundled into a blanket, lifted up and carried away.

Huw wasn't at home anyway, he was scouring the village for a missing piglet.

It was nowhere to be found and he was turning disconsolately for home when he heard Bess's brief cry.

He ran towards the sound and was just in time to see a hooded figure carrying a bundle into Solomon Sneck's house.

Huw ran to Sneck's door and tried to open it. It was bolted.

He thumped on the heavy oak. He kicked it and shouted and the noise he made disturbed all the cats and dogs of Kingswell.

'Open up, Mr Sneck!' he yelled. 'Let me in!'

Nearby another door opened very quietly.

Footsteps crept silently.

'Let me in!' Huw shouted again.

'As you wish, boy,' whispered a gruff voice. A hand rose. Huw hardly felt the blow. And being unconscious before he hit the ground he didn't feel himself being lifted up and carried into the house of the Kingswell enchanter.

chapter Sixteen

Potion

In the courtyard Big George was thinking, If I'm really going to help my friends I ought to *do* something. But what?

He wondered if the blind man with the tapping stick might have some ideas, and since hanging about a courtyard was as boring as becoming an icicle he set out for the hills in the hope of finding Biffin again. Besides, he liked the tapping sound of Biffin's stick, the lilt of his accent and the adventures that seemed to happen whenever they were together.

As he passed by the churchyard Huw's missing piglet came snuffling out and tagged along behind him, grunting gently.

Climbing into the mountains George watched the weather change again.

The dismal rain clouds sailed away eastward and in their wake stars pricked the sky like pins on a black pillow.

The comet, even lower and brighter than it had been before, pointed its tail directly at Kingswell.

The temperature plummeted. Soon frost was stiffening the ground again beneath George's striding feet and fingers of ice were exploring the edges of rain pools in the hollows.

The piglet, distinguished from its brothers and sisters by a black spot on its snout and a curious droop of its curly tail, trotted breathlessly at his heels.

As luck would have it Biffin was also out on the mountain, his sightless face lifted to the sky as he listened to the night.

Although Biffin couldn't hear the universe sing as George could, he had discovered that at night, when all the distracting noises of the day had been stilled, he could hear the music that *Earth* made.

He had found that Earth had its own orchestra, whose instruments were grass growing, worms turning, insects crawling, owls hooting, bats flitting – and even the ground itself expanding and contracting.

Lovely music, Biffin thought. Lovely, and very exciting.

Tonight what he heard was the sound of frost – and then of the ground shivering as if it was a drum being beaten by giant drumsticks.

Biffin knew what it was, and he was pleased. He liked the monster now and was no longer afraid of it. So he poked out his stick and set off in search of the grolyhoomp, tap-tapping his way down the mountain.

When he found George he sang, 'It is pleased I am to meet you again, George bach. Indeed to goodness, look you. Would you walk with me down to the village, please? I wish to examine you, see.'

*

All through that night the frost tightened its grip.

The fingers of ice crawled like spiders across the rain pools, touched and locked together.

Earth turned hard as iron.

While it did so, these things were happening.

Only twenty miles away from Kingswell the King of England's avenging army was camped in the hills and cursing the weather.

In Kingswell itself Big George lay flat in the square while Blind Biffin, trying to imagine what this monster looked like, measured him with his stick. The conclusion Biffin came to was that George was an impossibility. But that only made him more exciting.

Not far away Sarah and Rachel Evans were so worried about Huw they were hardly aware of the cold. Even so, little by little they sought comfort by moving closer and closer to the animals, finally dozing off dangerously near their hooves.

Inside Kingswell Manor, Sybil was very, very afraid for her missing young mistress. Instead of preparing Bess for bed she was lying on her cot whispering over and over like a prayer, 'Where are you, my angel? Why have you not returned to me, my lamb?'

Below Sybil, in the great hall, Sir Simeon

Griphook was gazing damply at the portrait of his departed wife and wondering about the candidate for the coronation of the Winter King in the morning.

Although he had appeared to trust the sorcerer completely Sir Simeon didn't trust him now. He felt uneasy about Sneck's proposal that his own assistant should wear the crown. There seemed a danger there, although at the moment the knight could not see where it might lie. In the end he was forced to admit that he himself could think of no suitable alternative – especially when you considered how the Winter King's short reign was going to end.

Sir Simeon marvelled at the deviousness of the plan. What a twisted mind that strange man must have!

Sir Simeon didn't know that his daughter was missing. Nobody had dared to tell him.

Meanwhile, in another part of Kingswell, Solomon Sneck was having a hilarious time concocting a new potion to send his two unwilling guests to oblivion.

As the mixture bubbled and steamed on the fire it gave off a kind of laughing gas, and every fifteen seconds Sneck roared and chuckled as he tossed in a new ingredient: fragment of tail or eyeball or sliver of sinew or poisonous toadstool.

When he judged the potion to be exactly right he scooped out a bowl of liquid stench. Then, holding it at arms' length and giggling as he went, he shuffled in flapping slippers down the corridor to the rustling rooms. At the third door he stopped, drew open the bolt and entered quickly. He saw Huw, eyes popping, pressed back against the opposite wall besieged by adders.

Sneck held out the bowl.

'Drink two sips of this,' he growled. 'No more than two, mind, or you'll be a very sick pig boy indeed.'

Huw peered at the steaming sticky lumps swimming in grease and found himself grinning. 'Why should I?' he asked suspiciously.

The magician leered. 'Because it will make you smell even worse than you do already, and the snakes will keep away from you.'

Huw risked a glance at the writhing mass at his feet and knew he had no option but to agree. Retching at the horrible smell, and in spite of grave misgivings, he took the bowl and forced himself to drink from it.

The effect was immediate: his body convulsed with laughter, then heaved, shuddered and vomited. Finally it slid helplessly down the wall to the floor.

Giggling away, Sneck left him there, and the last sounds Huw heard before he fainted away were the slamming of the bolt in the door and the soft slithering of snakes climbing over him.

Sneck entered the fourth chamber.

Here Bess stood frozen and trembling surrounded by hideous creatures. Huge rats jumped and squeaked and hissed at her with bared teeth. Deformed spiders humped about the floor. Wingless bats flopped in corners.

There was ceaseless movement everywhere with Bess rigid in the middle like the still eye at the centre of a hurricane.

She was so frightened she would do anything to keep these revolting creatures at bay and when Sneck offered the promising bowl she drank from it so quickly she gagged as she giggled. Purple slime dribbled down her chin.

The enchanter was only half way through the door when Bess followed Huw's lead and sank glassy-eyed to the floor.

Rubbing his hands with satisfied glee, Solomon Sneck returned to his kitchen knowing that his prisoners would be out of action for a very long time.

Too long, as it turned out.

chapter Seventeen

who will Be crowned?

The next day was Christmas Eve – that eager, anxious time when the world seems to be holding its breath in anticipation of a great wonder to come.

It was certainly a breathless time in Kingswell, because very early in the morning four important things with far-reaching effects happened in as many minutes.

First: a small grey insignificant-seeming cloud wandered out of the west. When it reached Kingswell it paused and hung and loosed a few spinning flakes of snow.

Second: Sarah Evans, so heavy with child she could hardly walk, visited the sorcerer's house to ask for a spell to help find her missing son. She knocked on Sneck's outer door just as, in the courtyard, the sorcerer was shoving his assistant Richard – 'who had unfortunately fallen and bumped his head', said Sneck – on to a decorated cart in readiness for the parade of the Winter King.

The magician peered through the door, listened impatiently and sent Sarah packing. 'Go into the forest,' he snapped, 'and look for wild pigs. Your son will be the ugliest among them.'

Third: As Sarah Evans turned disconsolately away a pair of hefty unpleasant-looking bruisers pushed past her with an unpleasant scowl. Solomon Sneck, who'd met them during a recruiting mission in the dark alleys of Shrewsbury, was expecting them. Looking furtively about him he beckoned them inside and closed the door quickly.

In the courtyard he looked them up and down and grinned. 'Scalding bluebottles,' he chortled, 'I chose well. You look as likely a pair of villains as ever put the frights up innocent citizens. You're just what I want. I hope you and your cronies are handy with your fists, for you're going to help me conquer Kingswell!'

Fourth: As if by magic Sir Simeon Griphook, Lord of the Manor of Kingswell, changed back from the weeping mouse he'd become to the gentle, kindly, brave knight he once had been.

He woke early, still pondering the choice of

Winter King, and found to his surprise that this morning the overwhelming sadness he had experienced at the loss of his dear wife felt just a little less unbearable now he had something else to worry about.

He left his bed, padded to the window, drew back the curtains and saw two things: a snowflake and a grolyhoomp.

The first he ignored; the second changed everything.

Dashing through his manor shouting, 'The King! The King! I've found the King!' Sir Simeon flew into the courtyard and gazed rapturously up at the most shocking and wonderful being he had ever seen – who just at that moment was trying to catch snowflakes for educational purposes.

Awed by Big George's size, neck, colour – by everything about him – the knight bowed and said, 'Sir, I honour you. You're a wonder and no mistake.'

George bowed back. 'Grolyhoomp,' he said.

'And the same to you.'

Blind Biffin came tapping across the drawbridge. 'That's a grolyhoomp, look you, sir,' he said.

'Ah,' Sir Simeon said wisely. 'A grolyhoomp, eh? Well of course that explains everything.'

Behind Biffin the population of Kingswell

streamed over the drawbridge, dressed in their very best finery for the Midwinter Feast and the Coronation of the Winter King.

Noisy and excited, they crowded into the courtyard around Big George, who beamed down at them and said, 'Can I belong here?

That was his second time of asking, and once again the people did not understand him.

But it seemed as if they did, because what happened next appeared to George to be the biggest vote of confidence he could imagine. Sir Simeon Griphook bowed low before him and then – smiling for the first time in months – turned to his people and said, 'Behold your Hero, your Spirit of Christmas, your Winter King!'

The villagers went wild, because this was exactly what they themselves had been hoping for ever since the moment when they first saw this amazing wonder frozen on a mountainside, and thawed him out and made him the clothes that had warmed him ever since.

They jumped for joy, and cheered.

They patted George on his legs and boots – the only bits of him they could reach.

They praised Sir Simeon for having such a wonderful idea – and for stopping crying.

A squinting friend of Biffin's handed him his

harp. Others had brought their instruments –
fiddles, tabors, bagpipes, viols, lutes, hurdy-gurdies
– and there and then, led by their blind harpist, they
played a happy jig and danced and sang, and so
started the wild party that was Kingswell's annual
Midwinter Feast.

George danced and sang too, and the people
cheered him all over again.

Then, to a loud fanfare of trumpets, Sir Simeon
produced the golden crown of the Winter King on
its blue velvet cushion.

He signalled to George to kneel.

George did, but Sir Simeon still couldn't reach

his head. So he asked George to lie down.

George lay down to please him, and Sir Simeon Griphook, Lord of the Manor of Kingswell in the Marchlands of England and Wales, stepped solemnly forward, and with the words 'I crown thee Spirit, Lord and Winter King!' set the golden crown into George's blue and green wiry hair.

Next the village priest, a tiny man with elfin ears and a dreamy look, was lifted up so he could sprinkle George with holy water. 'I baptise you Holy Fool,' he piped. 'May the Spirit of Christmas be with you and bless your reign with good things!'

George rose to his feet feeling pleased and happy without knowing why. As if echoing this uncertainty, his crown slipped sideways. But it stayed on his head.

'Long live the King!' the people shouted. 'Long live the Winter King!'

*

If you're wondering, 'Have the people of Kingswell gone mad? Have they forgotten that a vengeful army is bearing down on them?' the answer is – well, no, they haven't.

But since that prospect is too frightening to think

about, they have decided not to think about it. With a bit of luck, they're telling themselves, it might not even happen – why, those soldiers could march by on the other side of the mountain and not even realise that Kingswell is here!

Hope springs eternal.

Besides, very little in this world is absolutely perfect. You can find a flaw in most things if you look hard enough.

For Big George the flaw in his great celebration appeared when he looked for Bess and Huw to share his happiness and couldn't find them. Puzzled, he looked over the heads of his dancing subjects and called, 'Hoo-oo-oo! Bbeee-ssss!'

Everybody thought he was singing – except Sir Simeon Griphook. 'Bess?' he exclaimed. 'Yes, where is she? Where's my daughter! *Bring me my daughter!*'

In that heart-stopping moment the knight had found *his* flaw.

Sybil was brought before him, weeping for her lamb and wailing that it wasn't her fault she was missing.

'Missing?' cried Sir Simeon. 'Bess is MISSING?!'

Begging Fate not to be so cruel as to deprive him of *both* the creatures he loved most in the world, Sir Simeon ran into the manor and began to search it inch my inch. His desperate voice could be heard calling for his daughter even through the tumult of instruments and flying feet in the courtyard.

And now it was time for the people of Kingswell to find the flaw in *their* happiness.

It came rolling over the drawbridge towards them in the shape of a cart driven by two terrifying toughs. On the cart Solomon Sneck sat in his best sorcerer's suit with his arm propping up a sleeping youth who was so heavily cloaked and hooded as to be unrecognisable.

A cardboard crown trembled on the youth's head.

The Kingswell sorcerer was absolutely furious – more furious than he had ever been before in his furious life.

He was furious with the people of Kingswell for starting the festivities without him.

He was furious with Bess for making him late, and as they crossed the drawbridge he slapped her cheeks for the twentieth time and hissed, 'Come to, girl! Come to!', cursing her blank eyes and lolling face and the sleeping potion into which he'd clearly tossed too many thrushes' eye linings.

He was furious with the grolyhoomp for wearing the crown of the Winter King – how *dare* he? – and he was furious with that ninny Griphook for giving it to him.

Solomon Sneck was furious with everybody in the world except himself.

And now that his plan to install Bess as Winter King had been foiled, the presence of his knocked-out assistant was an embarrassment.

'Take the cart back to the house,' he hissed to his gap-toothed bully boys. 'Put this dozy object back where it came from and return quickly. It's time for us to make our move.'

Then, smiling a ghastly smile that looked as genuine as a pantomime horse, the magician jumped down from the cart and joined in the dancing with a clumsy skip.

Sneck's leer would have been even less genuine if he'd known his command had been overheard.

Once again the needle-sharp ears of Kingswell's blind harpist had pierced a private conversation.

Laying down his harp Biffin collected his stick from Squinter and followed the sound of the cart out of the courtyard.

chapter Eighteen

king for a Day or Two

Big George gazed in wonder at the strange things happening around him.

He saw more snow clouds sweeping in overhead, each heavier than the one before and loosing flakes that steadily grew bigger and fell faster.

He stored up impressions, looking, listening, learning, and saw the courtyard, the manor and even the people turning white before his eyes. He watched the world being transformed.

Looking up he saw millions of falling slivers of ice. Dozens of them stabbed his eyes and made him shiver.

He looked down and saw that the flakes were covering his mittens, knitting a white overmantle on his coat – and blanketing the bewildered snout of the oinking little piglet at his feet.

George picked it up and tucked it into his pocket, from where its two wide wondering eyes gazed curiously up at him.

Suddenly he became aware of another pair of eyes watching him. Beady, suspicious, piggier than a real pig's could ever be, they glared at him out of the snouty face of Solomon Sneck, sending out signals of pure hatred.

George instinctively understood. 'The sorcerer is my enemy,' he told himself. 'I'll have to watch him.'

He couldn't watch for long because suddenly the people, carried away by their excitement, grabbed hold of him, pulled him over the drawbridge and began the Parade of the Winter King through the streets of Kingswell.

Trumpeters blared one fanfare after another. All around George the villagers danced. The children clutched his legs and every dog and cat for miles ran squabbling behind.

'*Honour the Spirit of Christmas, look you!*' Squinter shouted, tossing Biffin's harp into the air like a flag.

'We honour him!' the people answered.

When they had circled the village twice they returned to the drawbridge. As they approached, George saw Sneck talking conspiratorially with the ruffians, who had brought along a dozen more thugs as ugly as themselves. They looked like a villainous private army.

When he saw the parade returning, Sneck ushered them all into the manor.

Across the drawbridge, through the courtyard and into the great hall the musicians, dancers, children, dogs and cats flowed – all with mouths watering at the prospect of the feast to come.

Everybody, that is, except one.

Big George could not get through the door and was left outside.

George was alone again.

Alone alone alone alone – he was always alone.

Yet this time not quite alone. The piglet in his pocket looked up at him and twitched its snout in a friendly fashion.

'Oink,' it said.

Then George saw Biffin approaching.

Tafth-tafth, *tafth-tafth* went his stick as it snuffled through the thickening snow. It stopped when it struck George's boot.

'That you, George bach?'

'Grolyhoomp,' said George.

'Oh, George, happy I am to find you. Come this way if you will, will you?'

The blind man tafthed away again, and George followed.

As they walked through the village George marvelled at the speedy transformation of Kingswell.

Already it was whiter than Biffin's eyes – the houses were festooned with whiteness, the mountains reared white all around – the very air was white with falling snowflakes. Everywhere George looked was dazzling.

This had an odd and unexpected effect. It pushed that door in his mind a fraction wider and lit up a scene in his damaged memory.

He remembered a landscape, also white, although its whiteness was not caused by snow but by sand and glittering quartz and pale, stricken stones that stretched away for ever in a limitless blinding desert.

Scattered about the desert were cities even more dazzling, great bubbles of glass, maybe, or shining metal – colossal at any rate – and dazzling because the glass reflected back the dangerous rays of a frozen, faraway sun.

In the whirling snow George paused and tried to look into the cities but Biffin snapped him back to Earth.

'Concentrate, George, please! Huw and Bess need you. Look at the house in front of you.'

Biffin too was looking through his memory – the

memories of a blind lifetime in Kingswell where every house and tree had become familiar to him through touch and smell and sound and echo. Now he pointed his stick at Solomon Sneck's barn.

George blinked, the glass cities vanished and the snow stung his eyelids.

'What I'd like you to do, George,' Biffin said, 'is demolish that building. Knock it flat. Can you do that?'

He kicked out a foot to show what he meant.

George understood.

He walked forward, measured the distance, drew back his boot and rammed it into the barn. Three of its four walls fell down.

Out of the dust snakes slithered, bats soared, spiders scuttled – and Huw and Bess stumbled like drunken ghosts.

'Hooo-ooo-ooo!' George shouted happily. 'Bbb-eee-ssss!'

They seemed to be having difficulty grasping what was going on – a feeling George knew very well – so he scooped them up and dropped them into his pocket beside the mirror-spoon, the rabbit's paw and Huw's long-lost piglet.

chapter Nineteen

Sir Solomon

Inside Kingswell Manor Solomon Sneck was making his bid for glory. Protected by his private army he burst without warning into Sir Simeon's personal chamber, surprised the lord at his desk, astonished Sybil who was making up the fire, arrested them both and locked them in the attic.

Then he marched into the great hall and announced to the feasting throng that their previous lord was a prisoner and he, Solomon Sneck, was the new owner of Kingswell Manor and their rightful lord and master.

He was, he said, to be addressed from now on as *Sir* Solomon. If anybody had any objections they were welcome to join sobbing Simeon in the attic and, when the King's army arrived, on the scaffold as well.

Nobody objected.

With their eyes popping, their mouths ajar and their fingers dripping gravy, the villagers could only gape in astonishment.

'You may show your appreciation of this great news,' said Sir Solomon, 'in the usual way.'

Imagining the spells and blows that would rain down on them if they disobeyed, his new subjects cheered and clapped and sang 'For he's a jolly good fellow' as if they had just heard the most wonderful tidings in history.

So when Big George returned to the manor he found that the world had changed again.

He was no longer the centre of attention. Far from it – as he put Bess and Huw gently down in the courtyard snow he saw the villagers prancing out of the manor chairing Solomon Sneck on their shoulders and singing praises to *him* instead.

They would have ignored George entirely if Sneck, his eyes burning with hatred, had not shouted, 'Arrest those three! And give me that crown!'

The procession stopped in its tracks. The people looked uncomfortably at each other.

'Well? Why don't *you* do it?' Sneck asked the ruffians whose looming presence had lent authority to his takeover. 'Get on with it!'

But while they had felt very big and brave in front of a bunch of helpless yokels, those toughs didn't feel half as tough in front of Big George. They felt jumpy as grasshoppers.

They looked at George and winced and asked themselves questions like, 'How can we arrest *that*? How can we take the crown off it? How do we reach it? We'll have to climb up it!'

Warily they moved forward.

What happened next was entirely unexpected, especially by Sir Solomon Sneck.

Bess and Huw positioned themselves between his bully boys and George.

'Go away,' said Huw.

'Go back in your holes,' said Bess. 'You ought to be ashamed of yourselves.'

Solomon Sneck lost all patience. Turning to his new subjects he screamed, 'DO SOMETHING!'

That was the moment when everything *really* went wrong for Bess and Huw. Scared silly by the sorcerer the crowd turned into an angry mob and surrounded them. Biffin was knocked down in the rush. 'There's bad manners!' he cried. 'What is going on, look you? This is rebellion against our true lord and rightful Winter King!'

Nobody listened to him.

Huw tried to pull Bess through the crowd. 'Come on,' he said grimly, 'We'll hide in the forest!'

But, as if a spell had truly been cast over them, the people who had once been their friends closed in.

'Leave us alone!' Huw shouted, butting a fat man's billowing stomach. The man grunted and lifted him off the ground by his collar. 'Gotcha!' he cried.

Then a woman with a broken nose elbowed Bess in the face as if she was trying to break her nose too. Bess saw stars and collapsed into the woman's waiting arms.

What was Big George doing while all this was going on? He was watching the world ending. Snow was suffocating it. What had been a breeze when the fall began had stiffened into a gale which hurled the snow like sling shot against his cheeks and eyes. It whipped up drifts and piled those drifts like barricades against buildings, trees and mountains alike.

There was nothing about this snow that was beautiful any more. It had become a wild thing, more dangerous and frightening than any animal, and Kingswell was foundering beneath its assault like a ship sinking into unknown depths of ocean.

Suddenly the gale doubled in ferocity. Anyone small or frail buckled at once beneath its force.

A girl, blown to her knees, tried vainly to tear the matting snow from her hair and eyes. 'We're going to die!' she sobbed. 'The storm will kill us!'

'Get back inside the manor!' Solomon Sneck commanded, wanting to be there himself. 'Bring the prisoners!'

Shielding their raw and bleeding faces as best they could, the villagers dragged Bess and Huw inside.

'George, we need you!' cried Bess, as the door closed behind her.

'Grolyhoomp!' Huw shouted, 'Help us!'

But George wasn't listening.

The manor door was bolted fast against the storm. The courtyard was abandoned except by the howling wind, the blistering snow and an awesome snowman who was big in every way and getting bigger by the minute.

Suddenly, for an extraordinary split-second, the clouds parted to reveal a star bright as the sun pointing down at the snowman and haloing his head with its light. It lasted only a moment, then the clouds merged again, the star vanished and the snow fell even faster than before.

Everything seemed the same, but, as if that light had been a signal, the snowman shook the snow from his head and strode out of the courtyard.

chapter Twenty

Reunion

Luckily there was one bright silver lining to the dark clouds pressing in on Kingswell that eventful Christmas Eve.

When Bess and Huw were thrust into the attic, what celebrations there were!

'Daughter,' Sir Simeon croaked, his eyes spouting like fountains, 'is that you? Is that really you?'

'Of course it is, Father!' Bess leaped into his arms. 'Though I'd be dead if your precious magician had his way!'

'I'll throw him in gaol!' Sir Simeon cried. 'I'll have him executed at once!'

'How can you? He's taken over the village.'

'He may think he has,' said Sir Simeon bravely, drawing himself up very tall and straight, 'but he has me to deal with first.'

The knight looked magnificent in his anger and Bess, who had quite forgotten how noble her father could be, felt tears surge into her eyes too. 'Oh, Father,' she sobbed, hugging him tight, 'you've come back to us!'

Sir Simeon frowned. 'When I thought I had lost you, child, I realised that one shouldn't mourn the dead at the expense of the living. I'm ashamed of myself.'

Sybil was also weeping tears of happiness. Crying, 'Lamb! My lambkin!' she bustled out of the shadowy eaves and clasped Bess to her billowy bosom. 'Dear girl, promise you'll never leave me again – I couldn't bear it!'

All was rapture.

Huw, hovering awkwardly in the shadows like the humble pig boy he was, smiled at their happiness and longed to be with his own family.

He wondered if he had a new brother or sister yet. How they needed him, he thought. But now here was Sir Simeon Griphook holding out his hand, beckoning him.

'Come here, boy,' the knight said. 'Have you been leading my daughter astray?'

Huw swallowed. 'No sir, I have not.'

Bess hurried to his side. 'No more he has, father,' she said stoutly. 'If anything it's the other way round. Huw is my friend.'

Sir Simeon's eyebrows rose. 'A swineherd dares to call himself my daughter's friend?'

'What does it matter what he is?'

The knight shook his head and smiled. 'It matters nothing, my dear child. Except that if Huw is your friend, then he's mine too.'

'And mine!' Sybil cried, embracing Huw like a friendly python.

'Give me your hand, boy,' said Sir Simeon.

And so it was that a lowly swineherd shook hands with a lord of the manor and was kissed by his daughter and her maid, and all four laughed as though they had quite forgotten that they were prisoners awaiting execution the moment the King of England's army should arrive.

chapter Twenty-one

George in Danger

Not half a dozen miles away, that army was in a sorry state. Its horsemen were no longer horsemen because their horses, having had quite enough of this fools' errand, had bolted during the night. So all Christmas Eve a miserable troop of exhausted foot soldiers – starving, soaking, freezing and weighed down by armour and weapons – struggled on foot through a snowy whiteout and drifts as high as their heads.

When they could struggle no more, they mutinied. They threw down their weapons, sat in the snow and refused to march a step further.

'I'll have you horse-whipped for this, you naughty men!' Captain Witless cried.

'Makes no difference,' the mutineers replied dully. 'We'll all be stiffs by tomorrow. We're going to die in this Godforsaken wilderness on Christmas Day!'

The Captain laid his head in his hands and prayed, harder than he had ever prayed in his life. Because he too believed that they were going to perish in the snowstorm, he prayed deep in his heart for help, even though he knew that in this alien country and unearthly weather there was no help to be had.

How wrong he was…

That small desperate cry from a desperately small soldier sent vibrations through the air which, in their own small way, were very powerful.

The Captain's prayer climbed the white windy mountains, slid down the snow-clogged valleys and slipped into Kingswell and Big George's ears at the very moment when Bess and Huw were being overwhelmed by the turncoat villagers.

It was that prayer which had distracted George from helping them. It was still distracting him when through that hole in the storm the comet momentarily reappeared and pointed – so it seemed to George – to the other side of the mountain.

It was a message which could not be ignored, so once again a grolyhoomp set out to follow a star.

*

Inside Kingswell Manor the Midwinter Feast was turning out to be like no other in the village's history.

Snow smothered the windows and darkened the hall. The villagers watched themselves being buried and completely lost their appetite for feasting and dancing.

Nor was Solomon Sneck as happy as he had expected to be, because already he was discovering what all rulers discover – that power is no picnic. All it does is bring responsibility.

The people of Kingswell lost no time letting their new lord know that he was responsible for them – for their present, their future and their very lives.

Questions stabbed Sneck from all sides.

'What will we do, sir, when the soldiers come?'

The sorcerer sneered. 'That's easy. Give them the fools in the attic.'

'But what if that doesn't satisfy them?'

'Give them the grolyhoomp.'

'Who's going to do that, sir?'

Sneck pointed to his henchmen, who backed hastily away.

'Don't look at us,' they said. 'Don't ask us to do anything with anybody tall. We've got no head for heights.'

The people's demands grew more and more outrageous.

'*What if this snow doesn't stop, sir?*'

'It will stop.'

'*But what if it doesn't? Will you make it stop?*'

'How can I prevent snow from falling?' cried Solomon Sneck, beginning to feel like a cornered animal.

'*You're a sorcerer, aren't you?*'

'*You **say** you're a sorcerer. So prove it. Make the snow stop now.*'

'*Yes, now.*'

'*Do it NOW!*'

Despairing, the sorcerer watched the people becoming an unruly mob again. He saw their faces turn ugly with fear, heard their voices whine like summer flies about the winter hall, and began to hate them.

'Why did I ever want to have anything to do with these peasants?' he wondered. 'Have I made another big mistake?'

Four miles away, Big George had made a very big mistake. He'd got lost.

George was used to being lost because he'd been lost ever since he landed on Earth, but this was different.

What worried him now was that he was as blind as Biffin. He could see nothing. His eyes were clogged with snow. So were his ears. He was alone in a blanked-out, whited-out, furiously swirling world. Twice he stumbled into drifts and almost fell.

The most worrying thing, though, was that with every passing snowblind moment the prayer he was supposed to be answering was getting weaker.

Then suddenly and unexpectedly another cry, coming from the opposite direction, clanged in his mind like an alarm bell. 'Save me!' it shouted.

George recognised Huw's voice.

What could have happened to *him*?

Chapter Twenty-Two

one Good Turn

Huw Evans had done a very foolish thing. Imprisoned in the attic he had been growing frantic to know how his family was faring in this most terrible of snowstorms. Was Rachel safe? Was his mother well, or ill? Did they have food, and a fire?

The questions whirled in his head and made him so dizzy that in the end he couldn't help himself. Without telling Sir Simeon, Sybil or even Bess what he intended to do, he waited until their backs were turned – and committed suicide.

Well, not quite, but he might have if it had not been for the snow.

He squeezed through a tiny attic window and slid down the roof above the kitchens to the battlements below. It was only snowdrifts slowing him down which prevented him rolling over the battlements into space.

The snow helped him in another way too. Because of it there were no guards on the battlements to see him. Everybody was in the great hall.

So, quicker and lighter than a wraith Huw slipped past drifted-up windows and down almost blocked stairways until he reached the ground.

There was a heart-stopping moment when he thought he heard Bess calling him, but the howling wind drowned it and all other sounds. Soon he was forging across the snowy courtyard and over the

almost vanished drawbridge to safety.

Or so he thought.

But Huw wasn't safe at all.

The storm's power astonished and frightened him. Beyond the drawbridge he turned towards his home but became confused almost at once. There were no landmarks any more, only wind-worried flakes that whipped and slashed his face. Everything was moving – falling, rising, spinning crazily.

The result was that when Huw thought he was approaching the cowshed he was actually following Big George out of the village.

Quickly his hands, feet, face and legs lost all feeling.

Soon he found he could not move at all.

He sank to his knees in the snow.

Hot tears melted the ice on his cheeks as he cried out, 'Mother! Rachel! Where are you!'

Slowly, like an axed tree, he toppled forward.

When his face hit the snow his mind was still searching frantically for inspiration. He had almost lost consciousness when it came.

'Grolyhoomp!' he cried, 'Save me!'

That put George in a terrible quandary.

'Help!' came the fading cry from in front of him.

'Help!' drifted Huw's weak cry from behind.

Even Big George could not travel in opposite directions at the same time. One must be sacrificed. But which one?

George knew that if he continued to plunge forward he might be able to rescue the stranger. On the other hand, if he turned back he might save a friend.

Which would *you* choose?

George didn't hesitate. He wiped the snow from his face, brushed it off his clothes and gazed at the white, blank, spinning world all around. Then he smiled. There was no contest.

He turned around and went back for his friend.

*

Huw, slipping towards death, dreamed of babies, cows and lost piglets. He was so far gone he did not see George loom out of the blizzard and gather him up as if *he* was a baby. Nor did he feel George's breath warm his face and body.

Huw did not realise that, just as a few days earlier he had helped save a gigantic stranger from an icy end, so now that stranger was saving him.

All he was aware of – and this too seemed like an extraordinary dream – was that one moment he was suffocating in snow and the next a distant owl was calling 'Hooo-oo-oo, hoooo-oo-oo!' Then he was falling into a dark comfortable shelter and landing on something soft and warm and noisy.

'Oink oink!'

'Oink!' it squealed.

As Big George turned round again, inside his pocket the piglet snuffled Huw's face with its hot little snout and began to revive him.

Chapter Twenty-Three

Action Grolyhoomp

Outside the door to the attic the first of the sorcerer's no longer brave henchmen hesitated. (Their colleagues, frightened by the storm, had fled while they could. These two heroes had stayed because they had nowhere else to go.) Each carried a platter of gruel for the prisoners.

They paused because, if there was one monster in Kingswell might there not be two? And might not the other one be in the attic, just waiting to pounce?

Bracing themselves and ready to run for their lives, they unbolted the door and faced the unknown together.

What faced them was a girl.

'Food for you,' they said, trembling with relief.

'You ought to be ashamed of yourselves,' the girl said.

The ruffians peered over Bess's head and sniffed. They could smell no monsters, They were safe. They became brave again.

In the shadows they saw Sir Simeon Griphook sitting on the floor and Sybil lovingly and hopefully combing his hair.

'Where's the other one?' they growled.

'What other one?' said Bess innocently.

'The boy.'

'Oh, him. He's gone.'

'*Gone*?' Their podgy fingers shook. 'What d'you mean, he's gone?'

'He escaped when you came in. That's what we'll say anyway.'

'Oh my. Oh my!' Pushing the platters into Bess's hands the ruffians bolted the door and tumbled down the stone staircase.

'We never heard that, right?' they panted. 'We never heard that at all. And now we're getting out of here.'

That's what they thought, but they weren't going anywhere. The snow wouldn't let them.

And what was George doing? George was getting excited. Action suited him. He was having an adventure and doing something useful at the same time and he didn't feel lonely any more.

Listening keenly for that ever-weakening signal, he forged through the driving flakes. Every minute he had to kick snow off his boots, spit it from his mouth and squeeze it out of his eyes.

Then he realised that the cry for help had stopped.

George pushed harder. His boots crunched and his breath rasped in the cold air.

He stopped to listen again.

No prayer.

No anything.

He was too late.

Then very faintly, so faint it was hardly more than a disturbance in the air, he heard a quite different sound. It seemed to come from somewhere just ahead.

Dat. Dat. Da-dat.

George had heard that noise once before, on his way here. It was the sound of a beating drum.

The drummer was a very young and very small soldier called William Tagg.

Sitting in the snow watching more snow covering his legs, William knew he was going to die because his companions had told him so. He looked round at them – little scattered humps like white bags in the snow. They had given up all hope.

But there was a difference between William and

them: he didn't know how to give up. Even now, with almost his last breath, a tiny flicker of purpose flared in him.

William was a drummer. Drumming was what he was trained to do. It was his reason for living. He couldn't stop.

So now, slowly and achingly, with the last spark of his energy he drummed. His hand lifted the drumstick and let it fall against the stretched hide.

Dat.

And again.

Dat, Very softly. *Dat.*

Hardly knowing what he was doing, William repeated the action like an automaton.

Dat. Dat. Dat.

Slowly his head slumped on to his chest. His eyes closed.

Now even William Tagg could do no more.

But what he had done was enough.

When he summoned his last remaining strength to open his eyes, he saw a monster ploughing through the snow towards him.

The thing approached, pushing through a swirling curtain of snow flakes and looking much as William had imagined a mammoth might look.

William sighed. His arm, acting entirely by itself, flipped.

Dat dat!

The mammoth towered over William, looked down, grimaced – and spoke.

'Grolyhoomp,' it said.

'Same to you,' William whispered – and passed out.

chapter Twenty-four

George Gets Mad

Christmas Eve drew on, blind as a mole in the storm. By afternoon what daylight had escaped the hanging snow clouds was fading fast inside the manor.

Torches were lit, and in the great hall their smoky light illuminated a nightmare scene.

Dogs, clearing the floor of scraps, squabbled over crumbs.

Blind Biffin tapped anxiously among them, worrying about Sir Simeon and Sybil and Bess and Huw – and even more about Big George, lost out there in the snow.

The old minstrel tried to chant the story of the Winter King all over again, but he was howled down by the people who, hungry and afraid, gnawed greedily at the remains of the morning feast. Their mouths slopped beer and their fists fought over pieces of piecrust and gristle from the trenchers.

Several of the more pious villagers knelt in corners with their hands pressed tightly together, faces raised, eyes closed and lips mumbling.

Others continued to harangue their new lord, demanding protection from every possible misfortune with which fate might attack them. Solomon Sneck regarded them all with scorn.

'Keep those fools away from me,' he commanded his henchmen who, as much as Bess and Sybil and Sir Simeon were imprisoned by the storm.

They were annoyed about that and fed up with the sorcerer.

'You're joking,' they said. 'There are scores of them and only two of us left. How do you suggest we do it?'

'Use your initiative!' Sneck snarled. 'Do I have to tell you how to do everything?'

'Not everything absolutely, Squire. But you might show some respect.'

'Respect!' Sneck roared with laughter and slapped his legs at the joke. '*I* respect villains like *you*? I respect a sheep's backside more than you!'

'Do you really?' they said. 'Well, well.'

They closed in on him and the sorcerer, eyeing the baying villagers below him and the mutineers in front, suddenly felt a little less secure.

'I'll put a spell on you!' he hissed.

'Try it.'

'Very well, I will!'

The enchanter raised his arms like a conductor and, staring them in the eye, intoned in his deepest, most ominous voice:

Hex, hex, toadlings two
Do whatever I tell you to do
When I snap my fingers
When I show you my hand
You will obey my every command!

He snapped his fingers and slapped each ruffian across the cheek. 'There,' he said triumphantly, 'now try to disobey me.'

They grinned. 'D'you want us to do it together or one at a time?'

'You incompetent ninnies,' the sorcerer screamed, 'you're so stupid you can't recognise a spell when it hits you in the face! Why, you're the thickest—'

The tips of two swords pricked his throat.

By now the only light in the courtyard was slanting down from the flaring window of the great hall and up from the pale, ghostly, luminous snow.

The snow was still falling relentlessly, deep enough now to reach a man's shoulder.

Solomon Sneck, with those swords threatening his throat, looked through the window for salvation – and gasped.

Something very strange was happening out there. An enormous tree branch pushed forward through the gateway and cleared it like a snowplough. Then it moved into the courtyard, sweeping left, right, left, right, powering away the drifts and making a passage through.

Into that passage there staggered a small figure whose arms rose and fell like those of a clockwork toy.

Dat. Dat-dat-dat. Dat!

With a final cheeky *Drrrrmmmm-dat!* the toy

sank to its knees. But then another clockwork toy came lurching stiff-legged behind and helped it to its feet again.

More shapes followed, and more and more until there were dozens of clockwork toy soldiers staggering about with their arms supporting each other like ghosts dancing.

Sneck laughed with delight as the figures multiplied.

'How's that for a magic spell, you dolts?' he beamed triumphantly. 'Here comes the English army! These are *my* allies and *my* friends, not rats for hire from the gutters of Shrewsbury. Now *you're* in trouble!'

The ruffians gaped. Their mouths opened even further when they saw a green moon on a stick come surging across the courtyard. The colour drained from their faces.

'Oh dear me,' they said. 'Oh dear oh dear oh dear!'

Sybil was also looking out into the courtyard, from the attic window. She too saw the pale green shining moon and her heart swelled with admiration.

'What a wonder!' she cried. 'What a hero! Oh, if only I could find a man like that!'

Bess, peering under Sybil's outstretched arm, felt

extraordinarily happy. 'What a grolyhoomp!' she laughed.

'What a phenomenon!' gasped Sir Simeon.

'HELP!' they shouted.

George, who knew a friend's voice when he heard it, cried 'Be-ee-sss!' at the top of his voice and started an avalanche.

The manor vibrated. Snow tumbled from its roofs.

Inside the great hall the villagers thought an earthquake had begun.

'Save us!' they cried.

George didn't know which way to turn.

Only Solomon Sneck curled his lips in contempt. 'Fools!' he taunted, 'you're all fools!'

In a fit of hysteria he raced to the door, dragged it open and screamed at George:

'Eeny meeny smidgy small,
A grolyhoomp's the biggest fool of all!'

George was certainly the biggest something, but he was not in any way a fool. Behind his lost memory he was very wise.

It seemed to him that almost every minute he was learning something new about life on Earth, and

the new thought which came to him now was that in every generation ordinary people were plagued by tyrants who rose to power at the expense of everybody else.

George didn't like that, and he did not in any way like Solomon Sneck, who seemed to him to be as wicked a tyrant as he'd come across in a long while. And now, when everybody should have been helping each other to survive the storm, the sight of that foul-faced, mealy-mouthed, fraudulent magician spouting venom from his sheltered doorway was too much to bear.

George felt irritated by Sneck, then angry – and then for the first time since he arrived on Earth he got really mad.

Grinding his teeth in fury George snatched up the suddenly shrieking sorcerer in his fist, carried him into the village squirming like one of his own snakes, and stuck him firmly down the tallest chimney of the tallest house in Kingswell.

Naturally, this being the coldest day of the coldest winter for years, there was a massive fire burning down below...

Chapter Twenty-Five

Miracle at Kingswell

George was also learning that we humans are subject not only to tyrants but also to our own changeable natures.

The fickle inhabitants of Kingswell were proving that now, because once again the grolyhoomp was a hero and saviour to be cheered to the snowy skies.

They weren't so sure about the army he had rescued but Huw, speaking from George's pocket like a very small preacher in a very large pulpit, explained that the soldiers were far too cold, hungry, frightened, frozen and grateful to be a threat to anybody. What they needed, Huw said, was a little human kindness.

The people looked at the soldiers standing only half alive in the never-ending snow and their hearts melted.

The soldiers looked at the people and, astonished, saw their stony suspicious faces relax and unexpectedly smile. They felt hands which a moment ago had been ready to strike reach out to protect and carry them into the safety of the manor.

It was the first gesture of friendship they had experienced since they left their homes and families a lifetime ago and it was too much. To a man they broke down in tears.

In a moment *everybody* was crying, the people with pity and the soldiers with relief.

Big George watched happily as the spirit of Christmas came at last to Kingswell. He felt moved himself, and liked that feeling so much he wanted to be kind too.

He looked around for things to be kind to – and found five.

Looking down he saw peering from his pocket the two trapped faces of a piglet and a pig boy who were both desperate to reach their families. And looking up he saw three equally pleading faces at a window high up in the manor.

'All right,' George muttered, 'here comes grolyhoomp kindness.'

He pushed a finger through the attic window, pulled the frame out of the wall and poked about inside.

'Bee-eess-sss!' he called.

Whooping with pleasure, Bess wrapped her arms around the great finger and encouraged her father and maid to do likewise.

Sybil flung herself across the first joint. 'What a lark!' she cried. 'What a digit!'

Sir Simeon Griphook gulped nervously and, telling himself that anything his daughter and her maid could do he should be brave enough to do as well, climbed on to the second joint.

Slowly and carefully George withdrew his finger and the three dangling figures entered a crazy world of whirling snow, howling wind and towering drifts.

But there – oh bliss! – was an open door through which a warm light shone and the faces of the whole village beamed an ecstatic welcome.

George put his passengers down in the doorway, then turned and plunged into the blizzard on his second mission of kindness – and on his way to a big surprise.

Christmas Eve was almost over as the grolyhoomp forged through Kingswell's deserted, snowbound streets. Deserted, that is, except for a

lunatic figure waving frantically from a chimney where it was stuck like a cork in a bottle. 'Oooohh!' it shouted, and 'Aaaahh!' as flames leapt up from the hearth below. The figure was also shouting nonsense about frogspit and wormbrains, but George could make no sense of that and didn't want to.

He pressed on.

Soon the village was behind him and in front was the cowshed, its roof sagging under the weight of snow. Huge icicles hung from its eaves and speared the drifts that had built up from the ground. Inside a woman cried out in pain.

Fearing the worst, as soon as Big George had

cleared the doorway and lowered him to the ground Huw ran inside with a thudding heart. The piglet scuttled after him, gurgling with happiness.

What George heard next was a jigsaw of sounds: cows bellowing, horses stamping, pigs excitedly welcoming their prodigal's return – and little Rachel Evans shrieking with joy as she jumped wildly into her brother's arms.

He also heard Sarah Evans gasp, 'Huw! Oh, thank goodness! You're just in time – help me, please!'

After that there was only the moan of the wind and the rustle of falling snow.

George waited.

Hours passed.

Then suddenly the jigsaw was enriched by two cries.

The first was Sarah Evans's shout of triumph.

The second was a thin elongated wail.

George could make no sense of that so he lowered his neck until his face hung upside down outside the cobwebbed window. What he saw inside was truly magical.

In smoky firelight animals were clustering round Huw, who was washing the face of the smallest living person George had ever seen. Rachel gazed at it adoringly and nearby Sarah lay on her pallet, pale but smiling.

'It's a miracle, George. A Christmas gift from Huw's father to his family.' George turned his head and saw Bess standing tiptoe beside him. Then, laughing, she hurried inside.

That was the moment when the snow stopped falling.

It happened quite suddenly, as if a spell had been broken. The wind died, the flakes dwindled and shrank and, as the snow clouds swept away eastward, in the west the stars and moon appeared. The comet dangled its tail above the cowshed and George like a bright chandelier.

In Kingswell, living began again.

Drawn by the comet's brilliant light the villagers left the manor and struggled across the courtyard. Solomon Sneck's thugs, feeling strangely as if a change was coming over them as well as the weather, went with them. 'We have seen his star in the west,' they breathed, 'and we'll never be wicked again.'

Then, thinking that was maybe a little drastic, they told each other not to get carried away. 'After all,' they said, 'it's only a bit of a shine.' But they crossed themselves just in case.

When the people reached the cowshed they saw the Kingswell pig boy, with their lord's daughter by

his side, waiting to greet them. In his arms Huw
held a tightly wrapped bundle.

'It's a boy,' he grinned. 'We're going to call him Little George.'

Big George beamed and stood protectively over them.

'Gg – e – oorr – gg – e', he said. 'Grolyhoomp.'

chapter Twenty-Six

The Spirit of Christmas

The villagers, with Sir Simeon Griphook, Sybil and Blind Biffin in front, clustered round the door to the cowshed like an audience at a theatre waiting for the show to begin.

George gave it to them.

He took the icy crown from his own head – how it was still clinging there was a wonder in itself - and placed it on Huw's shaggy locks.

'Kk – ii – nn – gg,' he said.

The people gasped with surprise and muttered among themselves, because of all the strange events which were happening was it not the strangest of all that the lowest among them should become the highest in a single moment?

Yet here was their own lord, Sir Simeon Griphook, falling to his knees and kissing the pig boy's hand and greeting him with, 'Your servant, Sire!'

Bewildering wasn't the word for it!

George had not finished.

Noticing the soldiers he'd rescued tottering at the back of the crowd, he beckoned them to come forward.

Captain Witless, who remained to be convinced that he wasn't dead and this wasn't Judgement Day, cleared his throat nervously.

'Er, on you go, men,' he sniffed. 'Don't hang about. Lead the way, Sergeant Moo.'

The villagers moved aside to let them through.

George regarded the troops very sternly, and pointed to the ground in front of Huw.

'Down we go, boys, and no messing,' said the Captain, throwing himself face down in the snow to show them the way.

The soldiers dropped like skittles and bowed before the Winter King.

Huw gave them a majestic wave.

George now beckoned Sneck's reformed bully boys, who were promising to be sweeter than angels from this moment on if only they were allowed to survive the next few dangerous seconds.

They closed their eyes and pretended not to notice, so George picked them up and dropped them in front of Huw.

They lay down at his feet.

'Sssttt-aaaa-nnndd,' said George.

'Oh lor',' they groaned, standing up and expecting the worst.

To their surprise, Big George very gently took Little George from Bess, held him out to show them, handed him back to Bess and pointed to the cowshed threshold.

'What's that about then?' the ruffians muttered nervously.

'It's very clear to me,' Bess said sternly, 'that the grolyhoomp wants you to guard the baby.'

'Does he?'

Huw smiled. His crown sparkled. 'George does,' he said, and it's the most important job in the world.'

'Oh, well, if you put it like that,' said the reformed thugs, 'we'd be honoured to do it.'

So like a jigsaw the pieces of our story have come together and the picture is complete.

Sir Simeon Griphook has regained his spirit, his village and, most important of all, his dearly loved daughter. He has a new motto: 'Honour the dead but love the living.'

Bess has recovered her father, her future and Huw, her much-loved companion. She has also made a very big and strange new friend.

Huw has altered beyond recognition. He's Winter King, Lord of the Swineherds and, even more exciting, he has a brand-new brother.

The **Soldiers** have their lives when they thought they'd lost them. Drummer William is their hero and Captain Witless their inspiration.

The **Villagers** have a Winter King and Lord to be proud of and a sorcerer they can throw snowballs at any time they feel like it. 'Serves him right,' they say as they pepper him - but they cross themselves just in case.

Solomon Sneck has run out of spells. Wriggle as he might he has become part of a chimney – which, when you think about it, is a better spell than any he managed when he could move around.

Finally, two cowardly ruffians have discovered that they're really quite exceptional characters: brave, bold, intelligent – and angelic. **Sybil** dotes on them.

So honour is satisfied and all's well that ends well.

A grolyhoomp has put a smile on the face of this small corner of the Marchlands and everybody's life has changed because of him.

We will let the good folk of Kingswell resume their interrupted feast and, under the midwinter wandering moon with snow lying deep all around, allow them to eat, sing, and dance the night away.

We can look at them for this last time through the upside-down eyes of a very large grolyhoomp, who smiles fondly at them through the manor window as his feet tap to their music and above his head a dazzling star shines down.

It is, of course, the Christmas star, for at last it is Christmas morning.

chapter Twenty-Seven

Something Has changed

George sees the dancers suddenly shimmer and move away from him. They come back into focus, but he knows what is happening. He's falling asleep again.

It's time to be moving, time to go back to bed. Yawning, he turns away from the manor, steps over the drawbridge and walks into the village.

Pausing among the silent houses he waves to the figure in the chimney, who might have been Santa Claus but isn't. This figure too is nodding with sleep, even though smoke is pouring out of its ears.

When he reaches the little church George pauses again and looks over the wall, where the smooth white expanse of the churchyard glistens under the Christmas moon. Beneath its snowy surface Alice

Griphook is sleeping a very deep sleep, but George doesn't know that. All around, the mountains rear to the starry sky, protecting her.

George marches on.

Half way up the first mountain he turns and looks back, just for a moment, at what he is leaving

behind. Under moon and star Kingswell crouches, a cluster of dark walls and shining roofs. Gleams of yellow light shine from its biggest building and George is sure he can hear the sound of Biffin's harp.

'I should have liked to belong there,' he tells

himself. 'But I can't, and that's that.'

Resolutely he sets off again, and this time he doesn't look back.

But as he climbs, George knows that something is changing inside him.

He's getting to like it here.

afterword

Inside his shelter, Big George sleeps again, with his hands thrust warmly into his coat pockets.

Clasped lightly in his right palm are three lucky charms: a spoon, a rabbit's foot – and a dried up piglet's dropping.

Well, anything can be a gift if it's meant kindly, and you never know when even a piglet's dropping might come in useful.

Life's a pantomime, isn't it?